In the Lion's Den

Barbara Taylor Bradford was born and raised in England. She started her writing career on the *Yorkshire Evening Post* and later worked as a journalist in London. Her first novel, *A Woman of Substance*, became an enduring multi-million-copy bestseller and was followed by many more, including the bestselling Cavendon series. Barbara's books have sold over eighty-five million copies worldwide in more than ninety countries and forty languages, and ten mini-series and television movies have been made of her books. In October 2007, Barbara was appointed an OBE by the Queen for her services to literature. *In the Lion's Den* is her thirty-fourth novel.

To find out more and join the huge community of her fans, find Barbara on Facebook, follow her on Twitter @BTBNovelist and keep up to date with her events, novels and tours at www.barbarataylorbradford.co.uk, where you can also register for the Barbara Taylor Bradford newsletter and receive regular updates.

Books by Barbara Taylor Bradford

Barbara Taylor Bradford

In the Lion's Den

HarperCollins*Publishers*

HarperCollins*Publishers*
1 London Bridge Street
London SE1 9GF

www.harpercollins.co.uk

First published by HarperCollins*Publishers* 2019
This edition published 2020
1

A catalogue record for this book
is available from the British Library

ISBN: 978-0-00-824249-7 (PB B-Format)
ISBN: 978-0-00-824250-3 (PB A-Format)

Set in Sabon LT Std by Palimpsest Book Production Limited,
Falkirk, Stirlingshire

Printed and bound in Great Britain by
CPI Group (UK) Ltd, Croydon CR0 4YY

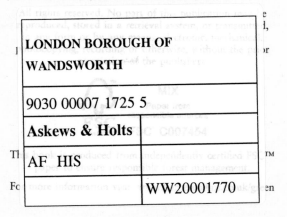

For my darling Bob, with my love

CONTENTS

CHARACTERS

<u>THE FALCONERS</u>
Philip Henry Rosewood Falconer, founder of the dynasty; a head butler.

Esther Marie Falconer, his wife and co-founder of the dynasty; a head housekeeper.

Their sons
Matthew Falconer, his eldest son and heir; a stall owner at the Malvern Market.

George Falconer, a noted journalist on *The Chronicle* daily newspaper.

Harry Falconer, a chef and owner of a café, the Rendezvous.

Their grandchildren (Matthew's offspring)
James Lionel, an ambitious young businessman on the rise.

Rosalind, known as Rossi, a seamstress.

Edward Albert, assistant to his father on the stalls.

Their daughter-in-law
Maude Falconer, Matthew's wife and mother of his children; a seamstress.

THE VENABLES

Clarence Venables, Esther Falconer's brother-in-law, great-uncle of James Falconer, owner of a shipping company in Hull.

Marina Venables, Clarence's wife and younger sister of Esther Falconer. Great-aunt of James Falconer. A noted artist.

Their children

William Venables, eldest son and heir, working at the Hull shipping company.

Albert Venables, second son, working at the Hull shipping company.

Their daughter-in-law

Anne Venables, Albert's wife.

THE MALVERNS

Henry Ashton Malvern, owner of the Malvern Company, a big business enterprise and real-estate company.

Alexis Malvern, his only child and heir; a partner in the business.

Joshua Malvern, his brother and business partner.

Percy Malvern, his cousin who runs the wine business in La Havre.

THE TREVALIANS

Claudia Trevalian, eldest daughter and heir of the late Sebastian Trevalian.

Lavinia Trevalian, sister of Claudia.

Marietta Trevalian, sister of Claudia.

Dorothea Trevalian Rayburn, an art collector and member of the Trevalian private bank's board. Sister of the late Sebastian; now the head of the family.

Cornelius Glendenning, Claudia's husband, a banker, now running the Trevalian private bank in London.

THE CARPENTERS

Lord Reginald Carpenter, a publishing tycoon and proprietor of *The Chronicle*.

Lady Jane Cadwalander Carpenter, his wife.

Their daughters

Jasmine Carpenter, a debutante.

Lilah Carpenter, a debutante.

Their twin sons

Sebastian and Keir Carpenter, born in March 1889.

THE PARKINSONS

Maurice Parkinson, a well-known biographer, journalist and academic.

Ekaterina Parkinson, known as Kat, his wife, descended from the Shuvalovs.

Their children

Natalaya Parkinson, eldest daughter, known as Natalie, assistant to Alexis Malvern, in charge of the arcades.

Irina Parkinson, second daughter, a dress designer.

Alexander Parkinson, son, known as Sandro, a theatrical designer of stage scenery.

(All three children are English born.)

PART ONE

Honour & Loyalty
London/Kent
1889

ONE

Dread. That was the feeling James Lionel Falconer was experiencing as he sat at his desk in his office at Malvern House in Piccadilly.

It was the afternoon of Wednesday 25 September 1889, and an hour since a packet of documents had arrived by courier from Paris. James had opened the packet hastily and read them immediately, shocked by the bad news they contained.

James looked down at his hands resting on the pile of documents, a chill running through him at the thought of giving them to Henry Malvern, who was an ailing man. Rocked by his daughter's breakdown and his brother Joshua's stroke and lingering death, his employer had been unwell all summer with a debilitating fatigue. But James had no choice. The head of the company had to know everything.

A deep sigh escaped him as he opened the top drawer of his desk, placed the documents inside, locked the drawer and pocketed the key.

Taking out his watch he saw that it was almost seven o'clock. At least he didn't have to face Mr Malvern until tomorrow morning, by which time his friend and colleague

Peter Keller would be in his office next door if James needed him. Keller was stalwart; they had shared interests and had become close friends. And Keller worked in the Wine Division and might be able to help solve this mess. Though it was hard to see how, since it now turned out that Percy Malvern, Mr Malvern's cousin, was not only a thief who had stolen millions from the Wine Division in Le Havre, but also a *bigamist*.

Striding across the room, James put on his coat and left his office.

When he stepped outside onto Piccadilly, it was drizzling after a day of heavy rain. The early evening light had dimmed, and there was a slight mist, but the street lamps were aglow. People were rushing home, dodging in and out and around each other, the pavements wet and slippery. James joined the throng.

He hurried toward Half Moon Street, wanting to get home as fast as he could. The sound of horses' hooves, the rattling of carriage wheels, and the general bustle of the traffic in the streets grated on him tonight. He turned up the collar of his topcoat and plunged his hands into his pockets. It was not only wet but also cold for September.

The moment he opened the door and went into the small flat he shared with his Uncle George, a newspaperman, James felt a great sense of relief. The gas lamps on the walls filled the room with a shimmering light and a fire burned in the hearth. In an instant his uncle's smiling face appeared around the kitchen door. 'Supper is almost ready!' he announced. Smiling, James hung his damp coat on a hook behind the door, then returned to the kitchen to help George.

His uncle was deftly carving a large piece of roast beef, and he said, without looking up, 'Your grandmother left this for us today, while we were at work.' Laughing, he added, 'And these two loaves of freshly baked bread. You see, she dotes on you, Jimmy lad.'

'And you too, Uncle George . . . you're her son.'

A smile slid across George's face, and he finally looked across at his nephew. 'She's the best there is, nobody like her.'

James nodded, and spotted the small glass pot with a white paper label stuck on it. *Horseradish sauce*, it read, in his grandmother's handwriting. He smiled inside. She always thought of every little thing, right down to the last detail.

Sitting at the kitchen table a bit later, eating their roast-beef sandwiches and drinking mugs of hot tea, James was quiet. His mind kept going over the problems dogging the Wine Division in Le Havre, problems that the documents he'd received today confirmed.

'I dread giving the terrible news from France to Mr Malvern,' James said, grimacing.

'Just give him the documents and tell him he won't like what he reads,' George had suggested. 'You may well find that he's been expecting bad news anyway.'

Sleep did not come easily that night. James considered it to be his saviour, the key to his health. Yet when it was elusive he did not toss and turn like some people might; instead he lay perfectly still. Reflection and analysis were his special friends during these wearisome, sleepless hours.

He was glad he had his uncle to talk to. He had always been particularly close to George, even as a child, and they had truly bonded on a different level when he moved into the flat on Half Moon Street in Mayfair. Not that they saw much of each other. George was a journalist working on *The Chronicle*, where his star had risen over the years. His hours at the newspaper changed constantly.

James appreciated George's wisdom and began slowly to relax, stretching his long legs in the bed, settling himself comfortably on the pillow. The dread had slithered away. Mr Malvern *had* to know everything, and perhaps he might not be too surprised after all.

Unexpectedly, and much against his will, thoughts of Alexis Malvern, Henry's daughter, crept into his mind, and for a moment he felt a rush of emotion, a sudden desire for her. But he squashed this when he focused on her lack of concern for her father and for the business she would one day inherit. He saw her continued absence as a dereliction of duty. And these thoughts damaged her image in his mind. He thought her behaviour didn't quite live up to his standards, just didn't 'fit the bill'. Then, quite unexpectedly, Georgiana Ward came into his mind, and he wondered how she was, how she was doing. He had only ever once asked his cousin William if he had any news of her. William had shaken his head, then told him, 'My mother has only heard from her once, letting her know that she was feeling better away from London fogs. That's all I know.'

James had remained silent at the time, not wanting to probe too hard. A small sigh escaped as he turned on his side. Whenever he thought of the older woman who had been his first lover, he realized how kind she had been to him, how much she had cared about him. One day, he thought. One day I will meet someone like her . . . I know I will.

He also missed William, who was far away in Hull. As he fell asleep, his thoughts were only about the importance of family and friends.

James sat up with a start, as if someone had shaken his shoulder. He was wide awake, and the room was very bright. He blinked as he got out of bed and went over to the window. The moon was riding high in the midnight-blue sky, and it was shining into his bedroom because he had forgotten to close the curtains last night. He noticed that the rain had stopped.

He was suddenly restless, wanting to be outside, walking the streets, as he sometimes did, thinking through his problems. And clearing his head. Within minutes he was dressed in his trousers, shirt and shoes; he pulled on a thick jacket for warmth and slipped out of the flat quietly. All he needed was his uncle to wake up and ask where he was going at two in the morning.

His answer would have been nowhere in particular, because that was the truth. Once outside, he walked along Curzon Street and turned onto Park Lane, heading down towards the Wellington Arch and on towards Buckingham Palace. It wasn't far away, and as he caught sight of it in the distance he noticed there was no Union Flag flying on its flagpole. Queen Victoria was at Balmoral, and the Prince of Wales, her heir to the throne, lived in his own home with his wife, Princess Alexandra. Now there was a beautiful woman, he thought, one who was elegant and regal. She was deaf, but did not appear to let that bother her. Uncle George had told him she was Danish and that her sister Minnie was married to the Romanov Tsar of Russia.

As he neared the palace walls, James slowed down and stood staring at the regal building, almost entirely in darkness, only a few lights showing through upstairs windows. During the summer, Princess Louise, daughter of the Prince and Princess of Wales, had been married there.

Married, he thought. I wonder if I will ever get married. He grimaced to himself. The idea did not appeal to him at the moment. He had other fish to fry. His career. He knew within himself that he was doing well, so lucky to work for the Malvern Company, to be close to Mr Henry.

Yet he was always aching inside to be on his own, to start his own retail business. Ever since his childhood he had longed to become a merchant prince. Too soon, he thought. It's too soon.

He sighed under his breath, slowly walking away from Buckingham Palace. He was still too young to go out on his own. He mustn't be impatient. His grandmother was forever reminding him of that. He headed down the Mall, his thoughts shifting to the days when he worked on his father's stalls in the Malvern Market. He had been eight years old, and fell into the work at once, loving every moment of the day. Stay calm and keep going. Slowly, he told himself. And one day you'll get to where you want to be.

TWO

The following morning James went to Malvern House very early. As he walked down the corridor to his office, he relished the silence, the closed doors, and the lack of lights. He was the first to arrive today.

He immediately unlocked his desk drawer and took out the batch of documents that had been delivered the day before. They had come from Philippe de Lavalière, a private detective in Paris, whom the company had hired to look into the fraud they had discovered. Swiftly, he went through them all, reading a number of them again, and then put them away.

Mr Malvern wasn't in yet, and so he studied some of the reports from Natalya Parkinson, who had been Alexis's assistant and was helping to manage the work in Alexis's continuing absence. He enjoyed working with Miss Parkinson, or Natalie, as her friends and family called her. She was efficient and had quite a flair for helping their tenants arrange the windows of their shops appropriately.

A bit later, when he heard Mr Malvern's footsteps in the corridor outside his office, James rose and strode out. 'Good morning, sir,' he said.

Henry Malvern turned, smiled at James. 'Morning, Falconer,' he answered. His employer was looking better these days, though he still tired easily.

'I wonder if I can come in and see you for a moment?' James asked. 'It is important.'

Malvern nodded. 'Of course.' As he moved on, he added, 'Come in now, Falconer. I have a meeting in half an hour with the accountants.'

'Right away, sir.' James rushed back into his office, took out the documents and hurried after his boss.

After hanging up his overcoat on the coatstand in the corner, Henry Malvern sat down behind his desk. Looking across at James, who was already making his way into his office, he said, 'Are those documents why you want to see me?'

'Yes, sir.'

'Not from Alexis, I don't suppose?'

James shook his head. 'No sir. They arrived late yesterday by courier just after you left. They're from the Paris office.' James stopped at the large Georgian partner's desk and placed the bundle of documents on it. 'I'm afraid it's not good news.'

Henry Malvern inclined his head and gave James a hard stare. 'I wasn't expecting good news, Falconer.' He began to read the documents, but then said, 'Please sit down, you know it makes me nervous when you're hovering.'

'Sorry, sir,' James replied, and sat down in the chair opposite the imposing desk, patiently waiting for his boss to digest everything.

At last Henry looked up, sat back in his chair and shook his head. 'A bigamist! I'm not too surprised he stole so much, but his romantic philandering does surprise me. My cousin is such a plain man, and rather short, with quite a reserved manner. But as my mother always said,

"Still waters run deep and the devil's at the bottom." I think her words may well apply to Mr Percy Malvern.'

The documents revealed that Percy Malvern had not only embezzled money from the company, but also had two wives. His English wife Mary, and a seventeen-year-old daughter, Maeve, were living in Nice. A second wife, Colette, a twenty-six-year-old Frenchwoman, was living in Beaulieu-sur-Mer, outside Monte Carlo, with a six-year-old son, Pierre.

Percy Malvern himself was nowhere to be found. He had disappeared into thin air.

In the letter he had written, Philippe de Lavalière had suggested that Percy might well have fled abroad, perhaps to somewhere like the French West Indies, where a man could hide forever. There was little chance of ever finding him.

James nodded. 'He must be very devious. It takes a special kind of skill to keep two families going. But then money helps, I suppose. Do you think we can recoup any of it, Mr Malvern?'

'I've no idea, Falconer. It doesn't sound hopeful. In the meantime, I shall have to plan on putting some of my own funds into the Wine Division in Le Havre. That's the only thing I can think of.' The older man frowned. 'It will be a long haul to get back into profit. I'll have to increase revenue from other parts of the company.'

James paused, and gave Malvern a quizzical look before saying, 'It might seem strange to suggest spending money at this point, but have you given any more thought to my suggestion that we build an arcade in Hull, sir?'

'The City of Gaiety, you say it's called.' Henry nodded. 'I have given it some thought. If you can find the right spot, one which you know people will easily frequent, then I might be persuaded. Fortunately, retail is in good financial shape in general, and I'm not against expansion.

We'll need something to make up for this disaster.' He gestured at the documents from France.

This response made James happy, and a cautious smile broke through. 'My cousin William Venables has several sites he wants us to look at, whenever you can spare the time to go to Hull, Mr Malvern. And when you're ready to give it your attention. Also, I've done a bit of research and come up with the plans you had made for the Harrogate arcade. They would work very well for the Hull project.'

'Very enterprising of you, Falconer,' Henry answered, with a small rush of pleasure. He had always known that this young man was clever; he had also proved to be a hard worker and extremely disciplined. Occasionally he was also fierce, a young lion marking out his territory. And now he had offered a way out of this hole. Henry Malvern thought for a moment then cleared his throat and said, 'We should go to Hull as soon as possible. Maybe we can make a start on this before the cold weather sets in. What do you think of that?'

James beamed at his boss. 'I'll start making the arrangements immediately, sir.'

Esther Marie Falconer was the kind of woman whom everyone liked, and many truly loved. To her family she was Mother Earth, compassionate, understanding, full of wisdom and kindness. To her employers, the Montagues, she was the best head housekeeper in London, calm, organized and discreet. And as her staff and her children knew, she could also be tough, relentless, and implacable, but by nature loving in her heart. And she loved her family to the very depths of her soul. They were her whole life.

Now, she sat in her small but comfortable housekeeper's parlour, which served as an office in the Montague mansion near Regent's Park. Five days ago her husband, Philip Falconer, the house's butler, had fallen down the stone steps leading to the cellar and broken his ankle. He had only just been discharged from hospital and she had some thinking to do.

She cringed yet again when she thought about the accident and how lucky he'd been. If he had fallen and hit his head, he might not be alive today. She closed her eyes, leaned back in the chair and thanked God for protecting him. Her devoted husband, her stay and her stand, had never had an accident of any kind before in his life. And she prayed that the first would be the last.

Opening her eyes, Esther glanced at the calendar once more, adding up the weeks the Montague family would be travelling through Europe. It was as she thought. They would not return until late October. Lucky again. Philip would be recovered by that time.

It struck her suddenly that she and Philip had always been lucky. In a certain sense they had led charmed lives.

Her thoughts fell backwards in time . . . to when she was twelve years old, growing up in Melton, a small village just outside Hull, one of the great seaports in England.

Even at twelve she had been clever and ambitious, and also quite pretty. She knew perfectly well that those were the reasons she had been taken into service at Melton Priory, home of Lord Percival Denby, the Sixth Earl of Melton.

Through her mother's connection to Lady Minerva Denby, Lord Percival's sister, Esther was trained to be a lady's maid in order to look after Lady Agatha, the sixteen-year-old daughter of the earl.

Esther had been with her mistress ever since, travelling with her when she was a young girl and staying with her once she married – for fifty years, to be precise.

How time flies, Esther thought, with a small shock,

13

remembering she was now sixty-two years old. Philip was four years older, almost sixty-six. Not that he looked it, and neither did she. But then they had been protected and well fed living with the Montagues, who appreciated their loyalty, honesty and devotion, and all the hard work they put in. As long as his ankle healed well, they would continue to serve. She rubbed her left hand absent-mindedly, where a niggling arthritis made it ache.

Over the years, Esther had risen in the ranks to become the head housekeeper at Lady Agatha's two homes – the John Nash-designed Regency house in London and the old country estate in Kent, Fountains Court.

Esther and Philip had met at the London house when Lady Agatha married the Honourable Arthur Blane Montague, who owned both of their homes. Philip, a Kentish man, had also gone into service when he was young, just sixteen. Having started out as a junior footman at Fountain Court, he was now head butler and devoted to the Honourable Mister, as he referred to Mr Montague.

Like his wife, Philip had remained with his original employer and was highly valued.

Just imagine, Esther thought, glancing around her parlour, I was married from this house and I am still here. She smiled as she looked at the small photograph of her husband with their sons and grandchildren and remembered the boy she had fallen in love with all those years ago.

We met, looked at each other and just clicked. Lucky. Indeed, I was. And so was he, she thought.

Pushing back her chair, Esther got up and went out into the corridor, walked down to the kitchen, pushed open the door. 'I'm going upstairs now, Cook, since we've settled everything about supper tonight.'

'It's all in hand, Mrs Falconer,' Cook answered, and

14

gave her a huge smile. 'I'm looking forward to cooking a few of your family's favourite dishes.'

Esther smiled back and retreated. She climbed the back staircase and crossed the hall, discovered Philip and their grandson sitting together in the conservatory, which opened onto the garden at the back of the house.

'There you are!' she exclaimed, hurrying across the room. 'Nattering away like two old codgers.'

'I am an old codger,' Philip said with an amused laugh.

'That's not so!' his wife answered, and went and sat next to James on the sofa.

'I'm so happy we can have our Saturday supper here downstairs in the servants' dining room, instead of at your house. Easier for your grandfather.'

James nodded, glanced at Philip. 'It was nice of the Honourable Mister to let us all come here, wasn't it?'

'Indeed it was, James,' Philip replied, and looked down at his left leg encased in plaster of Paris, stretched out and resting on an ottoman. 'He sent a telegram from Monte Carlo immediately after he received mine. He insisted that you all join us here for our traditional supper. Even told me to choose one of his wines.'

'Wonderful things, these telegrams,' Esther observed. 'I can't imagine how we ever managed without them. The Honourable Mister also insisted your grandfather rest in here as well, to benefit from some light and warmth. Anyway, James, I'm relieved to see you looking well. Your father told me you are working long hours.' She gave him a hard stare.

'Yes, I am, Grans, but I'm in fine fettle at the moment. And Mr Malvern is such a nice man to work for. We've been doing some reorganization of the whole company, and he's appreciated my help. He says he couldn't have done it without me.'

'James, whatever happened to Mr Malvern's daughter?

15

Is she not working alongside her father and you?' Philip asked.

James shook his head. 'No, I'm afraid not.' He looked from his grandfather to his grandmother, and continued in a solemn voice, 'It's rather a sad story, really. Miss Alexis doesn't seem to have recovered from the death of her fiancé. Just a week before they were to be married. She lives in Kent and hardly ever comes to Malvern House.'

Esther frowned, said in a low voice, 'I seem to remember you talking about her. She was a first-class businesswoman, one of only a few in London.' Esther paused and shook her head. 'Isn't she his only child? Mr Malvern's heir?' she asked, puzzlement echoing in her voice.

'That's correct, Grans. But she doesn't seem to be interested in the business. Or anyone. Not even her father. It's a shame. So sad to see the pain he's in. He's heart-broken, in my opinion.'

Esther leaned back, shaking her head again, looking nonplussed.

It was Philip who now spoke up. He glanced at James, a brow lifting quizzically. 'Is she physically ill in some way?'

'Not that I know of,' James answered, his forehead puckering. 'What are you getting at, Grandfather?'

'It sounds to me as if Miss Malvern is mentally disturbed. How long has she been acting this way?'

'It's over a year since Sebastian Trevalian died.'

There were a few moments of silence. Glances were exchanged. It was Esther who spoke first. 'It seems to me that she can't let him go, that she's hanging onto his memory. Very sad. I'm sure the sudden loss of the man she was about to marry was a shock. It would leave a terrible sorrow. However, to avoid society for so long appears abnormal, in my opinion. The way she is behaving is odd, to say the least.'

16

'She went to see a famous doctor in Vienna,' James volunteered. 'His name is Doctor Sigmund Freud. Seemingly he examines the mind, not the body.'

Philip suddenly was sitting up straighter and nodding his head vehemently. 'I've read about him! In one of Lady Agatha's science magazines. He is called a mind doctor. The patient talks to him, and he does an analysis of the things the patient says. I'm not quite sure how he cures the patient, though. But he is becoming famous.'

'She was treated by him for six months,' James confided. 'That is why Mr Malvern offered me a job as his . . . assistant, I suppose you'd call me. Miss Malvern had gone to Vienna.'

'I remember it now,' Esther exclaimed. 'Your father told me the story.' Esther looked off into the distance, as if she could see something far away. After a moment or two, she said, 'So what is going to happen, James? Is she ever coming back?'

'I've no idea. To be honest, I don't think Mr Malvern knows either.'

'But what is he going to do without an heir?' Philip asked.

Esther stared at Philip. 'Poor man. And whatever will he do with Malvern's?'

James said quietly, 'He has spoken to me about selling the company, once we've got it back into the best shape we can. We're working on that.'

'Do you think he *would* sell that old family company?' Philip asked.

James did not answer at first. A moment later, he said slowly, but in a firm tone, 'Yes, I do think he would, if the price is right.'

THREE

Esther was delighted when she opened the door and saw the rest of the Falconer family all together, standing on the step at the back.

'Come in, come in!' she exclaimed, pulling the door further ajar, a huge smile spreading across her face.

Once they were in the narrow lobby and the door was shut, there were hugs and kisses and greetings exchanged. She couldn't help thinking how smart her three sons looked, dressed in their best clothes.

Matthew's wife, Maude, was elegant in a simple cream linen dress which fell to her ankles, decorated with a black cotton rose on her shoulder.

Her granddaughter, Rossi, was likewise decked out in a summer frock, made of pale-blue crepe de Chine. Rossi's younger brother, Eddie, wore his one and only best suit.

'Let's go and see Dad, shall we?' Matthew announced, taking charge.

'Yes, come along,' Esther answered, smiling at her firstborn child. 'He's with James up in the conservatory.'

They clustered around Philip in his chair, fussing about him, making him feel well loved.

It was Eddie who pushed his way to the front, and said,

'I've brought a painting for you, Grandpa.' He handed him the package, and turned to Esther. 'And one for you too, Grandma.'

He stood and watched as his grandparents opened their gifts and praised his artistic talent; Matthew and Maude smiled with pride at their younger son.

Rossi had also brought gifts for her grandparents. 'A scarf for each of you.' She then explained, 'Silk summer scarves, because sometimes it does get cool in the evening.'

Esther and Philip gave more thanks and complimented their granddaughter. Then Esther turned to Matthew, Harry and George and said, 'Would you three come downstairs with me to the kitchen, please? Rossi and Maude can entertain Dad for the moment, and you can chat with him shortly. Will you come as well, James?'

The men nodded and followed Esther out of the room. Once they were in the hall, George asked, 'Is there a problem, Ma?' Concern echoed in his voice.

'No, no,' Esther answered swiftly. 'Let's go downstairs so that I can explain something to the three of you.'

Harry said, 'I'd love to see the kitchen, Mother. I haven't been in it for ages. And say hello to Cook.'

Esther led them down the back staircase and, once at the bottom, she turned to the others. 'Look at these stairs, tell me if you think a man with a cast on his leg can come down and go up easily, even with your help.'

'I don't believe he can,' Harry said immediately, then looked at his brothers. 'What do you think, George, Matthew?'

George shook his head. 'You're right. It would be a difficult task, even with each of us holding him on either side. The staircase is steep and narrow, with a turn in it.'

James exclaimed, 'But Grandpa thinks we're having supper in the servants' dining hall. Won't he be upset if we don't?'

'Perhaps,' Esther replied. 'However, I don't think we can let him anywhere near this staircase. In fact, I have already had the table set in the breakfast room. It's quite large, and we'll easily fit around the table.'

'He's not going to be happy about that,' Harry announced, staring at his mother. 'You know he's had those rules of his for donkey's years. Staff do not use the family's living quarters when they are absent. Dad calls it *trespassing*.'

'I know that only too well. He only agreed to sit in the conservatory because the Honourable Mister instructed him to. But thank goodness for telegrams. I sent one to Lady Agatha in Monte Carlo, explaining the problem. Her reply was simple. She agreed with my suggestion about the breakfast room.'

'It's a good thing you did that, Mother.' Matthew rested his hand on her shoulder. 'Once he's read Lady Agatha's telegram to you, I doubt there will be any problem.'

'I just wanted you to know this, because I need you to back me up, if that's necessary.'

'Absolutely, Grans,' James answered at once. Her sons assured her they too were on her side, and that there was no good argument to be otherwise. Their father could not navigate this staircase with a plaster cast up to his knee, even with their help.

'But how will you manage the stairs to your flat?' Matthew asked his mother.

'That's less of a problem – we can use the main staircase for now, while the family is away. And he does his paperwork in the conservatory.'

Esther thanked them, then added, 'Let's go to the kitchen with Harry. He's dying to see it and talk to Cook for a few minutes.'

They received a cheery welcome from Mrs Holmes, who had been the cook for the Montagues for twenty years.

She then said to Harry, 'I must congratulate you. I've heard all about your new restaurant and I'm happy it has taken off so well.'

'Thank you, Mrs Holmes.' He grinned at her. 'I'm glad you don't mind that I've pinched some of your recipes.'

Cook laughed. 'I enjoyed it when you slipped in to watch me doing my job when you were younger.'

'I've told them about eating in the breakfast room,' Esther now said, wanting to move on. 'And they will back me up.'

Cook nodded. 'It's a dangerous staircase for Mr Falconer to use. The breakfast room presents no problems, and the food goes up on the dumbwaiter as it does every day when the family is in residence.'

They stood talking to Mrs Holmes about the supper and Harry asked her permission to look at her beautiful copper pots, pans and moulds, admiring them as he did.

After leaving the kitchen, Esther took her sons and grandson to the breakfast room. They agreed that it was ideal for the family supper. The gas lamps were already glowing. The table looked inviting, with a bowl of fresh flowers in the centre.

When they returned to the conservatory, Rossi wanted to know where they had been and what they had been doing. 'Uncle Harry needed to check the menu, no doubt,' she said to her mother, grinning.

'Not really,' Harry answered. 'Mrs Holmes is a great cook, as we all know. She has made some lovely dishes for tonight . . . favourites.'

'I wanted to show the boys the back staircase,' Esther cut in swiftly, needing to get the problem out of the way. 'They agree with me it's very steep.' She stared at her husband and said to him, 'We are having the supper in the breakfast room, which is on this floor—'

'No, no, we can't do that, you know the rules,' Philip interrupted.

'Yes, we can. I sent a telegram to Lady Agatha.' Before he could object further, Esther took the telegram out of her skirt pocket and handed it to him.

Philip read it in silence and gave her a faint smile. 'You win,' he acknowledged. 'And you're right, actually. That staircase would be a problem for me in this plaster cast.'

Esther always enjoyed the Saturday night suppers and, on this particular evening, the gathering of their little clan over a meal was no exception.

As her eyes swept around the circular table in the breakfast room, she saw that everyone was enjoying themselves, and this pleased her.

She looked at her three sons, studying them one by one by one. They were rather handsome in their different ways, and certainly they were well put together. All three were neat and tidy in their dark ready-made suits, with their discreet silk ties – gifts from her, in fact. Each of them wore a floppy silk handkerchief in the top pocket of their jackets as a finishing touch. There was a flutter of pride behind her smile.

They had done well in their chosen jobs, and because she and Philip had brought them up with high standards, they were decent men, honourable, loyal and full of integrity.

Oddly, they had been rather mischievous, sometimes even naughty boys. They had had their differences, which led to quarrels and rows, occasional fist-fights, as well as heated verbal battles. Their father and she had taught them to sort things out fairly and quietly, not at high voltage. Eventually they had learned to do this.

When they were still quite young, Esther had invented

the Saturday night supper, a special meal where they were expected to be on their best behaviour. They enjoyed the delicious meals she concocted and made. It became a ritual the boys loved.

If they had misbehaved earlier in the week, they were banned. This rule brought them up short most of the time. It ensured a better attitude on their parts. None of them wanted to be excluded from the Saturday night get-together. It was a very special treat.

Her gaze settled on Maude, her daughter-in-law, wife to Matthew, mother of James, Rossi and Eddie. She and Philip loved this gentle and caring woman who had created a happy home for her husband and children. Very slender, more so than ever after a bad bout of flu some years before, Maude's burnished brown hair was shot through with fine threads of silver now, but her deep brown eyes were as expressive as ever and her face as loving.

She welcomed the extra money earned from her clever sewing and had a kind word for everyone. *We were lucky yet again*, Esther thought, *when Maude came strolling into Matthew's life*. She's added so much love to the family.

If only Harry and George could find lovely women like her. Esther's spirits dropped slightly when she thought of her two bachelor sons now sitting opposite her. It was her great hope this would soon happen, before they got too set in their ways. She didn't want them to be lonely, especially in their old age.

It will happen, she decided, and when they least expect it. Some young woman from somewhere will appear, and perhaps they'll fall in love. She sighed under her breath and pulled herself out of her reverie.

Now Kitty, the senior housemaid, was coming in with a tray which held three soufflés, followed by her two juniors, Fanny and Maureen, also carrying trays of soufflés.

'Thank you, Kitty,' Esther said, smiling at her and the other girls. 'They look wonderful.'

'Yes, they do indeed,' Philip added, and the rest of the family nodded in agreement.

'My mouth is really watering,' Harry said, wondering what Cook's secret was. The soufflés had not dropped, were still beautifully risen, even though they had been carried upstairs. Perhaps that was it. They had not been sent up in the dumbwaiter. *Rushed up*, no doubt, by the maids. Only in a very smart house like this with a cook as talented as Mrs Holmes would they taste something as fancy as a soufflé, and many complimentary comments were made as they ate them. When the roast beef arrived, served with Yorkshire pudding, roast potatoes and Brussels sprouts, the men broke into quiet cheers.

Esther laughed. 'I'm glad you're happy,' she said, looking at her three boys. 'You all asked if we could have a Sunday lunch on a Saturday night. Cook has obliged.'

FOUR

Alexis Malvern stood on the rise that looked down towards Romney Marsh. It was still shrouded in mist, images blurred, indistinct, but when she lifted her eyes and looked beyond, she saw the sea, and further still the faint outline of the French coast. A small smile tugged at her mouth as she recalled how Sebastian had liked to stand here at dusk, pointing out the lights of a foreign land just across the English Channel. This view at twilight had always delighted him.

For days Kent had been cloudy and wet, and Goldenhurst drenched, muddy underfoot in some areas, the last of the late-blooming flowers wilted and limp. Much of the gardens had suffered and been destroyed by the almost constant rainfall. Now, on this Friday afternoon in the first week of October, the sun was shining in a cloudless sky, the colour of their bluebells in May, and a light breeze brought freshness to the air.

Turning, she walked across to the corner of the gardens where she and Sebastian had liked to sit in the arbour nestled there. In summer, masses of blue flowers filled this part of the gardens, and invariably she would silently thank Magdalena Ellis, the talented gardener, who had helped Sebastian to create this oasis of natural beauty.

Leaning back against the bench, she closed her eyes, her grief rising up again. He should have been here with her now, as her husband of one year. Perhaps a baby too. The anniversary of his death had brought it all back again, stronger than ever. Her fiancé had been older than her, with grown-up children of his own, but he had been in the prime of his life and no one had expected pneumonia to kill him.

Shaking her head, she attempted to turn her mind to her imminent guests. She couldn't help wondering if it had been a mistake to invite Jane and Reggie to come for the weekend. There was no doubt in her mind that Jane would start lecturing her once again about why she was living down here in Kent. Or she would start wondering aloud if Alexis was ill and should revisit Doctor Freud in Vienna, asking if Alexis could be heading for another breakdown, perhaps?

A little shiver ran through Alexis at this thought, and she sat up with a jerk, glanced around, blinking.

I'll have to keep them really busy, she decided, as she slumped back, forcing herself to relax. Two days ago she had written a note to Sebastian's eldest daughter Claudia, with an invitation for her and her husband to come for the weekend, dispatching Gates, the new driver, to deliver it. He had returned with an acceptance, much to her relief.

At the thought of her friend, Alexis experienced a sudden lifting of her heart, a lightness of spirit that she rarely enjoyed these days. But then Claudia always brought happiness with her and a special kind of love, like that of an adoring sister. And in her lovely face, Alexis saw Sebastian and felt he was with them, which calmed her. Claudia had been the person who had introduced them and she shared in Alexis's grief for the dynamic man who had died too young.

'So Reggie's coming tomorrow afternoon, is that it?' Alexis asked, pouring more tea in Lady Jane's cup.

'That is correct, my dear. He does apologize, most profusely. However, he must see this American fellow, who owns the largest newspaper in New York City. It's important to Reggie. You know how men are when it comes to business.'

'I do, yes. And how are your girls? I suppose they must be in Italy by now? Claudia is arriving tomorrow, by the way.'

'That's nice. I haven't seen her for ages. Yes, Jasmine and Lilah are very much enjoying Florence and its treasures. My sister was so keen to take them once the Season finished.' There was a pause while Lady Jane took a sip of her tea, then asked in a gentle voice, 'And how is your father? Is he feeling better?'

There was a moment of silence before Alexis answered. 'Yes, he is. I think he has come to grips with his sorrow about Uncle Joshua dying. And shaken off that fatigue that brought him low. Although he's still somewhat angry about that awful betrayal by his cousin. However, my father is a practical man and accepts that life can be difficult.'

'Might we be seeing you in London soon?' Jane murmured, eyeing her friend carefully. 'Your father misses you, darling.'

Alexis laughed, shook her head. 'He's fine, and he doesn't miss me at all. He has Jimmy boy to keep him company.'

Staring at her, puzzlement apparent in her eyes, Lady Jane asked, 'Who on earth is this *Jimmy boy* . . . and why do you call him *that*?'

'Because that's the way I think of him. He's a poor boy

my father has always admired . . . he worked on his father's stalls at the Malvern Market in Camden, but has always had dreams of . . . *glory*, shall we say? Matthew, his father, has forever pushed Jimmy at my father, often suggested that Papa might one day give him a job in the Malvern Company. And naturally my father did just that . . . during the time I was in Vienna, actually.'

Taken aback, Lady Jane gaped at her, speechless for a moment. Finally she said softly, 'Doesn't it trouble you that this Jimmy fellow is there in London, working along-side your father, and you, the heir, are still out here in the depths of Kent?' Jane had wanted to say *doing nothing*, but she did not dare.

'Not really. I think Jimmy boy is a real opportunist, and in a hurry to rush up the ladder. But he'll only get so far. After all, Jane, it is *my* company.'

Lady Jane wanted to say: *But would you be able to run it, since you lack experience?* But Jane put that question to one side for later. Instead she asked in a neutral voice, 'So, tell me about Jimmy boy, Alexis. I'm curious that your father is so taken with him. And what's his real name?'

'James Falconer, and I admit he's talented, even clever. I met him when I went to Paris to help my father deal with the wine problem. But I find him bossy and arrogant. And very conceited.'

'*Conceited?* So he must be a handsome chap . . . is he, Alexis?' Lady Jane probed.

'Not particularly,' Alexis said, and changed the subject abruptly.

Lady Jane stood in the sitting room of her suite, staring out of the window. The view of the gardens was extra-ordinary, although she was not really seeing it. Her mind was caught up in the conversation she had just had with Alexis over afternoon tea.

The situation between Alexis and her father troubled her, and had done for a long time. Until today she had been reluctant to say too much. By nature she was discreet, diplomatic and only ever wanted to make her friend, all of her friends, in fact, feel happy. She did not wish to present their problems to them on a plate, so to speak, and dissect them.

Jane, born Cadwalander, was a handsome rather than beautiful woman, who dressed strikingly and stylishly to her advantage. Now in her thirties, she was the eldest daughter of the most renowned and brilliant barrister in England's Courts of Justice, Louis Cadwalander, long considered a great star of the courtroom. When Louis's wife, Estelle, died unexpectedly and very suddenly, it was to their eldest child he turned. This was his fourteen-year-old daughter, Jane. Very simply, he told her to take charge of the household and run it the way her mother had. Jane did so without flinching. She became the chatelaine, managed the butler, the housekeeper, the maids and the gardeners, and brought up her younger siblings. The children did as they were told and called her The General, at first behind her back and then to her face. And she didn't mind that, and laughed; she thought of it as a compliment.

When Reggie met her, it was love at first sight for them both, and soon he was calling her The General, too, in the most admiring way. He thought she was quite a marvel. And to him she still was. Now she was his private general, her siblings having grown up, but her own twin sons – their little miracles – were now her charges.

Moving away from the window, Jane settled in an armchair in front of the fire. Her thoughts focused on Alexis Malvern. Deep down inside, Jane was upset with Alexis. She believed it was time she pulled herself together and went back to London, worked alongside her father, learning to run the Malvern business. After all,

warming his hands against the flames. 'All I had to do was order the carriage and jump in.' Happiness flooded his face. 'So here I am, with the woman I love, sooner than expected.'

Jane reached out and grasped his hand. 'Did you see Alexis?'

He nodded. 'I said we'd see her at dinner.'

'Reggie, there's something I need to ask you,' Jane began and then stopped.

He looked at her alertly, catching the tone of her voice, but he replied mildly, 'Go ahead, ask away.'

'Does George Falconer have any relatives?'

'Well I'm sure he has a mother and father,' Reggie responded, smiling, suddenly looking faintly amused.

'I know *that*, of course! Please don't tease me. This is important. Can you tell me what you know about George? After all he is one of your favourites on the newspaper.'

Nodding, Reggie was thoughtful before saying, 'He has two brothers. One owns a café; the other, the eldest I believe, has stalls at one of the markets.'

'What about nieces? Nephews?'

'I believe he does have some. Actually, I met his oldest nephew some time ago. Bumped into them near the Bettrage Hotel in Mayfair.'

Jane sat waiting, holding her breath, her eyes riveted on her husband.

Lord Reginald was frowning. Eventually he said, 'Now I *remember* . . . they were coming out of the hotel and it was the young man I noticed first. Then suddenly, there was George, speaking to me and introducing the young fellow. I was taken aback, actually.'

'Why were you surprised?'

'I was startled by the young man. If I hadn't known better, I would have said he was the scion of some aristocratic family. Tall, good-looking, properly dressed.

32

He had impeccable manners, and what a voice . . . an actor's voice.' Reggie shook his head, and exclaimed, 'Come to think about it, he had a voice that resembles your father's. Mellifluous. Put him in a courtroom and – with those looks and that voice – he would be like your father. He'd win every case.'

Jane had a surprised expression on her face, could not speak. After a moment, regaining her equilibrium, she said, 'Are you sure it was George's nephew, not someone he was interviewing?'

Laughing, Lord Reginald shook his head rather vehemently. 'I'm sure. Why does this matter to you, Jane? You are being quite intense about this.'

'Did he say, "This is my nephew", or did George introduce him by name?'

'Both. He said this is my nephew, James Falconer.' Again Reggie asked, 'Look, why does this matter so much?'

'Because James Falconer is Henry Malvern's right-hand man. He's been working for him since Alexis went to Vienna to be treated by Dr Sigmund Freud.'

Lord Reggie was silent. After a moment, he took out a cigarette and a match flared. He smoked for a moment or two, then asked, 'Is she afraid of him? Or has she fallen for him?'

'Neither, in my opinion. I believe she dislikes him, looks down on him. Certainly she was derogatory when she spoke to me about him today. She thinks he's an opportunist. She's using him as a reason why her father no longer needs her help.'

'I see.' Reginald, a genius in the world of business and perceptive about people, took a moment before he addressed the matter. 'I have a feeling that James Falconer is a very decent man, if his uncle is anything to go by. I am quite sure he *is* ambitious – and what's wrong with that? He obviously wants to move up in the world. I bet he has been

33

a godsend to Malvern.' He blew smoke into the air and said, 'I'm afraid our friend has been something of a fool. Sitting around here *mooning* . . . for a dead man.'

'I agree, Reggie. However, I don't know how to handle this situation with Alexis any more.'

'She needs a *shock* . . . we have to shock her into coming to her senses. I'll put my thinking cap on.' Looking hard at his beautiful, sensible wife, he continued, 'Now I want to ask you a question, Jane.'

'I will answer you if I can.'

'What do you think about Alexis's view of James Falconer? I know you've not met him, but I've described his manners, his voice, his general appearance. Be honest with me.'

A reflective look came across her face and settled there. She said, 'I think Alexis might have felt a pull towards him, regretted that emotion, and grown afraid of him. Alexis ran.'

'And perhaps she felt guilty regarding Sebastian?'

'Maybe,' Jane agreed, and pursed her mouth. 'She was rather strong about his background; she called him a poor boy and mentioned that he'd worked on the stalls.'

'That's just the snob in her coming out. But truthfully, in my opinion, a relationship between them is out of the question.'

'Don't you think she's got to take her responsibilities seriously, Reggie? You've got to persuade her to go back and help her father, learn how to run the Malvern Company. It's *her* legacy.'

Jane was silent, thinking for a moment. After a pause she said softly, 'I love Alexis. I want to help her, get her better. You know that, don't you?'

'I certainly do. I feel the same, Jane. I really do.'

'What if she remains stubborn, won't budge?'

'Then we'll just have to leave her to lead the life she chooses. It is *her* life, after all. Not ours.'

FIVE

Early on the misty autumnal Saturday morning, before he went riding with Alexis, Lord Reginald promised his wife he would find a way to get Alexis to go back to London.

This promise had helped to relieve Jane's anxiety, and now she sat in front of the fire in the library, reading a book, relaxing, enjoying the quiet and being alone. Thus the unexpected knocking on the door startled her; she glanced across at it, frowning. Instantly it opened to reveal Mrs Bellamy standing there, her manner somewhat hesitant.

In an apologetic voice the housekeeper said, 'So sorry to disturb you, Your Ladyship, but Miss Alexis told me you would give me the menu for supper tonight. If you can spare a moment now, it would be helpful.'

Although she was surprised this task had been left to her, Lady Jane put down her book. 'Yes, of course, Mrs Bellamy. Do come in.' As she spoke, Jane stood and walked over to the small desk. 'Have *you* had any thoughts about it?'

Walking over to join her, Mrs Bellamy replied at once. 'I do know His Lordship likes my lobster and fish pie, and I had thought of that for the main course.'

Turning to her, Jane nodded. 'I like it too, so let's settle on that, Mrs Bellamy.' Writing this down on the piece of paper she had taken out of a drawer, Jane then added, 'It's a bit chillier today, so why not one of your delicious soups first?'

A smile of pleasure slipped onto the housekeeper's face. 'My carrot and ginger soup would be perfect before the pie, m'lady. I'll do some oysters as a between-course too. And what about a plum clafoutis as a dessert, with a cheeseboard to follow?'

'Sounds perfect to me. Thank you so much, Mrs Bellamy.'

'There's just one other thing, m'lady. What time will Miss Claudia and her husband be arriving this afternoon? In time for tea?'

'Oh no, they'll be here for supper. They have to attend an engagement party first, and—' Jane cut her sentence off abruptly. She glanced at Mrs Bellamy as the sound of carriage wheels rattling on the cobblestones outside in the courtyard was heard.

'Are you expecting someone, Your Ladyship?' Mrs Bellamy asked.

'No, I'm not,' Jane murmured. Excusing herself, she hurried down the hallway to the front door and opened it.

A look of enormous surprise crossed her face as she stood on the front steps. *Well, well, well,* she thought.

Walking toward her was a young man in his early twenties, tall and good-looking, with fine features and fair hair.

Lady Jane stepped out into the courtyard and walked forward, smiling at the young man. He extended his hand and said, 'Let me introduce myself, Lady Carpenter. I am James Falconer, and I'm here at the behest of Mr Malvern. I have a letter from him for Miss Malvern.'

Jane stretched out her hand to him. He shook it, and she said, 'I'm very pleased to meet you, Mr Falconer.'

'It is my pleasure, Your Ladyship. If I could speak to Miss Malvern and give her the letter, I can be on my way, Lady Carpenter.'

'She's not here, I'm afraid, but she'll be back fairly soon. You must come in and wait for her. Come along.'

James did not move an inch, although he did reach into his inside jacket pocket and took out an envelope. 'Could you please give her this when she returns? I will have to come back later because Mr Malvern needs her answer today.'

'Why do you say *come back*? You can wait here for her, Mr Falconer. Unless you have somewhere else to go?'

He did not address her question. Instead he said, 'I don't believe Miss Malvern would think that quite appropriate. However, there is one thing I would like if it's not too much trouble . . . could the driver take the carriage to the back, please, so the horses can drink some water? He knows Goldenhurst, and where the trough is.'

'Of course he can, and he might want a drink of water himself, or a cup of tea. And so might you, Mr Falconer,' Jane exclaimed in a brisk manner.

Before James could respond, Broadbent, the butler arrived. 'Can I help with anything, m'lady?'

'I think the horses might need water. Oh, and Broadbent, this is Mr Falconer. He runs the Malvern Company for Mr Malvern.'

Broadbent inclined his head and smiled at James, and said to Jane, 'I know this driver, Your Ladyship. It's Bolland. He works for Mr Malvern.'

'Very good, Broadbent. Thank you. Now that is settled, let's go into the house, Mr Falconer.'

James had no option but to walk alongside Jane and enter the house. She led him along the corridor and into the library. 'I won't be a moment,' she told him, and hurried off.

James looked around the library with interest, admiring the simplicity of the decor, which was clean-lined and soothing. Walking over to the window, he looked out, thinking how well the gardens had been planned. They must be a riot of colour in the summer, he thought.

A moment later, he turned around when Jane entered the room. 'Please, do come and sit down, Mr Falconer. Mrs Bellamy is making a pot of tea.'

'Thank you, Lady Carpenter. That is very kind of you.' He took a seat in the armchair opposite her, and smiled.

She smiled back and couldn't believe the colour of his eyes. They were as blue as cornflowers. Realizing she was staring at him, she said swiftly, 'I know your uncle George. Well, I've met him a few times, to be accurate. My husband likes his work, especially his editorials.'

'That's such a nice thing to hear. I know Uncle George loves *The Chronicle*. My grandmother is always saying he'll never get married because he's married to his newspaper.'

Jane laughed, fascinated by the ease, grace and confidence she discerned in this very good-looking young man. And wondering why Alexis had been so nasty about him. She suddenly knew it had nothing to do with Falconer, in the sense that he was more than likely innocent of any wrongdoing. The fault was probably with Alexis and her troubled mind.

James said, 'I grew up in Kent as a small child, and my great-grandfather, Edward, owned a grocery shop in Rochester. Anyway, it is a beautiful county, especially around here.'

'It is indeed. I love it too. Although we have a house near Cirencester, I still enjoy it here.'

'May I ask you a question, Lady Carpenter?'

'Yes, please do. I'll answer if I can.'

'I couldn't help wondering why you told Mr Broadbent that I ran the Malvern Company.'

'Because you do, don't you? I know Mr Malvern is not well at all, his brother Joshua is dead, his cousin Percy is missing. And his heir, Miss Malvern, is mostly here at Goldenhurst. That leaves *you*, as I see it, in charge.'

'I think Mr Malvern does very well, under the present circumstances, Lady Carpenter. I would prefer to say it's a joint effort, and we do have another good man, Peter Keller, who has taken charge of the Wine Division.' He leaned forward slightly, staring at her. 'I wouldn't want Miss Malvern to think . . . that I was . . .' His voice trailed off and he just shook his head.

Jane thought, oh God, he's right. She'll think he really is an opportunist, and I'm sure he isn't. After a moment Jane gave a small chuckle and, trying to make light of it, she finished his sentence for him. 'She might think you're getting too big for your boots . . . that's what you were going to say, isn't it?'

He nodded and leaned back in the chair. 'I try to do my best,' he said, and then added, 'Basically, I'm following in my great-grandfather's footsteps. I love retailing and I hope to open my own shop one day. A shop like Fortnum and Mason in Piccadilly. That's my ambition.'

'I love Fortnum's!' Lady Jane exclaimed, and thought to add, 'And I'll be your first customer.'

At this moment, Mrs Bellamy came in with the tea tray. Once she had poured for them, she left with a smile and a nod, taking with her the menu Jane had left on the desk.

Jane said, 'I hope I'm not intruding into your life, Mr Falconer, but it sounds to me as if you are planning quite a different career for yourself . . . what I mean is, it sounds as if you will be leaving Malvern's.' She raised a brow and gave him a penetrating look.

'You're not intruding, Lady Carpenter. Everyone knows about my dream . . . but I won't leave Mr Malvern until he's really well again. I wouldn't let him down.'

'I believe I already know that,' Jane said, and changed the subject, asking James if he had any hobbies.

He chuckled at the question and said, 'It's perhaps the same as yours, Lady Carpenter.' He glanced at the book on the desk. 'I love reading, and I'm especially devoted to Dickens. Are you enjoying *Our Mutual Friend*?'

Jane did not answer at once, thinking that James Falconer was full of surprises. Finally she said, 'Yes, I am. Who cannot love his marvellous books?'

The sound of horses' hooves clattering in the yard announced the arrival of Lord Reginald and Alexis. Jane nodded at the window and said, 'They have returned from their ride around the estate . . . Miss Alexis and my husband are about to join us.'

SIX

James, knowing intuitively that Alexis would be angry that he was here at Goldenhurst, immediately stood up. Reaching into his jacket, he took out the letter.

Lady Jane, her eyes fixed on him, saw how intelligent and clever he was. There was no doubt in her mind that he understood Alexis and her complicated mind, her ever-changing moods.

Clearing her throat, Jane looked at James, and said, 'That's the best idea. Give her the letter at once to prevent any aggravation on her part.'

He simply nodded and glanced towards the door as it burst open, and Alexis and Lord Reginald came in from their ride.

They were both obviously completely taken aback at the sight of James. Alexis stopped suddenly, her expression one of alarm. However, Lord Reginald, experienced man of the world that he was, hurried forward, his hand outstretched.

'Falconer, isn't it? How nice to see you again!' he exclaimed, shaking hands with James.

'Thank you, Lord Carpenter,' James said in a calm and steady voice. 'I came on behalf of Mr Malvern. He is quite well, but he wanted to be in touch with Miss Malvern.' He took a step forward, offering the letter to Alexis.

As she took it, she tossed her riding cane and hat to one side and said, 'You could have just left it with Lady Carpenter and returned to London. You didn't have to hang around here.'

Jane flinched at the undercurrent of anger in Alexis's voice, and glanced at her husband, who looked nonplussed at this rudeness.

James said, 'I had to wait for your answer, Miss Malvern. Those were your father's instructions, and he told me he wishes to have your reply in writing.'

This last comment appeared to surprise Alexis, her face changing. She simply answered, 'Oh, I see. I'll be back in a moment.' Looking at Jane, she added, 'Excuse me,' and left without another word.

Once they were alone, Lord Reggie stared at Jane and raised a brow. 'Bit abrupt, wouldn't you say?'

'Yes, indeed.' Turning to James, she went on, 'Let's not stand here waiting.' She motioned to James. 'Please, sit down, Mr Falconer, and you too, darling,' she finished, smiling at her husband.

Both men did as she suggested, and after a moment, pushing down his annoyance with Alexis, Reggie said, 'It's almost tea-time, Jane. Ring for Mrs Bellamy or Broadbent, would you please? Falconer must be hungry, and he's got a long trip ahead of him this afternoon.'

James shook his head vehemently. 'That is a very kind thought, Lord Carpenter, but I must leave when Miss Malvern comes back with her reply. Her father is very anxious to have her thoughts on a certain matter.'

'I understand!' Jane exclaimed. 'Only too well.' Rising, she continued, 'Please excuse me for a few minutes. I am going to ask Mrs Bellamy to make sandwiches for you and the driver, and bottles of hot tea. She'll pack everything in a small hamper and you can enjoy it on the return trip.'

'Oh really, Lady Carpenter, that's not necessary. You don't have to go to all that trouble,' James said, looking suddenly worried.

'Yes, I *do*,' Jane responded as she left the library, closing the door quietly behind her.

Lord Reginald moved to sit in a chair closer to James, and confided, 'For eight hundred years the Carpenters have been known for their generosity and kindness to others, and especially for their hospitality. You don't think I'm going to let someone else who's *not* a Carpenter besmirch our reputation, do you?'

When James merely nodded his understanding, Lord Reginald added, with a wry smile, 'I'm afraid some people, when they're upset, are not quite themselves, do odd things, even behave badly. Just put Miss Malvern's rudeness down to that, Falconer.'

'I certainly will, Lord Carpenter. I haven't taken offence.'

'Is Mr Malvern in good health?' Lord Reginald now asked, giving James a penetrating look. The urgency of the letter was troubling him.

'He is. Though he has been a long time recovering from his fatigue. But we're doing various new things in his business, and he urgently needs some signatures and approval from Miss Alexis. That's all I can tell you, sir.'

'I understand.'

Reginald Carpenter was a good judge of character, and he had been impressed with James's demeanour, his quiet steadiness when confronted with Alexis and her curtness. After a moment, he said, 'Do you like your job at the Malvern Company, Falconer?'

'I do, yes, sir.'

'If ever you want a change, come and see me on my paper.'

James smiled, obviously quite flattered. 'I'm afraid I can't write, Lord Carpenter. I'm not gifted like my Uncle George. But I do appreciate your very kind offer.'

'I know you're not a journalist,' Lord Reggie said. 'But we have a division called Management and I know you would fit in very well there. I think you are most probably a good businessman and could tackle any number of problems.'

'Thank you for this extraordinary gesture, Lord Carpenter. But I think it's best for me to stick with retailing.'

Lord Reginald inclined his head. 'Consider the offer always there, Falconer. You see, I like the cut of your jib.'

At this moment, Lady Jane came into the library, her face calmer and her eyes smiling again. 'Mrs Bellamy is doing her best to pack the hamper quickly—'

Jane broke off as Alexis followed her into the room, holding an envelope.

James was already on his feet, as was Lord Reggie.

'Here is the response to my father's letter, Falconer,' Alexis said, her voice not quite as strident as earlier, but her tone still cool.

James took it from her, and inclined his head. 'Thank you, Miss Malvern. I shall be going now.'

Alexis simply nodded, and walked to the other side of the library, where she stood looking out of the window.

Lady Jane glanced at her husband then said, 'Come along, Mr Falconer. I will take you to the stables round the back of the house, where your carriage is waiting.'

'Thank you, Lady Carpenter,' James replied with a smile. 'And thank you also for your kind hospitality earlier.'

As the two of them walked towards the door, Lord Reginald said, 'Wait for me, I'm coming with you.'

The three of them walked to the stable block in silence. It was only when they entered the cobbled yard that Lady Jane spoke. 'I'm so sorry that Miss Malvern seems out of sorts . . .' She let her voice trail off, not wishing to make apologies for her hostess, who had behaved badly.

Lord Reginald shook James's hand before he stepped up into the waiting carriage. 'Good to see you again, Falconer. Remember what I said.'

'Thank you, sir. I won't forget.'

Jane and Reginald, watching the carriage roll out of the yard, then finally turned and looked at each other as it went out of the gates.

It was Jane who spoke first. 'You like Falconer. You offered him a job, didn't you?'

'As good as. Told him to come and talk to me if he tires of Malvern's. I think he's first rate, Jane. His self-control, his confidence, his impeccable manners are everything I need in my executives, wonderful qualities. Don't you agree?'

'I do indeed. He's a very nice young man. Rather exceptional, in my opinion.'

'Damned right he is, and I can't believe how rude Alexis was to him. She was awful. I hope she doesn't behave like that at the Malvern Company.'

'You seem to have forgotten she doesn't go to work there any more,' said Jane with a laugh. 'I fully believe James Falconer runs the company, and that he's Henry's right-hand man.'

'Then she's a fool, not going to attend to her business . . . the one she'll inherit one day. However, would any woman truly be able to run such a company, with several different divisions?'

Jane shook her head. 'I don't know. She was very involved in it before she became engaged to Sebastian. And I do think she's getting worse, more introspective . . . she seems to be *hiding* down here, and she's still focused on Sebastian. Sadly.'

'As I said, we must find a way to *shock* her into thinking

of her future, get her to move on, unless you believe she should return to Vienna to see Dr Freud.'

'I don't think that would help. We must come up with something . . . *important to her* . . . something that might be at risk,' Jane said.

Lord Reggie came to a stop and turned to his wife to face her. 'I don't know what that could be, but I'll do some hard thinking. Right now, I'd like to go back to the house and up to the nursery. I haven't seen my heirs since breakfast.'

Jane smiled at him, her face suddenly radiant. 'This is the perfect time. They'll have had their afternoon nap, and be ready to smile and gurgle at you, and happily kick their legs in the air.'

Laughing, suddenly feeling much more cheerful, Reggie took hold of Jane's hand. Together they walked back inside, happily silent, and went up to the nursery to see their twin sons, Sebastian and Keir, whom Reggie often referred to as his 'little miracles'.

It was during supper, later that night, that Lord Reginald had a brainwave.

Claudia and her husband, Cornelius Glendenning, known as Connie to his friends, had arrived just in time for supper. Halfway through the main course, Claudia made a reference to a fact Reggie had forgotten.

She was explaining to her husband that her father had *loved* this house, and had built part of it himself. Like everyone else who heard this, Connie was taken by surprise.

'I can't imagine Sebastian on a ladder with a hammer or a paintbrush. He was far too elegant,' Connie said. 'Mind you he was full of surprises, often doing the unexpected.'

As Reggie listened to this brief discussion between

Sebastian's eldest daughter and her husband about Goldenhurst, the relaxed farmhouse that Sebastian had loved so much, it came to him. Reggie suddenly knew what to do, what would shock Alexis to the core. But not yet. The timing had to be right.

He felt himself relaxing, some of the tension of earlier dissipating. Both he and Jane worried about Alexis. What troubled them most was this change in her personality. Once full of charm, she was now often cantankerous.

That had certainly risen to the surface with Falconer. Perhaps it wasn't hatred for him at all. Two sides to a coin, his grandmother Carpenter often said, pointing out that love and hate went together.

The thought lingered in Reggie's head all through supper, knowing Alexis the way he did. If she was attracted to Falconer, she would also feel guilty because she had loved Sebastian so much. But Sebastian had now been dead for over a year, and he of all people would have wanted her to start a *new* life.

We shall see, we shall see, Reggie thought as he sipped the red wine, one of Sebastian's best. The first thing was to see if Alexis would give up this self-imposed isolation from society and immersion in her grief. It might have suited Queen Victoria, but it was quite the wrong course for a woman like Alexis.

SEVEN

'Well, that's that,' Henry Malvern said, looking across at James. 'She's not coming back.' He held the letter in his hand for a moment longer and then threw it in the grate.

The two men were sitting in front of a blazing fire in the library of Henry Malvern's house early on Saturday evening. The roads from Kent had been empty and Bolland had made it in excellent time.

It was James who broke the silence when he said, 'Does she mean never? Or maybe in a few months?'

'The latter, as ever,' Henry responded quietly, and then shook his head. 'But I'm beginning to think she will never come back . . . that she's stringing me along. How say you, Falconer?'

'It's hard to answer that question, sir. Deep down inside, I believe she will realize she has a responsibility to you. And I know she thinks of Malvern's as *her* company. Also, I have a feeling she might eventually get bored sitting in the depths of the Kentish countryside. And as the months pass she might start looking to the future, finally leaving the grief behind.'

'I hope so, for her sake. What kind of life is it, longing

for a dead man?' He sighed deeply. 'I thought she had started to recover after her spell in Vienna, that when she visited France with you on my behalf she was ready to return to the company. No one expected her to vanish again. When I wrote today, urgently needing her approval on the Hull plans and her signature, I thought I'd told her enough about the plans for the future, the things we were doing in order to encourage her, to excite her, to push her into coming back . . . but apparently not.' Throwing James another questioning glance, he asked, 'How was Alexis anyway? Did she look well? Was she dowdy or glamorous? Was she alone or did she have guests?'

'Yes, she did have guests, Mr Malvern. Lord and Lady Carpenter were there and she was expecting Mr and Mrs Glendenning. She didn't look dowdy, but she certainly wasn't what I'd call glamorous in her appearance. She had been riding and was dressed in the appropriate habit, still in mourning colours, of course. However, she appeared to be well . . .' James paused for a moment, wondering how truthful to be. He decided he was going to tell Mr Malvern exactly what happened.

James announced, 'I'm afraid she wasn't particularly happy to see me. She was a bit rude, actually. I let it float over my head, so to speak, and gave her your letter. I waited for her reply and she was glad to see the back of me, I do know that, sir.'

'I'm sorry she was rude, Falconer. You didn't deserve such treatment, since you were there at my request. But I've noticed those angry moods when she has been here in London. Not like her at all . . . not as she used to be, I mean.'

'It's surprising to me she wasn't excited about the idea of a new arcade in Hull,' James volunteered. 'Building something is always a great venture, even an

49

adventure. I can't wait for next year, when we start the construction.'

'Once we've found the site,' Henry reminded him. 'I hope we're ready for the trip up there next week, since your cousin William now has a few good sites for us to view.'

'I'll write to him, sir, and tell him to expect us next Tuesday or Wednesday. Which day do you prefer?'

'Tuesday, and if we have to stay on we will, and come back later in the week.' Henry sighed again and sadness slipped into his eyes. After a moment or two staring into the fire, he said, 'If Alexis doesn't want the company, doesn't want to come and supervise the running of it, even while we're in Hull, if she can't do that herself . . .' He stopped, seemed to choke up. But he shrugged and finished, 'I suppose I should think of selling it.'

'Don't sell it, Mr Malvern. I feel certain Alexis will come to her senses, be back here sooner than you believe.'

Henry rose and walked across to the drinks table, poured cognac into two balloons and carried them back to the fireside. 'Here you are, Falconer, a bit of good old Napoleon. I want to make a toast to the new arcade in Hull.'

James was not a big drinker, but he took the brandy balloon and clinked his glass to Mr Malvern's. 'To the new Malvern arcade.'

'In the City of Gaiety,' Henry added, and took a swallow of the brandy. 'And to all of our other projects,' he added.

James smiled, took a sip of the drink and felt a slight burning in the back of his throat. 'I suppose you are going to spend what's left of tonight with your parents,' Henry murmured, cutting into James's thoughts.

'Yes, I am, sir, when I leave here. I enjoy being at home with my family.'

A fleeting smile crossed Henry's face and was gone.

'I wish I could say the same,' he said in a wistful voice. 'Anyway, Bolland will drive you to Camden Town.'

Paying attention to him and listening to him carefully, James felt a sudden twinge of sadness for Henry Malvern, who was undoubtedly rather lonely. And then it turned into a surge of genuine anger about Alexis, who was being unkind to her father, strange in her behaviour towards him. It was as if she were unaware of his existence these days.

Finally he said, 'Thank you for offering the carriage, sir. I'm grateful for your kindness.'

Although he arrived late, Rossi was so happy to see her brother, she hugged him tightly for a good few minutes, before standing away and staring at him. 'You get better and better,' she said, laughing, holding onto his arm. 'You look like . . . a shiny new penny, James Lionel Falconer, and I'm proud to be your sister.'

'*Adoring* sister,' Eddie corrected her, grinning at his older brother. 'And I agree with her – you gleam, Jimmy, but maybe more like a brass button than a penny.'

James couldn't help laughing at Eddie's comment. After squeezing his younger brother's shoulder affectionately, he walked forward into the cosy kitchen. He stood with his back to the fireplace, enjoying the warmth of the fire blazing up the chimney.

He glanced around, loving everything about this room in which he had grown up: the copper pots, pans and moulds hanging on a wall, gleaming brightly in the light from the gas lamps. The long oak table under the window was set for supper, with ten chairs squeezed around it; closer to him were the big armchairs facing the fire. One of the old leather chairs was his father's favourite; it was where he sat and read the newspaper, enjoyed a glass of beer, finally relaxing after being on his feet all day in the

keeping the name Rendezvous, which was what his café was also called.

'Because everyone has loved the café, they'll recognize the name and come rushing over. You will be flooded with customers.'

Everyone laughed. Picking up his glass of red wine, which he always chose over the beer the other men drank, Philip toasted the women present. His wife Esther, his daughter-in-law Maude, and his granddaughter Rossi. The men joined in, full of smiles.

The stew had been relished, called the best they'd ever eaten, and seconds were served. Later, it was Maude and Esther who cut slices of apple pie and covered them with Bird's custard. The finishing touch was a cup of coffee for those who enjoyed it.

Surveying the table at one moment, looking at each and every member of his family, James Lionel Falconer understood how lucky he was to be part of this clan. In their different ways, they were all quite wonderful. And very special. He loved them and they loved him, and that was all that mattered. Whatever was unfolding in his work, they would support him. If he chose not to take up the extraordinary chance Henry Malvern had offered him, the chance to move on from working the market to being in business, he knew his family would champion him, however risky it might seem. And as for Alexis Malvern? His eyes rested on his parents, Matthew and Maude. The love they had was what he yearned for some day – a love that was kind and true. And nothing about Alexis Malvern made him believe he would find it with her.

PART TWO

True Friendship
London/Hull/
Gloucestershire
1890

EIGHT

James Falconer stood in front of the mirror in his bedroom, giving himself the once-over. He nodded and decided he looked correct, finally admitted he liked his new dark navy-blue suit after all. It had been an investment he'd felt he needed to make, but he'd had to save hard for it.

Straightening his dark navy cravat, he turned away from the mirror and left the bedroom, taking out his pocket watch as he did so. It was exactly five minutes to five. He realized he might as well go down to the street. His colleague and friend Peter Keller was picking him up in a carriage in a few minutes.

He locked the door of the small flat behind him and ran down the stairs. It was a lovely June afternoon. The sun was still shining in a clear blue sky above the tall thin Georgian houses that lined their street, many of them given over to lodgings and apartments like his uncle's. As he stood on the front steps of their building, he suddenly grinned at the sight of Uncle George walking towards him.

'Well, well, well, don't you look the toff,' George said, also grinning. 'And where are you off to, all dressed up and fit to kill?' Then he frowned. 'Must be somewhere special, you're usually working till midnight.'

'I'm going to a supper for Natalya Parkinson – Natalie, as we call her outside the office – who works at Malvern's, as you know. Her aunt is Mrs Lorne, the well-known philanthropist. She's giving a little celebration because Mr Malvern has put Natalie on the Hull team.' James winked. 'At my suggestion. She's going to work with me on the building of the new arcade, as my assistant.'

'Good for you, I feel pleased you know how to delegate. You got Keller promoted. I know that.'

James nodded. 'The Wine Division needed someone to take over. And he deserved it. Look, here he comes now. At least I think he's in this carriage coming down the street. We're going together.'

When the carriage came to a stop, the window came down, and Peter Keller looked out at them.

'Good evening,' he said, opening the door. To James he murmured, 'I didn't know your uncle was coming.'

'He's not. He's just arrived back from the newspaper.' James squeezed George's arm and said, 'See you later, Uncle George.'

'Have a good time, lads. Nice to see you, Keller,' George answered and went into the building.

Climbing into the carriage, James sat down opposite Peter Keller and pulled the door closed. Settling against the seatback, he said, 'I'm very glad you agreed to come. You seemed a bit hesitant at first.'

'I think I was. I don't know any of the other guests. Only Miss Parkinson.' He gave James a sheepish look, and added, 'Whom I like a lot, actually.'

James smiled. 'I know you do, and I suspect Natalie likes you too.'

'How do you know? Did she tell you?'

'In not so many words, but I picked up on it. Trust me.'

'I do. Implicitly.' Keller leant forward, frowning a little. 'Can you tell me something about the other guests? Of course, I know who her aunt is – Mrs Lorne, who does a great deal of charity work. I believe she gives a lot of time and money to good causes.'

'That's true. She's married to an American banker, who is of like mind. Also, they're both hospitable. But I think he's in New York at the moment. Irina is Natalie's younger sister. I know she designs evening gowns, and their brother is a scenic designer for the theatre. His name's Alexander, but they call him Sandro. The last guest I know of is Aubrey Williamson. He's a barrister.'

'So you can help me through,' Keller remarked. He sat back against the seat and explained, 'I'm always a bit shy socially, especially when I'm meeting new people.' He shrugged. 'I don't really know why, unless it's because I was an only child and we didn't socialize very much.'

'That's probably the reason. But you'll be fine this evening. Just stick close to me. We'll circulate, do the best we can.'

'That I will,' Keller told him.

James simply smiled and glanced out of the window. The carriage was going in the direction of Chelsea, where the Lorne house was located. He had only been there a few times. He was glad to have the company of Peter. Over the past year, they had become close friends, often had supper together, and went to the theatre or the variety shows. They lived in an overwhelmingly man's world, one in which men socialized together, and travelled abroad or in England, supporting each other, enjoying large or small get-togethers.

He himself missed his cousin, William Venables, who still lived in Hull and rarely came to London. He smiled inwardly. Now that the Hull arcade was under way, he would see more of William, he hoped.

Keller had had a sad life as a child, James knew that. His parents had been killed in an accident in India, and he had been brought back to England by his nanny. The two of them had lived with his maternal grandmother. She had loved him, looked after him well, but he had been a lonely boy. For all that, he was quietly friendly and was one of the best-informed people James knew. Keller was a voracious reader, devoured books and was always seeking knowledge. He had told James there had been a truly nice teacher at Rugby, who had mentored him, been a big influence on him in those years. 'Mr Parsons helped me to open up,' he had told him once. 'He gave me self-confidence and told me to value myself, to have the belief that I could do anything if I really tried.'

James was convinced that that teacher at Rugby had put Peter Keller on the right path and that was why he had done so well at Malvern's. Certainly he had got the Wine Division back on track this past year, for which James was grateful. Peter was twenty-three and would soon be twenty-four, but at times he seemed older than that. Perhaps because of his childhood years. Shorter than James, he had dark hair and a serious face.

How lucky I am, James suddenly thought. I have a big family around me, who have always been there for me, had my back and given me the greatest start in life. Last month, at the end of May, they had celebrated his twentieth birthday with love and generosity.

'I believe we've arrived,' Peter Keller announced as the carriage came to a stop.

Pulling himself out of his reverie, James agreed. 'Indeed we have,' he said. 'So, brace yourself Keller! Let's go inside and knock 'em dead!'

Francesca Lorne paused under the arched entrance to the drawing room, catching her breath in surprise and pleasure. The late afternoon sun was slowly fading, its last rays filling the room with sudden brilliant light, giving it a burnished look. Everything gleamed.

It occurred to her that the room looked different this evening and, of course, it did. Irina, her niece, had been at work. She had filled it with numerous vases of flowers, rearranged certain objects of art, and put new cushions on the sofas and chairs; done one of her 'fix-ups', as she called them. Irina could do wonders with quite ordinary things, bringing new life to any room in this house.

Francesca loved Irina and her sister Natalya, as if they were her own daughters. And, in a sense, they were. She and her husband Michael were childless and had brought them up for the past eleven years and had helped to make them who they were today.

When Francesca's brother, Maurice, and his Russian wife, Kat, had decided to move to Shanghai, the girls had not wanted to go. They had begged their parents to let them stay in London with their aunt and uncle.

Francesca and Michael were genuinely happy to become their guardians and to bring them into their home to live with them. Maurice and Kat had been relieved and touched by this generous offer, and the girls had been well educated and looked after with great care and affection. Natalie, at twenty-five the elder of the two, had sometimes mothered Irina to a certain extent. But it was to Aunt Francesca that they usually turned for advice. Now grown-up young women, they were lovely to look at and a joy to be around. They still lived at the Chelsea house with their aunt and uncle.

The sound of a carriage coming to a stop outside made Francesca turn around. She saw Violet, the housekeeper, hurrying across the hall to the front door. Natalie and Irina were coming down the staircase, as usual well dressed and perfectly groomed, Natalie wearing a fashionably cut dress in palest yellow silk and Irina a gown made from a pretty cream silk with tiny green sprigs.

The two of them were smiling broadly as they stopped next to Aunt Cheska, as they called her. At the same moment, Violet opened the front door to admit James Falconer and Peter Keller.

After introductions had been made, Francesca ushered them all into the drawing room. 'Let us wait in here for the other guests to arrive . . . I'm so pleased you are punctual. It always upsets Cook when we have latecomers – she doesn't like to have her best dishes ruined.'

Keller, wanting to join in and be sociable immediately, said, 'I understand how Cook feels. After all the great effort she must put in, it would be such a disappointment for her.'

Francesca smiled at him warmly. 'I like thoughtful young men. Now come along, Mr Keller, and tell me all about yourself. Let's sit over there by the French doors.'

James quickly glanced around the drawing room. He had seen great beauty and stylishness but had not yet had any time to take in the details. Primrose-yellow walls, touches of pinks and greens, a marvellous airiness and pale colours which were uplifting. He had never seen a room quite like this before, and unexpectedly he felt a sudden lightness of spirit. He was always aware of his surroundings. He preferred beautiful places, which soothed him.

Aware of someone beside him, he turned around swiftly. Irina Parkinson stood next to him. He stared at her, seeing her properly for the first time. She was tall and svelte, and her abundant brown hair was swept up into a mass of silky curls on top of her head. Her eyes were remarkable: very dark, framed by thick lashes. While she was not a great beauty in the current fashion, Irina had lovely features, and her dark eyes and high cheekbones gave her an exotic look that he found fascinating. 'I'm sorry, I don't mean to be rude . . . I'm afraid I got caught up with this room. It's lovely, Miss Parkinson.'

'I'm glad you like it, Mr Falconer, and you weren't rude, not at all.'

'So many flowers, so many unique objects.' He glanced at a mahogany table and asked, 'What are these objects here? I've never seen anything like them, not even at the estate sales I used to go to in the country with my father years ago.'

Irina stepped closer to the table and beckoned to him. 'They are icons,' she explained. 'Pictures of a sacred or sanctified person. They are traditional to the Eastern Christian church, especially the Russian church.'

'They are so beautifully painted, every detail perfect and in such rich colours. As for the frames, they are works of art in themselves,' James said, peering at the icons. 'And there are so many. Obviously your aunt collects them,' he finished, straightening, looking at her.

'No, she doesn't, actually. These icons belong to me and Natalie. They were given to us by our mother. She uses the name Kat, but she was christened Ekaterina. You see, she is descended from the Shuvalovs, as are we. We are half-Russian through our mother's side of the family.'

James nodded. 'Of course. Now I remember! Your sister did once make a remark to me about being from an old Russian family, but she never told me anything more, nor alluded to it again. It was something said in passing, and it never came up later.'

He felt a sudden pull to her, wanting to know her better.

Realizing he was staring at her, he went on quickly. 'So how did an old Russian family come to live in London?'

She was silent for a moment or two, gazing at him.

James said, 'I do apologize. I must sound very nosy and rude. It's just that—'

She interrupted him with a small, quiet laugh and shook her head. 'No, not in the slightest. I am happy to tell you the whole story. And I'd better make it quick before the other guests arrive.

'It was my great-grandfather, Konstantin Shuvalov, who first came here. He was a courtier in the Romanov court, and was posted here in 1850 as the Russian ambassador to London. My great-grandmother was called Zenia and they had one son, my grandfather, Nicholas Shuvalov. My great-grandfather had been educated at Eton and so he sent his son there too, ensuring he spoke excellent English. Nicholas was the father of my mother Kat and her sister Olga, who now lives in Russia.'

Irina broke off as she heard voices echoing in the hall and noticed her aunt hurrying across the room.

'Excuse me, Mr Falconer, but I have to go and greet the new arrivals. I'll tell you more about the Shuvalovs later.'

'I'll hold you to that!' James exclaimed.

Irina turned around and smiled at him. It was a lovely smile that filled her face with radiance.

James smiled back and felt his heart lifting, something he had not experienced for a few years.

After the three women went out into the entrance hall, Keller joined James, who had remained standing next to the mahogany table where the icons were displayed. Keller was immediately interested in them. After studying them for a moment, he said, 'What a splendid collection of icons! Many of them must be very old, I think, and highly valuable.'

'I didn't even know what they were,' James admitted, pursing his mouth, shaking his head. 'You are truly amazing, Keller. Your knowledge is extraordinary.'

'Mrs Lorne must enjoy collecting them,' Keller answered, as usual low-key.

'Oh, they're not hers, actually,' James informed him. 'I thought the same as you, but Irina told me they belong to her and Natalie. Their mother gave the icons to them. You see, through their mother's side of the family, they are descended from the Shuvalovs, apparently a well-known and ancient Russian family. Their great-grandfather was the Russian ambassador to London in the 1850s.'

'How interesting – so he was here during the Crimean War. He was probably glad to be well away from the area, just as many Russian intellectuals are now – fleeing the censorship that has been imposed by Alexander III.'

Impressed by his friend's knowledge, James fell silent as their hostess returned with her nieces, ushering three other people into the drawing room. Her nephew Sandro, the elder brother of her nieces at twenty-eight, was followed by a good-looking couple. James felt certain they were Aubrey and Rebecca Williamson.

After greetings and introductions had been made, Francesca Lorne led the Williamsons down to the far end of the room, opening the French doors which revealed the garden. They went outside together.

James stepped forward to speak to Irina's brother, greeting Alexander by his surname, as was the custom. 'I'm delighted to see you, Parkinson. Natalie tells me you're doing the scenery for a new play.'

'Pleasure to see *you* here tonight, Falconer,' Alexander answered. 'And I haven't quite made my deal yet. However, I am hoping.' Glancing at Keller, who was talking to Irina, obviously about the icons, he went on. 'Your colleague appears to be a nice chap.' Lowering his voice, he added, 'I have a feeling Natalie rather likes him, not that she's admitted that to me. Yet . . .' He raised a dark brow. 'What say you, Falconer?'

'She finds him rather shy, which he is in a way. I like him tremendously. He works hard; he's a good chap. And most definitely true blue.' A smile surfaced on James's face, and he said *sotto voce*, 'It wouldn't surprise me if they hit it off. He's her type.'

'And what's that?' Parkinson asked, his curiosity apparent.

'Serious without being stuffy, highly intelligent, honest as the day is long, and not a bad bone in his body. I appreciate him, and he's taken a great burden off my back. He's turned the Wine Division around and managed to bring it up to par in Le Havre, where we've had problems.'

Before Alexander could say anything, Natalie returned to the drawing room and, standing next to her brother and James, told them, 'Cook is happy. I'd even go so far as to say delirious . . . because all the guests have arrived. No spoiled dishes *ce soir*.'

'I hope I'm sitting next to you,' James said, as he noticed Mrs Lorne bringing the other guests inside.

'You must wait and see,' Natalie replied, and took hold of her brother's arm. 'Let us lead the way, Sandro.'

NINE

James followed Natalie across the front entrance hall, flagged in black-and-white marble, somewhat reluctant to leave the lovely drawing room. Although he had been to Mrs Lorne's house several times, he had previously only ever been entertained in the library opposite.

That room was rather masculine, with shelves full of books and dark-green leather sofas and chairs. He had had tea there once, and a meeting with Natalie on another occasion. So seeing the rest of the house today was a revelation to him.

Natalie paused at the doorway of the dining room and whispered, 'You're in for a surprise. Come on, you're going to see how clever Sandro is.' As she spoke she took hold of James's hand and led him inside.

He was indeed taken aback, and drew in his breath as he glanced around. What he saw were the most beautiful murals of garden scenes on all four walls, broken only at the window where narrow green silk draperies hung to the floor, neat and unobtrusive.

The scenes Sandro had painted were true to life: green trees, bushes and lawns. There was a blue sky filled with puffy white clouds and a wonderful mixture of flowers with the blooms in their natural colours: pink roses, delphiniums, daffodils, and tulips of varying hues.

Turning to Natalie, he exclaimed, 'What an amazing effect he has created! I feel as if I am really in the garden, in the middle of it.'

Natalie said rather proudly, 'My brother is probably one of the best scenic designers for the theatre in London.'

'If this room is anything to go by, I would say *the* very best,' James replied, his tone sincere.

'Please everyone, do be seated,' Francesca Lorne announced. 'There is a place card at every setting. It's easy to find your name.'

Within seconds the chairs at the round table were filled.

James was surprised to see he was seated next to Mrs Lorne, on her right, with Aubrey Williamson on her left, positioned between Mrs Lorne and Irina.

Irina gave James a smile as she sat down and then winked at him, which amused him. There was something about this young woman that touched him. It was not just her loveliness, but something else that drew him to her . . . perhaps her warm and welcoming personality. A deep kindness emanated from her. She had a certain aura he could not quite pinpoint.

Well schooled in manners by his Falconer grandmother, James turned at once to his hostess and praised her for her beautifully set table. Silver and crystal sparkled in the candlelight, and the large bowl of pink roses gave off a lovely scent.

'And I must compliment you on the overall beauty of this room, Mrs Lorne. Especially your nephew's murals, which are breathtaking. They are so lifelike I feel I have stepped into the garden, as I just told Natalie.'

'They are unique,' Mrs Lorne murmured. 'Everyone says exactly the same as you. There is no doubt about it, Sandro is genuinely gifted. His theatrical designs are much praised, you know.'

At this moment, the door to the kitchen opened and the housekeeper appeared. Addressing Francesca Lorne, she announced, 'Supper is about to be served, madam.'

'Thank you, Violet. You can all come in. I know we're in for a treat.'

Within seconds, Violet ushered in three young maids in black dresses, white aprons and starched white head-dresses. All were carrying trays laden with dressed crab arranged in well-scrubbed crab shells, decorated on top with sprigs of parsley. The trays were placed on two empty sideboards. The crab was served by two of the maids. The third maid carried around a large platter of sliced brown bread, already buttered.

Violet and one of the maids filled the crystal goblets with white wine, while another poured the water into silver beakers.

Natalie was seated on James's right. When the food had been served, she touched his arm. She said, 'I'm going to Hull on Friday. I wondered if you could come up. I have an idea.'

'What do you mean?' he interrupted, staring at her intently.

'Have you ever thought about Hull? As a way to start out, I mean. With a little shop, a beginning . . .'

He was startled and, for a moment, he couldn't answer. Then he shook his head. 'Aren't you the one? Looking out for me all the time—'

'As you do for me,' she cut in.

'Because you deserve it, Natalie. With Alexis gone to darkest Kent, you've really managed to fill the gap. Even more than that. I appreciate your efforts, and so does Mr Malvern.' He let out a deep sigh and a sudden look of sadness crept onto his face.

'Let's not go there this evening,' Natalie whispered softly. 'Anyway, I want to tell you something else. I'm going to create . . . *a posse* . . . for you.'

He frowned. 'I don't understand you.'

'A sort of . . . team, but let's say no more for the moment. And I think you should tell my aunt about . . . *your dream.*'

'Why?' He shook his head. 'She wouldn't be interested.'

'Yes, she would. She's a great believer in ambition, drive and determination – all that motivates you. Tell her you enjoyed the book she gave you. She's got another one for you, I think. So go on, speak to her, James. Aunt Cheska can be useful.'

As the first course was cleared, she engaged Sandro by saying, 'James says he feels he can walk right into your gardens. He's very impressed by your talent, which *I* call your "genius".'

Her brother laughed. 'You're the best flatterer I've ever met, my sweet girl. Anyway, it was nice of him.' Leaning closer, he asked in a low tone, 'Are you interested in Peter Keller? You can confide in me. I'll keep it a secret.'

Natalie gave him a long, cool stare. 'I think he's a little shy. Inviting him tonight was a way to get him into my orbit. I needed him to see me out of the office and in a different light. I hope he has.'

'I know it. He hasn't been able to take his eyes off you, although I must say he's been rather discreet, not too obvious. You'd better make the first move, though, or it might never happen.'

'I've thought of doing that. On the other hand, I don't want to look pushy, or like some of those predatory women we both know.'

'You can do it in your lovely ladylike manner. He won't take offence or misunderstand you. Actually he might be glad – relieved – if you make the first move. I can

70

guarantee that he is interested in you; I think he just doesn't know how to go from here. A lot of men I know are a bit afraid of rejection.'

'Yes, I realize that. Maybe I'll take Aunt Cheska into my confidence . . .' Natalie broke off and bit her lip; gazing at her brother, she dropped her voice as she abruptly changed the subject. 'Don't you think Michael has been away rather a long time? His trips to New York have always been fast – two to three weeks and then back here. He once told me it was like a quick skip and a jump. And he always seemed glad to be back.'

'You're right.' Her brother frowned and straightened a spoon in front of him. 'They haven't been getting along, from what I understand.'

'Oh no!' she stared at Sandro. 'How do you know?'

'I picked up on one or two things.'

Natalie looked across at her aunt, who was deep in conversation now with James Falconer. Surely her aunt's long marriage was not in danger?

It was a jolly evening. Everyone appeared to get on well, enjoying the company and the delicious food. James relaxed and, as he talked to Natalie and glanced across the table, he reflected how his life had changed. Only five years ago he had still been working on the market. Now, he was dining with the descendants of the Russian ambassador.

TEN

Although he liked to converse and exchange ideas and viewpoints at social gatherings, James Falconer was also an observer by nature.

Now, after the lovely supper, he sat in a chair near the French doors in the drawing room, enjoying his surroundings. And watching the other people present. Discreetly.

Coffee, tea, lemonade, cognac and water had been offered. He had taken a silver beaker of water, always wanting to be absolutely in control of himself. He rarely drank more than a glass of liquor or wine.

As he sipped the water, James focused his attention on Aubrey Williamson, standing at the other end of the drawing room, thinking again what a good-looking man he was. He was certainly dressed in the height of current style. The black suit he wore was so impeccably cut it could only have come from one of the great tailors of Savile Row. In his mind's eye, James could easily imagine Williamson in his flowing black gown and grey-whitish wig, holding forth in a court of law. Commander of all he surveyed, no doubt.

Francesca Lorne had told him quietly, during supper, that he was a much sought-after barrister, and that prosecutors were loath to confront him when he was defending a client. Williamson rarely lost a case. Francesca had chuckled then, and explained that the name of his firm was Saunders, Thompson and Browning and that the initials spelled *stab*. Which he was prone to do. *Verbally.*

James had laughed with her and paid attention to him for the rest of the meal, catching everything Williamson did and said when he could do so politely. The man had great charisma, an outgoing personality and was extremely eloquent as well. No wonder he won so many cases.

Williamson's wife was an elegant woman, and quite pretty in a cool, blonde way. She smiled a lot, nodded and joined in when engaged by her dinner partners, Peter Keller and Sandro. But she was obviously in total awe of her husband. James could see that; he noticed her deference. He was fascinated by the blend of personalities here – different, he knew, to the aristocratic visitors at the house in which his grandparents worked.

'Can I join you?' Irina asked, walking up behind his chair.

'Of course!' James exclaimed, jumping up, delighted to see her.

She laughed as she sat down.

'I looked around for you,' he explained, lowering himself into the chair. 'But you had disappeared.'

'I went to see Cook to thank her for the superb food, and especially the crab.'

'That was very nice of you,' James said, placing the beaker he was still holding on a small side table.

'Great cooks are hard to find,' Irina said. 'And Mrs Milligan has been very loyal and devoted to Aunt Cheska. But then my aunt is not a difficult woman. She also installed a gas range years ago. Those charcoal-fuelled stoves kill cooks. Their fumes are perilous. All cooks hate them.'

James exclaimed, 'Naturally they do! My grandmother is the head housekeeper for Lady Agatha Montague and she insisted those gas stoves be installed in all the Montague homes. I'm sure you know that the charcoal fumes cause lung disease.'

'Aunt Cheska was aware of it. And aside from saving lives, the gas stoves are cheaper and cleaner.' Irina leaned closer to James and said, 'To change the subject, I promised to explain the Shuvalovs to you.'

He nodded, his smile warm. 'I would love to hear about them.'

'They were . . . well, I suppose I should say they were like landed gentry back in Russia, but basically, they were a family who were loyal and devoted to the Romanovs. They were diplomats and ministers at the Romanov court through many generations. They were very taken with the English – Anglophiles – and many of the boys were sent to Eton. That's how they knew the language. My great-grandfather Konstantin was an ambassador here for many years. So my grandfather Nicholas came with his parents in 1850 and grew up here.'

'So your grandfather is still alive?'

'Oh yes, and so is my grandmother. Anastasia is her name. They are the parents of my mother and her sister Olga. But my aunt is living in Russia at the moment. They were born here. My grandfather only ever went back to Russia for visits. On the surface, he became very much the traditional Englishman.' She laughed. 'At least, I think that he is. He's Russian deep down, of course. He's a lovely man, and he was rather successful . . . in publishing. And that's all of it, more or less.'

Her laughter echoed once more. It was light, lilting and James felt drawn to her. There was something entrancing about Irina, who he knew was twenty-two.

The bloom is on the rose, he couldn't help thinking as he sat gazing at her, her translucent eyes holding his.

A moment later Natalie joined them, bringing Peter Keller with her. James immediately stood up, offering his chair to Natalie. Thanking him, she sat down and announced, 'Our colleague Keller will be part of your *posse*—'

'I still don't quite know what you mean by that,' James exclaimed, cutting across her.

'It means team, group . . . supportive friends. And we'll help you with your first shop.'

'I don't have one,' James shot back swiftly.

'You'll have one sooner than you think, I suspect,' Natalie assured him.

Peter Keller, grinning, interrupted. He said, 'I asked the driver to come back at ten o'clock. I think he might be outside. We have to go, I'm afraid.'

When they went outside, both James and Keller were surprised how bright it was, almost like daylight. The lamplighter had been around, attending to the gas lamps in the street. There was a full moon riding high in the star-littered sky that was as black as ink. It was this summer moon that gave the evening its beauty and brilliance.

'What a sight!' Keller exclaimed, turning to James as they walked down the front steps of the house into the street. 'And such a gorgeous evening.'

'It is indeed,' James agreed, glancing up at the golden orb, and then looking at Peter pointedly. 'Did you invite Natalie to have supper with you? Or accompany you to the theatre?'

'No, I didn't really get a chance,' Keller answered, as he walked towards the carriage.

The driver was standing by the horses and tipped his cap. 'Evening, guv'nors,' he said to Keller and James, and they both greeted him in return.

Once they were settled in the carriage, the driver mounted his seat and set off at a slow pace down the side street. When they were on the wider road, he increased his speed, heading towards Mayfair.

It was James who broke the silence when he looked at Keller, a reflective expression on his face. 'I'm going to speak to Natalie tomorrow and invite them all to supper, at a restaurant. And that includes you. By *all*, I mean her sister Irina, Aunt Cheska and her husband, if he's returned from America. It will be reciprocation for tonight's lovely do, and you'll be in Natalie's company once again – socially, I mean. I know you occasionally run into her at the office, but that doesn't mean a thing. I know she likes you, and I'm going to bring the two of you together.'

When Keller did not respond, James probed, 'Aren't you glad I'm doing this? Or shall I stop interfering in your business with Natalie?'

Keller laughed. 'I don't have any business with Natalie – at least not yet. But with your help, perhaps I just might.'

ELEVEN

As the carriage turned into the long, tree-lined avenue which led up to Courtland Priory, Alexis Malvern opened her reticule and took out Claudia's note again. She reread the most worrying line: *I have a problem that totally overwhelms me. I need your help. Please come to Courtland earlier than planned. I beg you. Love, Claudia.*

All the way here she had worried and wondered what had befallen her dearest friend, the woman who had introduced her to Sebastian in the first place. She had asked Yates, the driver of Claudia's carriage, if everything was all right at the house. He had said it was.

'We're almost there, Miss Alexis,' Tilda said, interrupting her thoughts.

Alexis looked across the carriage at her maid. 'Thank you, Tilda, for managing to get the rest of the packing done so quickly.'

'Since we were coming here for a week anyway, I had done most of it, Miss Alexis,' Tilda responded. 'I like this place.'

'I know you do. It's much more interesting than Kent. I realize how dull it is there for you.'

Tilda simply nodded, not wanting to upset her employer.

But Miss Malvern was right. There was much more going on at this great stately home which belonged to the Trevalian family. It was a huge house on a great estate, one of the grandest houses in England.

Servants galore and guests most weekends. Claudia – or, more correctly, Mrs Cornelius Glendenning – owned it now. She had inherited it from her father in his will. She had been trained to become the chatelaine years ago, after her mother had died, one of the cooks had told Tilda.

The maid thought of it as a fun spot to be, with plenty of footmen and male servants to flirt with. She usually enjoyed her visits with Miss Malvern.

The tree-lined avenue led into the cobbled courtyard of this truly beautiful house, Palladian in style. It was on a slight rise above green lawns which rolled down to a large artificial pond. Reflected in this pond was an image of the house. Not far from the house were the ruins of a priory. Monks had lived there centuries before. It was from this priory that Courtland, which had been built in the 1700s by early Trevalians, took its name. Nearby the priory was the village of Courtland, built for those who worked at the house. It was a charming little village, with a schoolhouse, a church and even a post office for the area. The villagers kept it pristine and pretty with flower-filled gardens.

Even before the carriage came to a halt, Claudia was out on the front steps, waiting anxiously for Alexis. She ran forward to greet her friend as Alexis alighted with the help of Yates, the driver. Tilda stepped out after her and followed the two women, who had linked arms affectionately, into the entrance hall.

Turning to Tilda, Claudia said, 'Miss Malvern has her usual room, Tilda, and you have yours on the floor above. No changes.'

Tilda smiled, thanked her, did a small bob, and looked

at Alexis. 'Shall I go upstairs now, Miss Alexis, and wait for the luggage?'

Alexis nodded. 'And I'm sure Cook will have a little something for you in the kitchen, if you're feeling hungry.'

'Yes, of course she does,' Claudia said. She then glanced at Alexis. 'I'm certain you need to freshen up. I'll wait for you in the conservatory.'

'I won't be long,' Alexis reassured her, and hurried towards the wide staircase which led to the bedroom floors.

Claudia made her way to the conservatory which opened onto the gardens. It was a lovely sunny June day, and brilliant light flowed into the windowed room, where a collection of flowering plants brought a sense of the outside indoors.

It was a comfortable room, with cream-coloured sofas and chairs and a flagged floor of terracotta tiles. On a table was a collection of the latest magazines and novels, and set against the one interior wall was a small mahogany desk that her father had put there years ago. He had liked to do paperwork in the conservatory in the summer, and so did she. Like father, like daughter, she thought.

Walking over to the sofa, Claudia sat down, smoothed the silk skirt of her long lime-green dress, thinking once again how relieved she was that crinolines were not so popular these days. They were rarely worn now, except for a dance or a ball. Madame Valance, who was still her favourite couturière, had led the way, pronouncing the crinoline outdated.

'Here I am,' Alexis exclaimed, hurrying into the room. She had shed her hat and her travelling coat and was wearing a light day dress, made from a muted mauve colour that was often chosen for half-mourning, but which did little for her complexion.

Claudia stood up and went towards her best friend, pushing aside a thought about Alexis's appearance. Her friend had put on weight, and was showing none of her usual elegance. The two women embraced for a few seconds, and then they stepped apart. They stared at each other intently.

It was Alexis who spoke first. 'I've been so worried since Yates arrived yesterday afternoon. There was no way we could leave immediately. I'm sorry, but Tilda was still packing for the week I'll be here.'

'I knew that you wouldn't be able to join me until today. Anyway, Yates did need to stay the night. Two trips would have been too much for him in one day.'

'Tell me what's happened, Claudia darling. Why are you so troubled . . . there's nothing wrong between Connie and you, is there?'

'No, not at all. In fact, this is not about me, but someone else. Let's go outside for a few minutes, and then we'll have afternoon tea. You must be hungry after the long trip.'

'No, I'm fine at the moment,' Alexis assured her.

Claudia opened the French doors and they went outside, following the gravel path that led towards the main lawn. Taking hold of Claudia's hand, Alexis asked, 'Why did you want to come outside?'

'*Privacy.* There's no one here . . . we can't be overheard.'

Frowning, Alexis stared at her. 'Whatever is it? You sound so very troubled.'

'I am.' Biting her lip, frowning, looking as if she was on the verge of tears, Claudia leaned into her friend. In a voice that was low, shaky, she said, 'I am certain that . . . that . . . Marietta is . . . expecting a child.'

'Oh no! Oh my God! How can that be?' Alexis was dumbstruck, stood there shaking her head at this shocking news about Claudia and Lavinia's younger sister.

'When has she been around any men? Why do you think she's got herself into trouble?'

'Lavinia told me last night that she has heard Marietta vomiting. *Morning sickness*, Lavinia suggested. And I have noticed a change in her body. She's put on a bit of weight, but it's mostly her breasts. They look enlarged to me, and also to Lavinia.'

'Has Lavinia confronted her? Have you?'

'No, she hasn't, and I haven't either. I wanted to speak with you first. You're so clever, in so many ways. I just need guidance on how to go about it. How can I make her tell me the truth? Or give me the name of the man?'

'I don't know,' Alexis muttered, alarm reflected in her eyes, her worry escalating. 'I don't think she'll admit to anything – not yet, at least. Not until she is forced to tell you because she's really showing. Oh God, whatever are we going to do? Perhaps she has to be taken abroad, hidden away for the next nine months or so. I could help with that for you, Claudia. Oh, does Connie know?' As she asked this, Alexis felt her chest tighten.

'No, he doesn't, because he's not here, and Lavinia only told me two nights ago. Thank you for offering to take Marietta out of the country, but what do we do about the baby?' Claudia's face clouded over with concern.

'I suppose we would have to get the child adopted.' Taking hold of Claudia's arm, Alexis walked her back to the house. 'Let's go and have a cup of tea and think about this a bit more . . . this is a horrendous dilemma.' She added, 'I have a headache. A cup of tea will help.'

Once they were back in the conservatory, Claudia pulled the bell rope for Kingsley, the butler, who appeared within a few seconds. 'Miss Malvern and I would like to have afternoon tea a bit earlier than usual today, Kingsley. If you could bring it to us now, please,' Claudia said.

He inclined his head. 'Immediately, Miss Claudia,' he answered and disappeared.

Claudia sighed. 'He's known me since I was fifteen, and he can't get out of the habit of referring to me as he did then. It's always *Miss Claudia*, instead of Mrs Glendenning.' She half smiled. 'But Connie doesn't mind.'

'Will you tell Connie?' Alexis asked as she sat down in an armchair.

'I'm not sure. In the meantime, I'd love to know who the man is, Alexis. I really would. We need to discover if he will marry her.'

'Who has she seen lately? Surely it must be someone she knows, not a stranger. Who's been here? Wait a minute, what about Connie's birthday party in February? Some of his friends were here, as well as his family and yours. And . . .' Alexis broke off, a strange expression crossing her face, a look of sudden comprehension in her eyes. '"The twerp" was at the party. I had a long conversation with him.'

'Of course he was there, he's always around. They're like brother and sister; they grew up together. They wouldn't be interested in a . . . *sexual relationship*. I'm really quite certain about that.' Claudia's voice was strong, very firm, her expression positive.

Alexis shook her head vehemently. 'Don't say *that*! Things can suddenly happen. Unexpectedly. A look exchanged, a revelation, a different attitude settling in . . .' Alexis nodded, as if reassuring herself of something. Her eyes narrowed slightly when she gazed at her friend, and reminded her, 'Don't forget why we've called him "the twerp" between ourselves.'

A frown furrowed Claudia's smooth brow and instantly her dark-brown eyes widened. 'Because he is so eager to please, so kind and nice. Too good to be true, Lavinia and

I thought. So we gave him a funny nickname, called him something he wasn't.'

'That was it,' Alexis answered. 'But Anthony Gordon is who he is, very natural, and a very nice young man. And in the three years I've known him, he hasn't changed one iota. And that's why I'm changing my mind. You're right. He would never do anything to risk hurting Marietta. She *is* like his sister – and anyway, he's a gentleman.'

'Gentleman or not, whoever the man is didn't think to protect Marietta. He has taken her virtue and done nothing to prevent this scandal. He couldn't have used any sort of protection,' Claudia pointed out.

'Obviously. Let's strike him out. The twerp, I mean,' Alexis said.

'Done. Now, how are we going to get her to tell us who she lost her virginity to? Please tell me that, Alexis.'

'I will think it through, think of the right way to do it, what to say and how to approach her. And I will speak to her, Claudia. Don't forget, I spent six months being treated by Doctor Sigmund Freud.' Alexis smiled. 'I learned quite a lot from him, how to talk through difficult issues. Just trust me.'

'Oh I do, I do,' Claudia replied, unexpected tears misting her eyes. 'That's why I sent Yates to bring you sooner. Thank you, thank you so much, Alexis. This will ruin her if it comes out.'

TWELVE

The very first time Alexis had come to Courtland Priory with Sebastian, she had gone for early morning walks every day, acquainting herself with the gardens and grounds, and with the rolling Gloucestershire countryside. The estate was beautifully landscaped. She had also enjoyed sitting amongst the ruins of the monks' priory. Ever since, as she had this morning, she had walked over to sit amongst the ancient stones.

She and Claudia had been disappointed last night when Marietta did not come to supper because she did not feel well.

The message was delivered by Lavinia, who actually thought Marietta was being truthful. 'She looks pale, a bit depleted, and thinks she has caught a cold,' Lavinia had explained.

Before Lavinia's arrival, Claudia had warned Alexis to behave as if she knew nothing. 'I just don't want it mentioned at all. Little pigs have big ears, and so do walls.'

Alexis had agreed. The less said the better at this moment in time. And God forbid if any of the staff overheard anything.

Now, leaning back against a piece of broken wall, Alexis

closed her eyes, thinking about the problem, yet at the same time just enjoying the warmth of the sun on her face.

Today was 19 June, a Thursday. Tomorrow Sebastian's sister, Aunt Thea to the girls, would arrive in the afternoon to spend the weekend at the house. Claudia's husband Connie was going to be caught up in a bank event in London and would not be at Courtland until Saturday, Claudia had explained.

Alexis realized the easiest thing to do would be to speak to Marietta today, or early on Friday, before the others arrived. But how would she approach the matter? How to even bring it up? Claudia was depending on her to get the truth, and Alexis did not want to let her down. She believed Marietta might be more likely to confide in Alexis than her older sister, who had brought her up. Less embarrassing, perhaps.

'Good morning, Alexis.'

Alexis sat up with a jerk, and saw none other than the subject of her thoughts standing there in the priory ruins.

'Goodness, Marietta, you startled me! I didn't hear you coming,' Alexis exclaimed, sitting up even straighter, and smiling at her. Marietta looked pretty in a crisp white cotton blouse and a navy skirt that fell to her ankles. 'Please, come and sit down with me. It's been ages since I've seen you. I was sorry to miss you at dinner last night.'

Smiling back, Marietta stepped towards the broken stones and seated herself on a small wall opposite Alexis. 'I know. You've been in Kent, and I miss you, too. I am worried about you, Alexis. I hope you're feeling better.'

'I am, yes . . .' Alexis paused, let out a sigh. 'I'm afraid I do still miss your father though.'

'So do I,' Marietta answered quietly. 'But he's here, you know, deep in my heart, as I know he is in yours.'

Alexis simply nodded, her throat suddenly choked up.

Marietta said, 'I feel his presence here at Courtland at times, and I think he's just in another room where I can't see him. It's comforting.'

Alexis stared at Sebastian's youngest daughter, who looked so like him with her fair hair and large grey eyes, amazed by her comments for a moment. Then she said, 'You've just explained that you feel as I do, Marietta.' Alexis blinked back the incipient tears and noticed that his daughter did too.

Changing the subject, Marietta said, 'Aunt Thea is coming tomorrow, but perhaps Claudia told you already.'

'Yes, she did. And she's hoping that Lady Jane and Lord Reggie will be able to make it over on Saturday for supper, and stay the night. It will be nice to see them.'

'Like old times,' Marietta said, and regretted the remark when she saw the tears welling in Alexis's eyes. Clearing her throat, Marietta asked, 'When will you start living in London again?'

'I don't know. In a few months, perhaps. Maybe not until next year. I miss certain things in London. On the other hand, being in the quiet countryside has been healing, very helpful.'

'I hope you come here more often, Alexis. I love you and I feel you're part of the family.'

Touched by her words, Alexis reached out and took hold of Marietta's hand. 'And I love you, too.' She sat gazing at the seventeen-year-old girl, thinking how lovely she was. She would have been this girl's stepmother had Sebastian lived. In which case the current situation would certainly have been her concern. She studied Marietta and kissed her cheek. It was hard to see any obvious signs she was carrying a child. Had Lavinia been mistaken? Maybe she had had a bout of food poisoning?

'You're staring at me,' Marietta said, half smiling. 'Do I have soot on my face?'

'No, of course not, darling. I was just thinking how beautiful you are. And I've just remembered it's your birthday next month. You're going to be eighteen! How time flies.'

Marietta nodded. 'Claudia wanted to give me a birthday party here at Courtland, perhaps even a dance. But I'm not sure.'

Now, suddenly, Alexis saw an opening to get to the subject of men in general, although she did not believe she could accost this gentle, loving girl and ask her about her life and the possibility of being pregnant. She was so sweet, vulnerable. Alexis just didn't have the heart to probe or accuse her.

Finally, Alexis said, 'However, your sister does know how to give a wonderful party, especially a supper dance. Better than anyone. I loved being at Connie's birthday party in February. I do believe you did too, Marietta. You certainly appeared to be enjoying yourself.'

'Yes, you're right. Everybody had a good time.'

'I must say, you were gorgeous in your pale-blue taffeta gown and those superb aquamarines, with every young man falling all over you, asking you to dance.'

Marietta suddenly turned bright pink, and exclaimed, 'They did, and I felt a little awkward . . . they made such a fuss . . . so silly. I thought all the other girls would hate me.'

'Oh, I don't know about that. Anyway, sometimes it's rather nice to be the centre of attention – rather flattering, actually.'

Alexis eyed Marietta intently, but there was not a flicker of worry in her eyes. Her expression had not changed. Normal, Alexis decided. She's herself, no sign of worry, and certainly there seems to be no extra weight on her.

Alexis felt some of her concern easing away. Perhaps

Marietta had really had food poisoning, or just an upset stomach, not morning sickness at all. Maybe Lavinia had made an error. After all, Claudia's sisters were not worldly, wise or sophisticated. They had led quite a protected life, and had been in mourning for their father, with little socializing until recently.

Realizing that Marietta was staring at her, Alexis swiftly said, 'I was just wondering whether you would be going with Aunt Thea to Scotland this year? You've always enjoyed your holidays with her, haven't you?'

Marietta nodded, and said, 'Yes, Lavinia has, too.'

Standing up, Alexis straightened her grey skirt. 'I think perhaps we ought to go back to the house. Claudia may well be already downstairs in the breakfast room, waiting for us.'

'We had better go,' Marietta agreed, and also rose.

As the two women walked back towards the house, Alexis suddenly said, 'Thinking of Scotland reminds me of the Gordons. Is Dukey coming on Saturday?' Marmaduke Gordon had been one of Sebastian's closest friends.

There was a moment of silence before Marietta spoke. 'Claudia hasn't mentioned him.'

'Perhaps he will, and perhaps Anthony will come with his father. I like Anthony very much; he's such a nice young man,' Alexis confided.

'He has to go to India,' Marietta suddenly said. 'With his father.'

Immediately noticing the slight wobble in Marietta's voice, Alexis glanced at her. She saw the sudden paleness of Marietta's face. Oh my God, she thought, could there be something between her and the twerp after all?

Alexis and Marietta walked into the breakfast room to find Clarence and Lavinia eating boiled eggs and drinking tea.

After greetings were exchanged, Alexis and Marietta helped themselves to the same breakfast as the others and poured themselves some tea. The pretty bone china and gleaming silverware made a welcoming display on the highly polished mahogany table.

Marietta turned to Claudia with an apologetic look. 'I went for a walk earlier and found Alexis sitting in the priory ruins. I had forgotten her fondness for early walks too. So I sat with her and we had a lovely chat. I'm afraid we lost track of the time. Sorry we're late.'

Claudia smiled. 'You're not really. Papa's rule was breakfast from eight to ten, no need to wait for anyone else and everyone serves themselves.' She glanced at Alexis. 'I'm glad you had some nice company.' As she spoke, she raised a brow questioningly.

A little later that morning, Claudia went looking for Alexis and soon found her in the library reading. As she came into the room, she said, 'Can we talk?'

'Of course.' Alexis put down her book.

'What happened in the ruins – I mean, was anything else discussed?' Claudia asked, closing the door, walking over to join Alexis.

'No, it wasn't, I'm afraid. She's such a lovely girl, so sweet and understanding. I just couldn't start probing, asking the relevant questions. It just seemed too awkward.'

'I know what you mean. She's vulnerable and seems very innocent.'

'To be honest with you, Claudia, I'm not sure she *is* pregnant. Perhaps Lavinia has made a mistake . . . made the wrong assumption.'

Claudia sighed. 'Maybe you're right. I certainly hope so.'

After a moment's hesitation, Alexis told her about the way Marietta's voice had wobbled and how she had

89

paled when she spoke about Anthony and his father going to India.

'Oh God, don't tell me it's the twerp! How could it be? Maybe she's just upset because her closest friend is going so far away. What do *you* think, Alexis?'

'Anything is possible. And I won't let you down. I just have to find a nice, gentle way to talk to her, perhaps tomorrow. I have to handle this carefully and with tact.'

'You might not have to do it at all. His father is coming on Saturday night to join Aunt Thea. You know how close Marmaduke and Thea are – always have been, for donkey's years. Then after Belinda, his wife, died, they became inseparable. For eight years now. I know for a fact he's asked her to marry him several times.'

Alexis looked puzzled and said, 'What are you getting at?'

'Knowing Marmaduke Gordon the way I do, because he was one of my father's close friends, and knowing his nature, I think he might be able to help. He's a decent man.'

'Are you suggesting Anthony might tell his father about Marietta's plight? Has already told him?'

'No, not yet. We don't know if the twerp even knows, and I don't think he will confide in his father straightaway. No boy is going to want to own up to this, when it's not what anyone would hope for. But if it is him, we need to ensure Dukey can help us.'

'So what shall I do?' Alexis sounded perplexed.

'Well, if you find the right opportunity to speak with her, you might plunge in. However, if Dukey Gordon has any inkling of it—' Claudia stopped abruptly as the door opened and the butler appeared.

'Excuse me, Miss Claudia, but Cook is ready to see you now about Saturday's supper menu. If it's a convenient time, that is.'

'Thank you, Kingsley,' Claudia answered. 'I will come to the kitchen in a few minutes.'

The butler inclined his head and left the library.

Claudia gave Alexis a very pointed look when she said to her quietly, 'Be prepared for anything on Saturday. I think we might be in for a rocky ride.'

THIRTEEN

'I would jump up and down and clap my hands in the air with joy, if I weren't such an old fogey,' Henry Malvern cried, his sudden laughter filling the air, echoing around the building site.

James Falconer laughed with him and exclaimed, 'But you're not an old fogey, sir, if you don't mind me saying so. And I have the same feeling.'

Malvern smiled, looked around at their surroundings, the shell of what would be shops and a central promenade, and observed, 'And what a really good feeling it is to stand in the middle of this arcade and realize it will be finished in a few months. It's a miracle on your part, James.'

'Not really, Mr Malvern. The builders up here have been great and have kept to their timetable – better than any we've had down south. The architect hasn't let one thing slide, and we mustn't forget Miss Parkinson's constant attention. She has an eagle eye.'

'I know. And I'm aware how hard everyone has worked.'

The two men stood in the centre of the arcade in Hull, which was indeed almost ready. They planned a winter opening. The solid outer brick walls and the roof were in place, as was the wide alleyway down the middle, already covered in flagstones.

There would be ten shops, five on each side of the arcade. Mostly they were for women's day clothes, evening gowns, shoes, handbags, jewellery and hats. Men were catered for with a shop for ready-made tuxedos and evening suits, another for evening dress shirts. The tenth shop was to be for James's sister Rossi, who had now finished a whole new collection of shawls, scarves and capes. James was paying the rent for her and hoped it would allow her to spread her wings.

The architect who had designed the shops had made them the same size. The builders were now working on one side, had five structures that were almost finished. James had asked the construction company to put on extra men for speed, and they had obliged.

A woman's voice called, 'Cooee! Cooee! Here I am. Sorry I'm late.'

Both of them swung around to see Natalie Parkinson hurrying towards them. Wearing a grey tailored coat, and with a feather in her neat hat, she looked smart and respectable. She had a bright smile on her face, as cheerful as usual. That was one of the many things that James liked about her. She was never in a bad mood, always ready to get to work on a project. It was obvious she enjoyed what she did and wanted to excel.

She shook their outstretched hands, and then addressed Mr Malvern. 'It's coming along very well, isn't it, sir?'

'That's almost the understatement of the year, Miss Parkinson. You and James have worked a miracle, which I just told your colleague. I want to thank you for being so devoted to this new asset. I am very glad I came to Hull with James last night. This latest arcade is a sight for sore eyes, really cheers me up. And how lucky that you have your cousin to advise you about Hull, James.

William certainly found us a prize location right in the centre of everything. I'm just sorry I won't be able to come to his supper tonight.'

Natalie glanced at Henry Malvern, looking surprised. 'But I thought you had accepted his invitation, sir.'

A smile touched Malvern's eyes, and he suppressed the laughter bubbling in his throat. 'It's actually other members of the Venables family I'm dining with tonight, Miss Parkinson. William's parents.'

Natalie had the good grace to smile. 'You have such a lot of family up here, Mr Falconer. It must be very special for you.'

James simply nodded. He had very much enjoyed spending time with his aunt and uncle, as well as his friend and cousin William. But not everything in Hull was idyllic. No one ever discussed his cousin Albert. He was the black sheep of the family.

Malvern said, 'Shall we go to our office and go over a few matters? Then I would like to take you both to lunch at the Metropole Hotel.'

James nodded, and Natalie asked, 'Are you definitely leaving tomorrow morning, Mr Malvern?'

'I am, yes. Bolland brought James and me up, and he'll drive me back to London on Saturday. I do believe my carriage is a better means of transport than these steam trains, which are so dirty and uncomfortable.' He shook his head: 'Sometimes newfangled things just don't work as well as the old.'

James and Natalie shared a knowing look but remained silent as the three of them walked down the arcade to the main entrance on the busiest shopping street in Hull.

Whenever she was in Hull, Natalie Parkinson lodged at a comfortable bed-and-breakfast which was close to their small office. The bedrooms were neat and clean, and the beds comfortable. Furthermore, Mrs Pullman, the owner of the B&B, had plenty of good food for breakfast. Natalie was always accompanied by either Lucy Charteris, a young widow, or occasionally by her sister Irina, to ensure her travels were viewed as respectable.

There was a knock on her bedroom door, and Natalie turned away from the mirror and went to open it. Her sister stood there, lovely to look at in a pale lilac silk frock with a fitted bodice, square neckline and short sleeves. The long skirt was straight at the front, with side panels and a small bustle at the back.

'You look ravishing,' Natalie said, admiring her sister. 'James is really going to fancy you tonight, no question about that in my mind.'

Irina appeared puzzled when she repeated, '*Fancy me.* What do you mean?'

'I saw the way he looked at you the night you were at the supper Aunt Cheska gave for me. I think he'd like to pay court to you.'

Irina stood there, silent for a moment, and then she felt the heat rising in her face. She knew she was blushing.

Natalie smiled at her and drew her into the room, making no further comment about James Falconer. After glancing in the mirror once again, she said, 'Just let me get my reticule, and I'm ready to go. Do you like this dress, Irina? Is it the right colour for me?'

'Perfect,' Irina answered. 'I've always liked you in purple, and we sort of blend together, don't you think?'

Turning, staring at her younger sister once more, Natalie nodded. 'We do, and certainly you're very much in fashion. Lilac is the new favourite colour these days.'

Within a few minutes the two young women were out on the main street, walking toward the Tamara restaurant. Irina had never been there and she was looking forward to the evening. Natalie had explained that it had a special flavour, a slightly Russian feeling about it, and that some of the dishes were Russian in origin.

James and William had arrived early, were at the Tamara when the two sisters walked in. It was Natalie who spoke to the head waiter; a moment later he was leading them through the restaurant to the best table. The two men jumped to their feet at once.

Natalie had met William before, as part of the arcade work. Although James's cousin was busy with his own role in his father's business, he had helped them with the site. He was a fair-haired, pleasant-looking man, often eager to show them the sights of Hull. As she greeted William and introduced Irina to him, Natalie couldn't help noticing how James was gazing at her sister, obviously unable to take his eyes off her.

Once they were all seated, William said, 'I have ordered a bottle of French champagne . . . it's a sort of celebration tonight. James just told me how impressed Mr Malvern is with the arcade and the hard work you've both done.'

Natalie smiled at him. 'I don't often have champagne, so this is a real treat, William. Thank you.'

She then looked across at her sister. Irina was glancing at James from under her eyelashes, clearly as fascinated with him as he was with her.

He deserves to find someone, Natalie thought, after what he's been through with Alexis; working closely with Mr Malvern's daughter, she had begun to know her well. Like everyone, Natalie was saddened by her indifference to her father's plight.

James finally took his eyes off Irina and addressed Natalie. 'He's a good chap, you know, Mr M. Very appreciative, and I'm glad he's starting to get better. I just want to please him, help him get on his feet, and he really was happy today. The arcade will be a huge success. I know it in my bones.'

William said, 'Here comes the waiter with the bucket of champagne, and I shall order their best caviar to go with it. What do you think?'

The two sisters smiled and nodded their approval.

After the champagne and caviar had been enjoyed, the four of them perused their menus. It was Irina who suddenly exclaimed, 'Oh, they have borscht! I do enjoy beetroot soup. You told me the chicken Kiev was excellent, Natalie. Shall I try them both?'

It was William who answered first. 'If you feel like enjoying a lovely supper with a Russian flavour, do have them. I am.'

'Yes, I will,' she responded.

'So will I,' Natalie said.

'And I will too,' James announced, and looked again at Irina, mesmerized by her dark eyes. She had a beauty that was very different from the English girls he was introduced to here in Hull, or down in London; her face had a watchful quality, with her dark arched brows and her high cheekbones.

Irina gazed back and slightly parted her lips, running her tongue over her bottom lip. He felt a sudden rush of longing. He also recognized at once that he hadn't felt so titillated by a woman for years.

William and Natalie were talking about Hull, and Irina watched James, wondering why he wasn't engaging her in conversation. He now seemed far away, as if in a dream.

Eventually she leaned in a little and said to him, 'When we get back to London, I shall send you something I bought for you. A gift. It's an icon, a very old one, James, which I found in one of those continental antique shops in Mayfair.'

'A gift,' James repeated, coming out of his reverie. 'A gift for me?'

She nodded. 'I know you were fascinated with them, when you saw ours at Aunt Cheska's.'

'Yes, I was, and that is very generous of you, Irina. I am hoping to invite you and Mrs Lorne to supper once I'm back, if you are both available.'

Irina smiled. 'Thank you so much. I'm sure we can find an evening that would suit us all.'

James glanced at Natalie and, not wishing to be rude or leave her out, he invited her as well. 'You will be back in London early next week. I shall take you all to my uncle's new place, which he recently opened. Uncle Harry will reserve the best table for us at the Restaurant Rendezvous.'

'Thank you, James,' Natalie replied. 'It is so kind of you to invite me. I shall be there.'

They ordered their food, enjoyed every morsel, and finished the bottle of champagne. William was genuinely happy, glad that everyone was having a good time. They laughed and chatted about many things and, as Natalie remarked at one moment, they all got on so well together.

Suddenly, James sat up straighter and exclaimed, 'Oh look, William, the musician who plays the balalaika has arrived.'

'Where?' Irina asked eagerly, glancing around.

'He's just sitting down in the corner over there,' James answered. And as he was speaking, the man began to play his instrument, which sounded like a mandolin.

Natalie and Irina were entranced, listening attentively to the Russian song the musician had begun to play. The four of them relaxed, their attention fully taken, all of them lost in their own thoughts.

Suddenly a harsh voice said, 'Well, well, if it isn't Mr Fancy Pants himself!'

William jumped up at once. He walked around the table,

aiming to silence his brother Albert, who had appeared as if from nowhere.

He spelled trouble; William knew that only too well. He must be controlled at once.

James knew this too. He immediately rose and went around the table, stood next to William, ready for any threatening move Albert might make.

'Good evening, Albert,' James said politely, touching William's arm, wanting him to stay calm.

'So here *you* are in Hull.' Albert glared at his cousin. His jealousy did not seem to have diminished. 'Get out, go away. This is *my* town, not yours,' Albert snarled. He stepped a little closer and lowered his voice. 'You're a rotten sod. You turned my own family against me. Get out of town. If you don't, I'll get you, Falconer.' He laughed harshly. 'I'll get you anyway, one day. Better watch your back, you stinking bastard.'

William, alarmed, not knowing what Albert might do, said in a firm voice, 'Let me escort you back to your table, Albert. We don't want a scene here. Think of the family's good name.'

He took hold of Albert's arm, who instantly shook it off. 'You're a bastard – no brother of mine,' he hissed, his face contorted.

He looked up at James, and sneered, 'I see you're with a juicy pair of tarts as usual, Falconer—'

'That's enough,' William said in a low, hard voice, cutting him off. 'Come along quietly, or Father will hear about this tomorrow morning.' He took hold of Albert's arm hard, and James held the other. Together they frogmarched Albert to a table at the other side of the room, where his wife Anne sat with a well-dressed man and woman.

William nodded to his sister-in-law, who was bright red and obviously embarrassed. 'Hello, William,' she murmured softly. The couple remained silent, but looked appalled.

Albert was wise enough to sit down quietly without causing any more trouble. In his fury and arrogance, he hadn't noticed that everyone in the Tamara was staring at him, disgust on their faces.

William inclined his head to Anne and the couple. 'Have a nice evening,' he said and, taking hold of James's arm, led him back to their table.

Once they were seated, Natalie said, with a frown, 'I didn't know that man was your brother, William. I've seen him before.'

Surprised and suddenly worried, William asked, '*Where?*'

'Hanging around the site . . . months ago, and then quite recently. About two weeks ago, I think. I didn't pay much attention. I thought he was just a local.'

William threw a swift look at James but made no comment. Neither did James.

Irina looked at William and shook her head. 'He's not a bit like you. I would never have guessed he was your brother.'

When no one spoke, Irina blushed. 'Oh, I do hope I haven't said the wrong thing.'

'No, you haven't,' William reassured her, smiling at her, snapping back from his thoughts. 'Everyone says the same thing. Now, let's relax and finish the evening on a happy note. He won't trouble us again, I'm quite certain of that.'

'Yes, relax, Irina, and you too, Natalie. We won't hear a murmur from him,' James said confidently, and thought, *But I will.*

FOURTEEN

Dorothea Trevalian Rayburn, the only sibling of the late Sebastian Trevalian, had been born at Courtland Priory, had grown up there, and had married from there. She considered it to be her home and had always had her own full suite on the bedroom floor.

Since Sebastian's death she had become head of the family, although she did not intrude on Claudia or the role she played as chatelaine. Her niece had run the stately home ever since her mother's death some years ago.

Now, as Thea walked down the grand central staircase and went into the blue-and-white room, created by Sebastian when he had inherited the house, she wondered for the umpteenth time why Marmaduke Gordon had sent a note yesterday. He was asking to come an hour earlier to the supper party. He needed to speak to her privately, the note had said.

The carriage clock on the mantelpiece struck six as Thea walked into the room, glancing around, thinking how beautiful it was this afternoon. Like her late brother, she loved this room, with its play of different blues against the white; in the late-afternoon sunlight, it seemed to sparkle. French doors led to the terrace. She opened them, went out, and stood staring at the lush gardens, a smile of pleasure touching her face. Her favourite pink roses, which opened their buds in June, were in full bloom. Suddenly hearing voices behind her, she swung around and went inside.

The head butler was showing Marmaduke into the room. Inclining his head, he said, 'Mr Gordon has arrived, madam.'

'Thank you, Kingsley,' she replied, and smiled at Marmaduke, who was striding towards her. He did not smile back. She understood at once that this most remarkable tycoon, undoubtedly one of the most successful in England and revered by some, feared by others, was not here on a social call. He needed her help.

Although he moved elegantly and was as usual in control of himself, she instantly saw anxiety in his light-blue eyes, stress reflected on his face.

When the door clicked behind the butler, Marmaduke took her hand and raised it to his lips. Straightening up, he said in a low voice full of tension, 'We've got trouble, you and I, Thea. Bloody awful trouble.'

Stepping away from him, staring hard, she asked, 'You and I? Are you finally leaving me? Is that it?'

A hollow laugh escaped, and he shook his head. 'You'll never get rid of me, and one day you *will* marry me. No, this is not about us. If only it were.'

'What's wrong, Dukey? I know you're keeping yourself in check, but I can see that inside you are very agitated. Please tell me.'

He did not answer her. He simply took hold of her hand and led her out onto the terrace. 'Let's sit over there in the corner where it's quiet, secluded.'

Once they were settled in chairs facing each other, Marmaduke said, 'How're things in this house? Everything all right, is it?'

Slightly puzzled by the question, Thea gave him a hard stare. 'Why yes, of course. When I arrived yesterday I received a warm welcome. I believe all is well, but why are you asking? Do you know something I don't?'

'I think I do.' There was a moment's silence, and then he plunged in. 'As you are aware, my son and your niece have always been in each other's pockets. Seemingly they are now in bed together.'

For a split second, Thea thought she was not hearing him correctly, and then, aware of his grim expression, she felt a cold chill flowing through her. She turned ashen as she assumed the worst. 'You're not telling me Marietta is . . . that they have been intimate, are you?'

'I am.'

'Oh no, that can't be!'

'It is. They slept together. And have been doing so for several months. Since February, in fact. This new development in their relationship started the night of Connie's birthday party, apparently. Here in this very house. In her bedroom, actually.'

'Oh my God! This is scandalous. Whatever were they thinking?'

'They were overcome by desire. So Anthony told me.' Marmaduke shook his head. 'And there's worse.'

'You're not telling me she's . . . expecting?'

He nodded. 'I've drilled it into him to be careful, to protect the women he sees. I told him not to go anywhere near prostitutes. I thought he might get entangled with an eager married woman, or a lonely widow. It never occurred to me it would be Marietta. After all, they grew up together; they are like brother and sister. Or so I thought.'

'He told you this?' she asked, her mouth dry.

'Indeed he did, and at great length,' Duke sighed, rubbing his face with one hand.

'When?' she managed to ask, her voice now shaking. She felt slightly dizzy, completely taken aback, and certainly at a loss about what to do.

'He came to see me on Monday,' Duke told her, 'late in the afternoon. Actually, he said he had come to let me know he couldn't go to India with me, as we'd planned, that he had to remain in London. When I asked him why he had to stay behind, he said to get married. I suppose I looked so staggered that he quickly added he was marrying Marietta because she was carrying his child.'

Thea blew out air, shaking her head. Sudden tears blurred her vision; she blinked, went on, 'What an appalling situation we have on our hands. But at least he told you truthfully, openly.' She pursed her lips. 'And he is being honourable.'

'He's my son,' Duke said in a clipped tone.

'And he's very like you, Duke.'

'Sebastian used to say that Marietta resembled you, Thea. If that's the case, I suppose they were bound to end up with each other, just as you and I have.'

'Whatever are we going to do? How do we solve this?' she asked urgently.

'There will be no sending her away. Or worse, consulting some quack to get rid of it. I don't approve of that and he doesn't either . . . he wants their child.' A slight smile played around Duke's generous mouth. 'My grandchild,' he added. 'And your great-niece or -nephew.'

Leaning forward, pulling herself together, gathering her swimming senses, Thea said, 'We can't let them do this *now*. Get married, I mean. They're terribly young. And it could be ruinous to both our families. A scandal. Everyone will think it's a shotgun wedding. There's been no courtship.'

'I agree with you. On the other hand, they *do* have to get married, you know. And I'm glad it's Marietta, aren't you?' He actually gave her a half-smile for the first time since his arrival.

'I have to admit, I am, because I've always loved Tony . . . but they just can't get married *quickly*. We can't let the world know. Remember Sebastian's distaste for any kind of scandal?'

'I remember it, and I think I might have a halfway decent plan. I came down to the country on Tuesday night, with the two boys, and we talked everything through. I've got an idea that might work. That's one of the reasons I wanted to see you, to tell you about it and hopefully get your approval.'

'You know I trust your judgement implicitly. So explain things to me, darling.'

'I will.' He reached out, took hold of her hand, and squeezed it. 'Just being with you, talking to you about this problem has helped ease the burden, Thea.' He dipped into his jacket pocket and took out a blue leather box, opened it, and showed her the large diamond ring inside. 'This was his mother's engagement ring, which I gave to Helen. Tonight Tony is going to put this ring on Marietta's finger. I want Claudia to announce their engagement this evening, to explain that the supper is a celebration for them. She wanted to surprise us by not telling us in advance. Will she do it?'

'Of course she will. She has no option, really. If not, I will announce it.'

'The second step is *The Times*. The announcement of their engagement will be in the paper early next week. I also aim to ask Reggie to have one of his journalists do a special story on the two of them for *The Chronicle*. It will be a story of a family romance, childhood sweethearts. That kind of story validates them, in a sense, and makes it seem that the sudden engagement is not really sudden at all. I call it saving face. What do you think?'

'It's extremely clever, Duke, and *The Chronicle* is a very respected newspaper.'

'I don't want anyone to think this is a rushed engagement.' Taking a deep breath, Marmaduke continued, 'Next week, let's say the *end* of next week, we must all go to Scotland, where Marietta and Tony will be married in the little church on my property. I trust the vicar who comes to us from the village church. It will be a secret marriage, one which only our two families will know about. And the vicar, who is discreet.'

'But I don't understand why you want that? They can be engaged for a while, surely. And then they can retreat to the country, lead a quiet life until next year. We can have a big wedding a couple of months before the baby is born. Gowns can be made that hide a pregnancy. She's not the only woman who has been in this predicament.'

'I understand that, Thea, and that is also part of my plan, but there is an important reason behind my thinking. Hear me out, please.'

'Yes, of course. Tell me everything.'

'We live in a dangerous world these days, and Tony and I travel to France and various other European countries for business. We might have to go to India. What if something happened to him? Or to both of us? Where would Marietta be if anything happened to my son and they weren't married? Just look at what happened to Sebastian three weeks before he was due to marry.'

'You want the secret marriage now so that she's protected in the event of any . . . tragedy.'

'Correct. I want her legally married to my son as soon as possible so that she's safe no matter what. And my grandchild is safe also.'

'When you travel to India, how long will you be gone?'

'To be honest, I'm not sure. That's why I'm seriously considering a trip next year instead. I might be able to get my Indian partner to come to London.' Duke nodded, as if making a decision. He said, 'Perhaps you'd better work out with Marietta when we could have the public wedding, find out when she's due.'

'I will do that . . . so you mean they would have a proper white wedding here at Courtland, a little later.'

'Exactly.'

'Where is Tony?' Thea asked, her gaze quizzical. 'Did he drive over with you this afternoon?'

'Yes, my dear Thea. He is waiting with his brother in the breakfast room.'

'Perhaps you ought to bring them in here, and I will go upstairs to find Claudia so that you can explain everything to her and Connie.'

'We should do that, darling.' Rising, Marmaduke went over to Thea and offered her his hand. She took it and stood up.

As they crossed the blue-and-white room together, Marmaduke suddenly stopped, stood still and turned Thea to face him. A half-smile played around his mouth and, leaning closer he said, 'We could have a double wedding. Once again, will you marry me, Dorothea?'

She couldn't help laughing. 'I will. One day, Duke, when I'm ready. But not the same day as Marietta and Tony. Certainly not. A bride needs to be the star.'

'But a double wedding would distract everyone, don't you know? Everyone would be looking at *us*, not them.'

Laughing again, Thea led him out into the entrance hall, telling him not to be so silly, as she headed to the staircase.

Claudia stood near the window in the yellow drawing room, her eyes sweeping around her family and guests.

Naturally, all of the men were herded together, making a little clique near the door. Her husband Cornelius was in deep conversation with Marmaduke Gordon, while his sons Anthony and Mark were engaged with Lord Reggie, obviously also in a serious discussion.

A few steps away from her, close to the French doors to the terrace, Aunt Thea and Lady Jane were chatting, whilst Claudia's sisters Marietta and Lavinia were listening to Alexis, who was holding forth about something or other.

For a moment her eyes rested on Marmaduke Gordon – Duke or Dukey to his friends. He had been very close to her father and still was with Reggie.

They had been a threesome, always together in their free time. Marmaduke wasn't an Old Etonian like her father and Reggie, although most people would perhaps think he was. Certainly he had all the right standards, mannerisms and habits, and he was a gentleman.

Marmaduke Gordon, businessman *par excellence*, considered the greatest tycoon in the country at the moment, came from humble beginnings. He was a self-made man who had reached great heights and now held the world in the palm of his hand. And because he had brought his sons up with discipline and love, and given them proper standards to live by, they were honourable young men.

Anthony had stood by Marietta, gone to his father and given him the facts. What a relief it was to Claudia that he wanted to marry her, would marry her without being forced. And the brilliant Marmaduke had come up with the proper solution. One which would work.

Claudia was sure that Alexis would be relieved she didn't have to question Marietta, probe her about her private life. She was well aware that Alexis had been dreading it, especially since she had failed to bring it up earlier in the week.

Now, walking towards the centre of the yellow drawing

room, Claudia cleared her throat several times and then clapped her hands lightly, attempting to get everyone's attention.

'Please, all of you, I have something special to tell you,' Claudia announced, raising her voice slightly.

Instantly everyone stopped talking and turned to look at her.

'Thank you,' she said, and beckoned to Aunt Thea and Cornelius.

They both joined her, stood on each side of her. With a huge smile, Claudia said, 'I didn't explain the reason for the supper tonight, because I wanted to make it a surprise. We all did.'

Turning to her aunt, she slipped her arm through hers, and did the same with Cornelius, drawing him closer to her. 'We would like you to know that this afternoon Marietta and Anthony became engaged to be married.'

There was a collective gasp of surprise and, before anyone could utter a word, Claudia exclaimed, 'Marietta and Tony, please, come and join us.'

As the engaged couple moved forward, Claudia beckoned to Kingsley who was standing to one side, accompanied by two footmen. All three came forward, carrying trays of crystal flutes filled with champagne.

'We thought a toast would be most appropriate,' Cornelius said. 'Before we go in to dinner.'

Aunt Thea added, 'Now that Marietta has Tony's beautiful ring on her finger, there will be an announcement in *The Times* next week . . . but we did want to celebrate tonight before the public announcement.'

Everyone raised their flutes and then they slowly walked to the middle of the room to join the engaged couple. Smiles, loving words, kisses and handshakes. And all the women were admiring Marietta's diamond engagement ring.

Standing slightly away, watching her family and friends, Claudia experienced a rush of emotion, and wished her father were present. But then she let that thought slide away. Instead, she focused on the solution to a huge problem, a scandal averted, and walked over to Marmaduke to whisper her gratitude to him.

She didn't notice Alexis, standing, shocked, her face stricken. Nothing could make it clearer to her that she was no longer central to this family. The engagement had come as a complete shock to her. The role she had been entrusted with – to talk to Marietta, and encourage her confidence – was now redundant. The Trevalians had taken care of their own – and, without intending to, had made clear she was not one of them. Turning, she excused herself. Where, now, did she really belong?

PART THREE

Unexpected Revelations
London/Hull/Kent
1890

lovely man, but I never got to know him. He died when I was five.'

'She did a good job, that's all I can say.' James had great admiration for Peter, who seemed to get better at work every day and was willing to put in long hours.

It occurred to James that perhaps that was the real reason Peter hadn't done anything much about starting a relationship with Natalie. Despite them both seeming interested at the dinner party the previous year, nothing had developed. At the supper next week he would seat them together.

James now said, 'Make the most of my supper next week . . .' He smiled at his friend. 'I'm seating you next to Natalie Parkinson.'

Peter looked at him, his eyes serious. 'Whatever you might think, I do want to get to know her better.'

'Glad to hear that. Do you think I ought to ask Mrs Lorne's husband?'

'I suppose you should. That would be the proper thing to do. However, he was in New York when we went to her house, and I understand he travels extensively.'

'Natalie will be back from Hull tomorrow. I'll check with her then.'

Peter nodded. 'I'd like to go up to Hull with you sometime. I've heard so much about it. You call it the City of Gaiety, so I'm sure I'd enjoy it.'

'That's not a problem – I know we'd have some fun.' A mischievous glint settled in James's eyes, and he went on, 'It must be a weekend when Natalie and Irina are there. We can take them to supper and to one of the summer dances afterwards.' As he said this, James remembered hearing about the summer dances in a park in Kensington. He made a mental note to take the group there after dinner at the Rendezvous next week. He couldn't wait to hold Irina in his arms.

The two of them sat talking a little longer about this trip to Hull, and had just started to discuss the Malvern Company, when Esther came out into the garden and interrupted them.

'It's getting cooler,' she said, as she approached them. 'Will you please come inside now, James, Peter?' Glancing at James, she told him that his grandfather was asking for them. 'I think he might want to have a talk about wines with Peter, and it would be nice, anyway, for him to have your company.'

'We'll come right now, Grans,' James said, getting to his feet.

Peter followed suit and went over to Esther. 'Thank you for a lovely Sunday lunch, Mrs Falconer. I haven't had one for ages and I really enjoyed it.'

Esther smiled at him, linking her arm through his. 'You're always welcome, Peter. My husband and I think of you as being part of the family now. And perhaps you'll come to one of the Saturday suppers. James, don't you think that's a good idea?' As she spoke, Esther glanced over her shoulder at her grandson.

'Yes, I do,' James answered as he followed them into the conservatory and along the corridor which led to the Falconer flat. Esther and Philip had lived there for many years. It was at the end of the Montague house, comfortable and welcoming, their beloved home. It was full of their personal treasures and photographs of the family.

'James, I'm glad to see you looking well. Are you still working long hours?' Esther gave James a severe stare as she poured tea into the delicate bone-china cups that were her pride and joy.

'Yes, Grans, I am, but it's not so bad,' he hastened to reassure her. 'I'm learning a great deal from Mr Malvern.'

'Working with him is extremely good training for you,'

Philip agreed. 'For when you go out on your own. When you're a bit older, of course.'

James attempted to swallow a laugh rising in his throat, but he couldn't. When his laughter subsided, he said, 'You'll not believe this. I might almost be ready to open my own shop. It'll be small, of course, and it's in Hull, not here in London. But I shall hope to take the first steps very soon.'

Both of his grandparents looked startled, and Esther cried, 'How did you find it? And, more to the point, how would you pay for it?' She sounded concerned.

'I would rent, and I have just enough money saved to pay for six months,' James explained. 'I still need to find the perfect premises.'

Philip then asked, 'What about stock? The crucial entity?'

'I'm thinking of selling shawls, capes and scarves made by Rossi and my mother. She'll also have some of the women who work part-time for her make a few daytime dresses eventually. So I think I'll manage. Anyway, it's a beginning of sorts.'

'It certainly is,' Esther agreed. 'Bravo, James! So you are leaving Mr Malvern and going to live in Hull to run a little shop?'

James and Esther knew each other well, and he caught the laughter underneath her words. He said, 'No, I'm continuing to work with Mr Malvern. I have met a young woman who lives in Hull. She could work with me. She is also a designer and has some of her own items she wants to sell. In my shop. As for a wage from me, she's agreed she would work on a commission basis.'

'Well, that's a godsend,' Philip exclaimed. 'I'm relieved you don't have to pay her a wage. Who is she?'

'Her name is Felidia Spelling and she's very nice.' He turned to Esther and added, 'It was your sister, my lovely

Great-Aunt Marina, who recommended her. Felidia does alterations for Great-Aunt Marina, and she gave Felidia a good reference.'

'That's nice to know,' Esther murmured, a smile flickering. 'And congratulations, you seem to have been rather enterprising.'

Over lunch, the family had discussed many things – their employers, neighbours, the slow progress on the new Tower Bridge over the river, as well as Harry's new restaurant.

Now James turned to his Uncle George. 'You must tell everyone where you're going next week, Uncle George, and what it is you're covering for the newspaper.'

'Oh yes, do tell us, Uncle George!' Eddie cried, always eager to ask questions, to be the first to speak out.

'Oh, it's not all that important,' George said in his usual modest way. 'I'm only going to Scotland. To Balmoral, actually.'

'How will you get there?' Eddie asked.

'On a train to Ballater Station and, from there, along with other members of the press, we will be taken to Balmoral Castle.'

'To see Queen Victoria?' asked Eddie, his eyes wide with wonder.

There was a little burst of laughter from the others present, but George answered in the same serious voice. 'No, not exactly. I am covering the arrival of the Prince of Wales, who will be visiting the Queen. They're not always on friendly terms, so my editor thinks it's worth showing Prince Bertie arriving, because obviously they are on speaking terms again. My editor wants to show that mother and son are well disposed to each other.'

'But it's exciting,' Eddie pronounced, smiling at his uncle, whom he much admired.

'It's good for me, for my career on the paper,' George

117

admitted. 'I am standing in for the chief royal correspondent, who is suffering from a bad attack of gout. He has trouble walking and is in great pain.'

'You must tell him to remove all acidic food from his diet and to eat alkaline food,' Esther remarked. She then added, 'No red meat and no alcohol. I can give you a list, if you wish, George.'

Her middle son shook his head. 'I wouldn't dare pass it on,' he answered with a laugh.

Harry said, 'I have always been aware you know an awful lot about food, but I would like that list, Mother. If you'd make it for me, please. It's useful information for a chef.'

'Of course I will,' Esther responded, wondering what he had done with the same list she had given him several years ago.

Once the discussion had finished about the trip to Scotland, the men spoke about politics, comparing Gladstone to Salisbury. They also wondered about the Queen's long residency in Scotland, plus other matters to do with the royal family.

As they parted, they were all still talking, and James walked away from the Montague mansion with a smile on his face. His family meant so much to him. Yet he couldn't help thinking about Irina. He was so drawn to her, so wanted to be in her company. Since the trip to Hull he was beginning to realize he was fascinated by her exotic beauty. This posed a dilemma for him because he was not sure how she felt about him.

Perhaps he would find a way to assess her feelings next week. He had invited her for dinner and he couldn't wait to see her again.

SIXTEEN

Peter Keller's favourite restaurant was called Chez Simone and was named after the owner's wife. She came forward to greet them as they walked in; hurrying behind her was her husband, Gaston.

The couple greeted them effusively. Peter responded in perfect French, which he had learned at boarding school.

As Gaston led them to one of the best tables in a quiet corner, James glanced around. He had forgotten how charming it was, the decor similar to a French country kitchen, according to Peter.

After giving each of them a menu, Gaston said, 'I shall return with a small token of our appreciation.' He had spoken in English for James's benefit, but usually he and Peter conversed in French.

Settling back in the chair, James said, 'I'd forgotten how cosy and cheerful this place is, and very French.'

'Don't forget how good the food is too,' Peter answered, glad that he had invited James here and not taken him to one of his other preferred watering holes.

James and Peter both chose sole meunière and steamed vegetables, but promised Gaston they would let him select a special dessert for them. This brought a smile to the proprietor's face as he hurried towards the kitchen.

Gaston had poured each of them a glass of champagne and, as they sipped it, James and Peter talked about various matters. Henry Malvern had put his cousin Percy's betrayal behind him, and moved on. He was a man who refused to dwell on the past. Soon, however, James leaned closer to Peter and said in a quiet voice, 'To pick up about Malvern's again, I hate to be the bearer of bad news, but I think we'll soon be facing problems in the Property Division.'

Peter was so startled he sat gaping at James without saying a word. Finally he found his voice. 'But the Property Division is showing up very well on the books. I know Edgar Robinson recently audited them. Obviously he didn't see anything wrong.'

'And you won't either, and neither will Mr Malvern. But the Hull expansion, and my own long-term dream, means that I study the real-estate markets very diligently. Soon there is going to be a fall in the prices of houses, flats and especially shops. As for warehouses, they'll be selling at rock bottom. Especially those on the docks in the East End.'

Peter was troubled; he sat shaking his head, a stark expression in his eyes. Eventually he said, 'How can you be sure of this, James; how do you know it's going to happen?'

'I told you. I study the markets. Imports and exports are lower and continue to drop, although so very slowly it's not that noticeable at the moment. Houses in Wimbledon, Kensington and in the Hampstead area will start dropping, losing in value. But it's the warehouses on the docks that will suffer. And we own quite a few. Don't forget *that*.'

'Oh my God, we do! When are you going to tell Mr

Malvern? And what are you going to do about our property holdings?'

'Hopefully Mr Malvern will see the sense in selling a few buildings. Certainly I shall attempt to persuade him to go along with me. If we retrench a little we will protect ourselves.'

Peter frowned. 'How do you focus in on all this? I think you must have some kind of spirit helper whispering in your ear.'

James couldn't help grinning. 'I have a pair of eyes and a strong gut instinct. That's what works for me. I've seen a drop in retail sales in my favourite store, Fortnum and Mason. And we are a little down on sales in our arcades in London. Not in Leeds and Harrogate because the North is doing well. Now, because exports are down, manufacturers are producing fewer goods, which means some workers have been laid off. I know there are a lot of people in need of money. And then there're the farmers. Their profits are down for the same reason. People are skint, can barely afford the necessities of life. England may look booming but it is in the doldrums.'

'I've just lost my appetite for dessert,' Peter muttered, staring at James. 'So how is the Malvern Company going to survive this, might I ask?'

'I don't know yet, but I'll come up with a few ideas. I think we can weather the oncoming storm.'

After leaving Chez Simone, James and Peter walked through the streets of Soho. They'd talked longer than planned and it was later than they'd intended: they would have to go to the second show at the music hall. But they didn't care – they were young and often stayed up late, and the shows were always great at any time.

They were still talking about the difference between the North and South of England and how the North seemed to continue to prosper no matter what, when Peter exclaimed, 'Look! That little street over there. It's a shortcut. I've taken it before. It will save us time, and we'll get to the music hall much quicker.'

James followed the direction of his gaze. 'You know best, since you frequent this area more than I do. So come on then, let's go.'

The two men crossed the road and entered the street. James realized at once that it was dark, more like an alley, narrow and quite long. He wished there were street lamps.

There were no other pedestrians; it was empty. They walked on at a steady pace, their steps sure despite the pitch darkness.

Suddenly Peter grabbed James's arm. 'Don't look round. Keep walking. I believe there's somebody following us.'

'Why follow *us*? It could be someone walking slowly, that's all,' James replied. However, his mind instantly went on total alert. He became fully aware of his surroundings.

'Two men,' Peter said in a low voice. 'It might be ordinary folk or it could be thieves thinking we're an easy target. When I say *now*, I want you to swing around to face them with your hands up, as if you're ready to punch them. Before they hit us.'

'I understand. Go on the attack at once.'

'Yes. And I'll be in the same position. I've studied martial arts and I have a few good manoeuvres.'

'Got it. We'll take them by surprise.'

'Let's walk a few more steps and then we'll make our stand when I say the word.'

James did as Peter said, although inside he was now feeling nervous, remembering the bruisers who had attacked him and his childhood friend Dennis several years ago. Denny had died from his wounds.

'Now!' Peter hissed and swung around.

James followed suit.

They were facing two men dressed entirely in black, barely visible in the dark alley. They were close on their heels. Probably ready to assault them, but Peter's unexpected swivel and his lurch forward had taken the men by surprise. He ran towards the bigger of the two men, shouting tauntingly, 'Come on. Come and get it.'

The heavy-set man took the bait and headed for Peter. The other assailant was not far behind but was panting heavily, seemed less robust.

Just as the first attacker drew closer, ready to punch Peter and start to fight, Peter kicked his right leg in the air. The front of his heavy boot hit the man in the crotch, and very hard. Right on the mark, Peter thought.

The man screamed and bent double, clutching himself, still crying out in pain.

His partner, infuriated, made a dash for James, who was standing to one side. But James had been taught how to fight by his uncles.

He moved swiftly, dodged the punches and skipped out of range. The two men danced around each other. Then James saw his chance. He managed to give his assailant a sudden right-handed punch on the jaw. He kept on punching until the man went down. But the man jumped up quickly, unexpectedly full of vigour, fighting mad.

He attempted to tackle James, but Peter intervened and pulled the mugger away, smashing him on his shoulders and the back of his neck and head. The man crumpled.

Just at that moment, there was the sound of a woman screaming, and then a man's voice shouting, 'Police! Police!'

James glanced down the alley towards the Soho end and saw the couple. They were agitated and gesturing wildly. Then the man ran towards James, obviously determined to help. Before he reached them, the sound of police whistles heralded the arrival of the two coppers on the beat, doing their nightly rounds.

The bruiser Peter had kicked in the groin still lay in a huddled heap on the cobblestones, doubled over and holding himself, groaning. His partner in crime was slumped against a wall. At the sight of the bobbies carrying truncheons and running hell for leather down the alley, he slid down onto the cobbles and covered his face with one arm, trying to protect himself.

When the policemen came to a stop, one of them looked intently at James. Frowning, he stared again, peering at him in the darkness.

'Mr Falconer?' He spoke hesitantly, as if uncertain. 'Surely it can't be you? Surely not.'

James was as surprised as the police officer and stepped closer. 'I'm afraid it is, Sergeant Owen. And here *you* are, come to my rescue yet again.' He stretched out his hand, and the sergeant shook it. It was the same officer who had dealt with a street attack on James three years before.

'This is my new partner, Constable Jerry Cookson. Soho is now my beat.'

James shook hands with Cookson and introduced Keller. 'So, what's happened here, Mr Falconer? It looks as if you've been subjected to an assault.' The sergeant raised a brow.

James nodded. He then stepped towards the man who had come to their aid after shouting for the police. 'Thank you,' he said, glancing at him, offering his hand.

The young man took it. 'It's the least I could do. I wanted to get them.'

Turning back to Sergeant Mick Owen, James explained who the young man was and how he had come running down the alley wanting to assist, to help rescue them.

Sergeant Owen inclined his head. 'Brave of you to do that,' he observed. 'Not many would intervene in the middle of a melee like that. May I have your name and address, please, sir? Just as a witness.' He pulled out his notebook as he spoke.

'My name's Billy Watters, sir.'

Sergeant Owen was taken aback. 'Not *the* Billy Watters, the lightweight boxing champion?'

'That's me.' The young champion grinned.

'Good heavens!' the sergeant exclaimed.

James said, 'I thought I knew your face, but I couldn't quite place you. Nice to meet you.'

The young man said, 'And you too, Mr Falconer. Look, I left my wife standing at the far end of the alley. I'd like to go to her, take her home.' He gave Sergeant Owen a questioning look. 'Is that all right?'

'Yes, go and look after your wife. You might be called as a witness at *their* trial. My constable will take your details.' He glanced at the two assailants, inert on the cobblestones. 'And thank you for being a good citizen.'

'I'll be available, Sergeant Owen.' He looked at Constable Cookson and smiled. The bobby nodded, his expression friendly. He had always admired the boxer.

'So what happened here, Mr Falconer?' the sergeant asked.

'Keller and I had left a Soho restaurant, Chez Simone, and Keller, who knows the area, suggested we take a shortcut down this alley.' James glanced at Peter. 'You can explain the rest, Keller.'

Peter did so. The two policemen listened carefully. When the story was told, Sergeant Owen asked, 'And neither of you knows these two assailants?'

'I've never seen them before,' James answered.

'And I haven't either,' Peter Keller said firmly. 'They're total strangers.'

Constable Cookson said, 'Were you targeted?'

'I don't believe so,' Keller answered.

'And I don't think so either,' James agreed.

'So you were spotted leaving a good restaurant and followed by these two thieves, in all probability, who thought you were easy prey. Is that it?' Sergeant Owen asked, a worried look in his eyes.

There was a moment of silence. James shrugged. 'I think that is the only possible scenario. We're both presentably dressed, obviously had a bit of money on us, and they tracked us down here. That was our mistake and might have been a serious one, if Peter hadn't sensed their presence and come up with a plan.'

'And there was great luck that Billie Watters saw the attack and was courageous enough to get involved,' Peter remarked.

Sergeant Owen nodded vehemently. 'It was a woman screaming that caught our attention. We were nearby.'

'And we heard a man yelling for the police and so we ran,' Constable Cookson explained.

'We'd better cuff these two,' the sergeant announced. He and the constable did so.

The two attackers were then propped up against the wall, and the sergeant addressed them. 'You'll be taken to jail in the police wagon when it comes. You will be tried in a court of law. I am now charging you with assault and battery, with intent to rob. Give me your names.'

Neither man spoke. The sergeant stood waiting, notebook in hand. 'Your names!' he finally shouted, a snarl in his tone.

'Sid Puller,' the heavy-set man muttered.

His partner said, 'Johnny Clark.'

'Give me your addresses,' Sergeant Owen demanded.

'We live on't bleeding streets,' Puller replied. 'We ain't rich, yer knows.'

The sergeant glared at them and stepped away. He beckoned to the constable and said, 'Go to the station and come back with a police wagon. These two need to be behind bars. They're not going to talk.'

'Right away, Sergeant.'

Mick Owen added, 'I'll wait here with Mr Falconer and Mr Keller. It'll be nice to chat for a few minutes. But make it quick, Cookson.'

Once they were alone, Sergeant Owen frowned at James. 'Don't use this shortcut ever again, and don't go down dark streets. They are dangerous. London is the greatest city in the world and it draws people. Good folk, yes, come to enjoy it. But there are bad people, as well. A city like this is a magnet for people from all over the world these days.'

'We know that, Sergeant Owen,' James said. 'We'll be careful.'

'That's good to know. Beware of those who are very bad – foreigners who head here, such as the crooks, criminals and the anarchists out to make trouble – and especially look out for thieves.' He glanced at the two handcuffed assailants. 'Like these two.'

SEVENTEEN

On their way home, James Falconer and Peter Keller agreed not to mention the events of the night before, or talk about it between themselves in the office. It would cause too much chitter-chatter. Also, they did not want Mr Malvern to hear about it because it would undoubtedly upset him. So they put their heads down the next morning and got on with their work, dismissing all thoughts of their assailants, now in police custody.

By four o'clock in the afternoon James felt tired, and his neck and shoulders ached. He was not used to throwing punches and dodging around like a boxer. It was unlike him to leave the office early, but he felt weary and needed to be at home.

Walking down Piccadilly on this lovely July afternoon helped him. He adjusted his posture in an effort to stand taller, and made his way to Half Moon Street. Once inside the flat, he relaxed, took off his jacket, and sat down with *The Chronicle* in the living room.

His hand ached and he rubbed it, closing his eyes for a moment, reliving the rush of adrenaline he had felt on realizing they were being followed. He still carried the scar of the street attack that Sergeant Owen had referred to, which had cost his childhood friend his life. London was a violent city, but he was troubled by this second attack. James's thoughts turned for a moment to Hull.

Opening his eyes, he read the front page and flipped to the inside. He did not look for his uncle's by-line because he had only just left for Scotland. Uncle George was joining the press corps on their jaunt to Balmoral to cover the arrival of the Prince of Wales.

Leaning back in the comfortable armchair, James let the paper drop on the floor and closed his eyes again, his thoughts on the Queen's heir.

He had always had a soft spot for their future king and shared his uncle's opinion that Prince Albert Edward had never been treated properly by his mother.

Seemingly she blamed her son for her husband's premature death after he caught a chill.

Not valid, his uncle had said at the time, and they both still believed this to be the truth.

Unexpected knocking on the front door of the flat caused James to jump up and walk across the room. When he opened the door, he was totally taken aback. Standing there was Irina, looking lovely in a russet-coloured day dress and a matching hat, a vibrant silk shawl hanging from her arms. She had a bright smile on her face.

'Irina,' he exclaimed. 'What a surprise. How nice to see you. Do come in.'

'I'm so sorry to intrude like this,' she said, stepping into the room as he opened the door wider and ushered her inside.

She went on, 'I did go to the Malvern office, only to discover I had just missed you. I spoke to Natalya, and she gave me your address. She suggested I come here, to give you this.'

Opening her handbag, she took out a small package

wrapped in silver-coloured paper and tied with silver ribbon. 'It's a gift for you.'

Surprise flashed across his face. He smiled to himself as he looked at the gift, at the same time telling her to sit down in a chair. He took the other one. He opened the package and found himself holding in his hands the most extraordinary icon. It was the face of the Madonna, beautifully painted, and set in an ornate, gold-painted frame. It looked valuable to him.

'Irina, this is just wonderful,' James said, admiration clear in his voice. 'Thank you so much. It is very kind of you to give me something so unique. I will treasure it.'

Her face was ringed in smiles. 'It's my pleasure. I'm happy you like it. I found it in one of those old-fashioned antique shops in Mayfair. Most of them have unusual treasures, mostly from Europe. I understand this icon's provenance is Russian.'

'Then it is even more meaningful,' he said, his voice full of warmth. He had been drawn to this young woman from the first moment they had met. She was younger than her sister and quite a different type altogether, a little softer, rather enigmatic, yet at the same time outspoken when she wanted to be.

For reasons he didn't quite understand, she reminded him of his ex-lover, Georgiana Ward. They did not look very much alike, and there was a big difference in their ages, but they exuded femininity and a quiet sexuality that was most appealing.

He knew at this precise moment that he wanted her. He was hoping her visit meant she felt the same way. Yet he was also aware he must be cautious, go slowly with her.

Irina said, 'By the way, I must explain something to you. Our aunt would like to bring Aubrey Williamson to the supper on Thursday. He is alone in London and

130

available. She feels she needs an escort, you see. Mr Lorne is still away. Is that all right, James?'

'I would be happy to invite him to the supper, and I understand quite well how your aunt feels. No woman wants to be alone at a dinner. Anyway, it balances the table better. Now we will be six.'

'How shall we handle it?' Irina asked.

'Your aunt can tell him, say he is very welcome, and I will send him a written invitation by hand tomorrow, if you give me his address. That is the proper thing to do.'

Irina answered, 'I will write it down for you, and then I must leave. I have imposed on you long enough.'

'Oh no, please don't go just yet. I so enjoy your company. Or perhaps you have another engagement.'

'No, no, I don't actually,' she answered swiftly, wanting to be here with him, although she did not dare say that. She had fallen heavily for James Falconer, wished they could be together.

'It's settled then, you'll stay for . . . I'll make some tea.' He jumped up. 'Excuse me a moment. We only have a woman who comes in to clean – we fend for ourselves with food. My uncle is often out.'

'My mother says a kitchen is a woman's place and men are not allowed.' She began to laugh, and he laughed with her.

James walked towards the kitchen, and she followed him in, glancing around. 'What a nice size it is,' Irina exclaimed, and headed towards the large window. She continued, 'It's so light. I loathe dark rooms.'

James filled the kettle, picked up a box of Swan Vestas, struck a match, and put it to the gas ring.

Turning around, he walked over to the window. 'It's funny, I feel the same way. I too hate dark rooms. I prefer all the lamps blazing.'

'And this happened when you were in Russia? I know you and Natalya went there a lot with your Aunt Olga.'

'Yes. Vladimir and I came together at his dacha. He had come to check on the estate, and he came to see Aunt Olga. When he left, I asked if I could walk with him back to his dacha. He agreed, and when we arrived, he told me we had to say goodbye because he loved me. He said I was too young and also he was married. But Aunt Olga had told me he was in the middle of a divorce. His wife had left him for a *woman* so I picked a rose in the garden and I gave it to him. I told him I had loved him since I was a little girl. And so we went into the house, and talked, and I just stopped him at one moment because he was afraid. I said goodbye and left the dacha.'

'I suppose he ran after you, didn't he?' James observed. 'And he made you his.'

'That is true. And we were together in his bed. We were . . . very close for one year, lovers, and then he fell ill. It was tuberculosis. Very infectious. Fortunately, I had never lived at the dacha. I couldn't. Our relationship was a secret. Aunt Olga never knew. I couldn't – there would have been a scandal. Anyway, he went into hospital. No one could go and see him. I never got to say goodbye. Vladimir died.'

Her voice cracked a little and then she sighed. 'He was like you, in a sense. He worried about taking my virginity.'

James was silent. At last he said in a low, gentle voice, 'I am glad he was a considerate man, and thank you for telling me. I'm sorry for your grief. It must have been a hard time.'

'Thank you. But I was eighteen when he passed away, and now I'm almost twenty-three. Have you had many lovers in your life?'

'No, only one. Her name was Georgiana. She was older than me, a young widow. She was lovely in every way. She had dark hair and violet eyes, and like your Vladimir, she was kind and loving. She made me happy.'

'Is she dead?' Irina asked.

'No. She left where she was living and moved to London, but has left here now because of her health and the pollution from the coal fires. She went to live in the country to look after her sister, who was ill.'

'And you never see her any more?' Irina probed softly.

'No. And I've never heard from her.' He took hold of Irina's hand. 'You remind me of her, in certain ways, in your personality. She made me feel comfortable and so do you. You arouse me as she did.'

He put his arm around her and pulled her closer. They began to kiss each other, their excitement growing. It was Irina who pulled away first. Looking deeply into his blue eyes, she whispered, 'Let us stop now. We understand how we feel, that we want to make love. But it can't be hurried, because the first time must be perfect. And I must have protection.'

His disappointment showed on his face, and she was well aware how hard he was. She said in a whisper, 'It will be tomorrow, James. Tomorrow I will be yours.'

EIGHTEEN

Detective Inspector Roger Crawford sat at his desk in his office at Scotland Yard, checking off the appointments he had kept that day. It had been unusually busy. But when wasn't it? Criminals never slept.

Only one left, he thought, staring down at his engagement book. It was Monday 7 July, and the appointment was for eight o'clock. Sergeant Mick Owen would be on time. To the exact minute. Punctuality was his middle name.

A half-smile flickered on the inspector's face for a split second and was gone. He had no idea why Owen wanted to speak to him so urgently, but he had agreed to see him tonight . . . because he was able to do so. Anyway, he had great respect for Owen, who was a superlative policeman: dedicated, diligent and clever at his job. If he could help him in any way, he would.

Crawford glanced at the alarm clock he kept on his desk. It was one minute to eight. As the hand moved, there was a knock on the door. 'Come in,' he called out, and Mick Owen did so.

Roger Crawford stood up, walked around his desk, and shook hands with Owen, greeted him warmly.

The sergeant responded in kind. They went back at least fifteen years.

'So what's this all about?' Crawford asked, stepping back around his desk, adding, 'Take the weight off your feet, Sergeant.' He motioned to the chair facing his.

Once they were both settled in their chairs, Mick Owen said, 'There was a strange event last night when I was on patrol in Soho with my partner. We might have missed it, me and Jerry Cookson, if a woman hadn't started screaming at the top of her voice and a man hadn't called out for the police.'

'And so you both ran to help. What was happening?'

'Two men were being attacked in a nearby dark alley. Imagine our surprise when we reached the man who had shouted for help. It was Billy Watters, the British light-weight boxing champion of the world.'

Crawford nodded, wondering what was strange about this event. Surely not meeting the boxer.

Before he could ask this question, the sergeant continued, 'We ran down the alley, only to discover that the young men had already dealt with their attackers, who were odd-looking blokes. Dressed entirely in black. It was dark a' course, but I recognized one of the young men. It was James Falconer, Inspector Crawford.'

Crawford was momentarily startled and instantly sat upright in his chair, leaned forward, his expression alert. 'Don't tell me he had been beaten up again. I couldn't bear to hear that, not after what happened to him a few years ago.'

'No, no, fortunately Falconer was not injured, and neither was his colleague, Peter Keller. The latter had kicked one of the assailants in the balls with his boot. Falconer had punched the other bruiser on the jaw, and quite a few times. They were down and out of it.'

137

'I'm relieved to hear that. You cuffed the attackers, took them off to jail, I presume, to be charged?'

Owen nodded. 'I needed to come and tell you about it, Inspector, because it was so like that last attack on Falconer. I worried about it all night, couldn't sleep, in fact. Do you think someone really *is* out to get Falconer, sir?'

A concerned expression settled on Crawford's face, and he was silent for a moment, his mind racing. 'I don't know, Sergeant. But it's strange. I agree with you there. Didn't Falconer's friend, Dennis Holden, die from his head wounds?' Sudden rage swept through Crawford and he exclaimed, 'Damn and blast! Why wasn't that case ever solved? I can't believe it! That some rotten buggers got away with murder – and of a young lad, no less.'

'That's what I thought. I had to talk to you because it's been bothering me so much.'

Crawford nodded. 'I need to know as much as you can find out about these two assailants. And I've every intention of opening that cold case, making it active immediately.'

'Where would you start, sir? Quite a lot of time has passed,' Owen said cautiously.

'It has indeed, but I've a mind to start with that bar, Tango Rose. And, by the way, what are the names of those two attackers of last night? And how much did you get out of them?'

'Their names are Sid Puller and Johnny Clark, but who knows if they were telling the truth. I questioned them at the scene and in the jail. They didn't talk at all. Told me nothing. Clammed up, they did.'

'What about James Falconer and his colleague, Keller? For instance, what the hell were the two of *them* doing in a dark alley in Soho?'

'They said they'd had dinner at Chez Simone earlier,

and Keller had led them into the alley, because it was a shortcut to the music hall they were headed for.'

'Bad choice,' Crawford said, and grimaced. Standing up, he looked across at Owen. 'I'm glad you came to see me, Sergeant. Are you on duty now?'

'No, Inspector, I'm not. It's my night off.'

'Then come and join me for a pint. I for one need a beer after what you've just told me. And incidentally, I *do* think Falconer is being targeted. I aim to find out who is behind this and put the bastard behind bars.'

'With my help, sir. And I wouldn't mind a pint in a cheerful pub.'

On this Tuesday morning, the inspector sat at his desk at Scotland Yard drinking a mug of tea and running Owen's memories through his mind yet again.

Over a few pints of bitter at the Pig and Whistle last night, Mick Owen had told the inspector everything he could remember about the attack on James Falconer, now approximately two years ago. And he had a good memory, even for small details.

For the umpteenth time, the name Milly Culpepper loomed large. And he knew the reason why. She was the only person who was friendly with Falconer and Holden. In fact, she had gone out on dates with Denny Holden several times. No one else who frequented Tango Rose on a regular basis had paid much attention to the two young men.

She was the link.

Whichever way he looked at the pages of information in the folder of this cold case, he always came back to her. She knew them, chatted to them, and even saw Denny alone. And more than likely she knew what they were doing and where they were going when they were not at the bar. There was nothing wrong with that. It was quite normal, chatting with friends. What was dangerous was who this information was repeated to.

And so he kept coming back to the idea that Milly Culpepper might well have fingered them without even realizing she was doing that. Totally innocent of any wrongdoing. Yet Dennis Holden had died from his severe head wounds. He had never come out of the coma which had enveloped him in King's Hospital.

Somewhere out there was a murderer. Chief Inspector Roger Crawford did not like that at all. The monster had to be found, charged, tried and found guilty. If Crawford managed to solve this cold case, he would make sure that murdering bastard swung at the end of a rope.

Drinking the last dregs of the tea, Crawford decided he would find Milly Culpepper no matter what, even though Mick Owen had told him last night that she no longer worked at the popular bar near the Thames. Somebody would know where she was or know someone else who did. He was an old hand at finding people.

Once outside in the bright sunlight, the inspector cheered up. He threw off the sense of defeat that surrounded this cold case. He set his mind on its resolution. Unexpectedly, he suddenly felt full of piss and vinegar, as he was wont to call it; bursting with energy. He was also in a hurry because he kept wondering if the attack last night was linked to the attack two years back. If so, it made it all the more deadly. Whoever it was who had it in for James Falconer was obviously not going to give up. At least not until Falconer was dead. And that must not happen. He couldn't let it.

When a hansom cab came by, Crawford hailed it immediately. He gave the driver the name and address of the bar and climbed inside. The cab moved forward at a quick trot and in no time at all he was being dropped off on the Embankment overlooking the River Thames.

It was noon and the bar had opened. Within several minutes Chief Inspector Roger Crawford of Scotland Yard was involved in deep conversation with the owner. She was a statuesque, well-put-together woman called Rose Sinclair.

Tango Rose herself, in full blazing colour, he thought as they shook hands. She was made up, dressed in a deep-magenta velvet gown and heavily bejewelled. Quite a sight at noon on a Tuesday.

She spoke swiftly, in a well-modulated voice. She would tell him anything he wanted to know; she had never had trouble in her bar. Every member of her staff would cooperate. She was a great admirer of Scotland Yard, she said, and ended up congratulating him on the courage and dedication of his brave and talented officers of the law.

Once she had finished her speech, such as it was, and then looked at him questioningly, he explained why he was there.

She seemed surprised that the cold case was open again, and told him she was certain Milly Culpepper was blameless of any wrongdoing. She was just an innocent bystander. After all, she was only a young girl.

'I am inclined to agree with you, Mrs Sinclair. But she knew those two young men quite well, and there might be something she's forgotten – or not thought important enough to mention – that might help me, give me a clue, a way to move forward.'

'I see what you mean, Chief Inspector, and please call me Rose. The whole world calls me Rose. Milly never really chatted to the other customers, who were older men, more . . . worldly, more sophisticated, shall we say? The boys were familiar to her. She came from their world, their class.'

Something clicked in Crawford's head when she made

that remark, but he moved on without making reference to it. 'I was hoping you could tell me where Miss Culpepper works now, Rose.'

'Of course. I am happy to help. When she left my employment, Milly went to work at a bar in Covent Garden. It's called Grape on the Vine. It's a nice place, mind you. I have no idea if she is still there.'

'Thank you very much, Rose. You have been very helpful.'

Crawford walked across the Embankment and stood leaning against the wall, looking out across the River Thames. He knew from the sergeant that Milly Culpepper had only stayed at the Grape on the Vine for about two weeks and had quickly moved on. Mick Owen had named four other bars where she had worked within the year after the attack on Falconer and Holden.

The inspector stood thinking about his next move. According to Owen, Milly had just disappeared. Even her mother claimed she had no idea where her daughter was working, because she had moved away, gone to live in the country.

Making a snap decision, Crawford took out his notebook and found Mrs Culpepper's address. He would go and visit the mother. Two years had passed, and no doubt she now knew where her daughter was residing.

He walked up to the Strand, hailed a hansom, and was soon on his way to Camden Town, hoping to get the information he needed.

NINETEEN

'So what you're telling me is that we are going to have problems with our Property Division, is that it?' Henry Malvern asked, his dark-brown eyes resting on James Falconer intently. But his expression was guarded.

'I'm afraid so, yes,' James answered. He pushed his hands into his pockets and winced. His right hand was still tender.

'Have you spoken to Marvin Goring about this? After all, he's in charge of the warehouses.'

'No, sir, I haven't. I thought it would be wiser to speak to you first. I don't want him to think I'm poking my nose into his business. He's very good at his job, and he works hard. This is not a criticism of him, Mr Malvern. It's just a statement of the facts, as I see them.'

'I surely know that, Falconer, you're not made that way. I agree that Goring is conscientious, does a good job.' There was a momentary pause before Malvern said, 'What about Harold Clayton? How's he doing now that he's running the Property Division?'

'He's cut from the same cloth as Goring, very diligent and smart, and everyone likes him much better than his predecessor.'

'Could you just explain again exactly why you think there's going to be a change in property values, please?' Malvern leaned over his desk, still focused on James, anxious.

'There is a slowing down of business in general, especially in retailing. People are not spending enough money in shops. So that affects the manufacturers of goods who are making fewer products, and letting employees go because of that. It's like dominoes falling. House prices are dropping, and I have a feeling this slowdown might turn into a Depression. I hope not, sir. To sum up, the whole country is in a mess,' James paused, then finished. 'Except not everyone knows that.'

Henry Malvern was silent for a moment or two, looking off into space. Finally he spoke. 'How is it you know and no one else does, Falconer?'

'I don't believe I am the only person, Mr Malvern. Other people read newspapers as well as me and study the situation. However, I spotted the changes in property values because I try to read between the lines. Let's just say I'm looking for changes and problems, and maybe others aren't.'

'So how do we handle the warehouses?'

'I suggest you bring Goring into the picture and instruct him to put the warehouses in the East End up for sale.'

'What about those on the docks?'

'We need most of those, Mr Malvern. Keller runs the Wine Division very well, and I'm positive it will continue to flourish.'

'When do you wish to advise Goring of the situation, Falconer?'

'Later this week. I know he went to Bradford to check on the warehouses the company owns there. He told me he would be back on Thursday of this week.'

'So we'll talk to him then. And why Bradford? There's nothing wrong up there, I hope.'

'All is well. The warehouses are full of shoddy. No problems at all. Wool is always a safe bet. So don't worry about that.'

'I suppose we had better have Clayton in on the meeting with Goring, don't you think?'

'Yes, I do, sir. I was just going to suggest it. We can assess their opinions and decide what properties to keep and what to sell. We'll come out all right, I'm certain of that. Providing we move quickly.'

Henry Malvern nodded, wondering what he would ever do without James Falconer. Also wondering how to persuade him to stay at the company. He knew full well that Falconer was ambitious, wanted to go out on his own. He couldn't let this brilliant young man do that. Where would *he* be if Falconer left? Lost, Henry thought. I'd be at sea swimming with the sharks. Once again he felt the pang of loss over Alexis, who had once worked so closely with him.

James Falconer stood up. He said, 'If you don't mind, sir, I have to leave now. I have a meeting. Some personal business out of the office which I have to attend to.'

'Of course, Falconer, go and get on with it. God knows you stay here far too long most days.'

'Thank you, Mr Malvern. I'll see you tomorrow.'

James hurried down the stairs and pushed the heavy door open out to Piccadilly. He started to walk along the busy pavement towards Mayfair, mulling over the conversation they'd had. The same slowdown he had described to Mr Malvern was an opportunity. An opportunity for someone wanting to start out – to rent premises for less; premises that big companies would be offloading. But for now he was still run off his feet at Malvern's.

Once he reached Half Moon Street, he managed to freshen up and check out the flat to make sure it was tidy.

Ten minutes later he was opening the door and ushering Irina into the living room.

She smiled and greeted him warmly, and he smiled in return, and took the cloth bag she was carrying.

'Goodness, this is heavy. Whatever's in it?' he asked.

'Our supper,' she answered. 'Let's take it into the kitchen. We can unpack it together. I've made everything in advance, James.'

'Oh, I thought you would be cooking it here. I was looking forward to watching you.'

Her light laughter echoed around the kitchen as she began to take out items from the bag he had placed on the table. 'That is a jar of borscht soup with meat, our main course. There should be another jar.' She reached into the bag and took it out. 'And these are the blinis I made, to go with this, the caviar, and a packet of pirogi—'

'I've never heard of these,' James cut in. 'What are they?'

'Delicious little pastry rolls filled with meat.' She opened the packet and took one out. 'Look, they're a bit like sausage rolls except smaller.' She offered the pirog to him.

James took it, bit into it, and nodded. 'You're right. It *is* delicious. Did you make it yourself?'

'I did. I cooked everything in my aunt's kitchen this morning. All from my grandmother's recipes. She's the one who taught me how to cook Russian food.' Irina paused. 'Speaking of Aunt Cheska, I'm afraid she won't be able to come to your supper on Thursday.'

'I'm sorry to hear that. It's a good thing I didn't send an invitation to Aubrey Williamson. I didn't have time.' He was suddenly aware of the troubled look on Irina's face, and asked, 'What is it? Is there something wrong?'

'Yes, I'm afraid so. Her husband returned from his latest trip to New York yesterday. He'd arrived when I was here with you. Anyway, to make a long story short, Uncle Michael says he wants a divorce. Aunt Cheska is devastated, and he seems very upset, too. So that's why she won't be able to come. And I won't come either. I'm so sorry, James, but I think my aunt needs my support. And, of course, she needs Natalie as well.'

'I do understand. Please don't worry about cancelling. I can give the supper another time.'

'Thank you.' Irina was quiet for a moment, and then turned to look over her shoulder. 'Dinner, then. I think we should put the caviar, the lemon cake, the blinis and the pirogi in the pantry where it's cool, don't you?'

'I do, Irina. Let me show you where it is. And I must say this is quite a feast you've made . . . thank you.'

'I hope you'll enjoy it. Anyway, I was glad to be down in the kitchen. There was a lot of disagreement upstairs, and tears. Oh, it was awful. Uncle Michael eventually left for the bank, and Natalie and I tried to console Aunt Cheska. She was so tearful, and hurt, I think.'

'I'm so very sorry to hear all this. She must have found it hard.' He hesitated, before saying gently, 'Was this the first she'd heard about it? His wanting to get divorced from her?'

'No, I don't believe so, but he hadn't pursued it, and so it was quite a shock.'

'I bet it was,' James said. 'She's so beautiful and such a lovely person, I can't believe any man would want to leave her.'

'I can't understand either. I mean, she's really the innocent bystander in my opinion, and I can't help thinking there must be another woman. I've often suspected he was seeing someone, that he had a mistress, just from his peculiar behaviour at times.'

'Peculiar in what way?' James asked.

'His late nights at the office, lack of punctuality and odd trips to Paris, Rome – always called business trips, naturally. Natalie often said he had a guilty look about him.'

147

James nodded but made no response. He went and opened the pantry door. 'Shall we put these items away?' he suggested. 'And then I'm going to open a bottle of Uncle George's champagne, because you think it's a treat.'

'Being here with you is a treat,' Irina answered, smiling as she carried the blinis and pirogi to the pantry.

James looked at her and knew that they shared the same attraction.

James opened a bottle of champagne and took two flutes out of the cupboard. After filling them with the champagne, he turned to Irina and said, 'Shall we go into the living room where it's more comfortable?'

'Yes, let's do that,' she responded, stopping to reach into the bag and taking out a small silk pouch.

James frowned and asked, 'What is that?'

'It's a caftan, a house gown I wear to be more casual and relaxed. Actually, it is Moroccan in origin and the women in Morocco wear it instead of a dress.' She held up the silk bag. 'It's folded up in here.'

She placed it to one side and went on, 'I'll put this on later, when I start to prepare our food,' she explained.

'It's beautiful, Irina.'

Sitting down on the sofa, Irina took the glass he offered her.

James seated himself in the chair and, leaning closer, he clinked his glass to hers, 'Cheers!'

'Cheers!' she repeated. 'And here's to success with your first shop.'

'Thank you . . . I don't want to appear rude,' James went on, 'but why do I think I had heard a few rumours lately about your aunt having problems in her marriage?'

'Because there has been some talk and I think information has leaked out. People see things, hear things, and gossip with each other. You know that, I'm sure.'

She sipped the champagne, sat back on the sofa, a reflective look settling on her face.

He wondered what she was thinking, what she was about to reveal. He really felt sorry for Francesca Lorne, who was one of the nicest women he had ever met. Her husband must be weird to dump her in this way. And a marriage with a mistress was one thing; asking for a divorce would cause a scandal.

At last, Irina said, 'I have a feeling Natalie won't be able to go to Hull on Friday and neither will I, James. I'm sure my aunt is going to need our support. She's not taken this lightly.'

His face fell, and his disappointment showed at once. 'That's a shame. I was looking forward to your company,' he told her. 'However, as it happens Peter Keller is coming. He's longed to see the City of Gaiety, so he'll keep me company. But I will miss you.'

'I know. I feel the same.' Placing the glass on the table, Irina stood up and reached for the silk bag. 'I should start the supper. May I use your bedroom to go and change into the caftan?'

James nodded. 'It's this way,' he said.

Once she was alone in his room, Irina took off her long skirt, tulle petticoat and her white blouse. She laid them on a chair, then removed all of her underclothes except for a thin silk slip. Taking out the pale-blue caftan, she put it on and went to look in the mirror. The exotic clothing suited her, but she also knew she was completely covered, looked properly clad. After sliding her feet into a pair of soft leather mules, also from Morocco, Irina went into the living room.

James couldn't take his eyes off her as she walked towards him. He exclaimed, 'I do like your caftan. It's beautiful. You're beautiful. I bet I could sell quite a few of those. They're so becoming.'

149

She laughed. 'You surely could, and they are easy to make. It's just a long-sleeved straight dress, falling to the ankles, with some embroidery on the front.'

He followed her as she went into the kitchen, where she began to bring out the food, at the same time asking him to find her pans to heat the borscht. James did so, and put them on the gas stove.

He sat down in a chair, continuing to gaze at her while she prepared the food. As she moved around the kitchen, the caftan clung to her enticingly. He could see the outline of her shapely figure, the movement of her breasts against the silk, her nipples. He tried to look away but was unable to do so. She was lovely, mesmerizing and ravishing. He'd never met anyone quite like her.

Unexpectedly, he stood up and went over to her, took the spoon out of her hand, and turned her to face him. His expression was intense with desire.

He said, 'I can't stand it. I need to be with you, Irina. Now, not later.'

'I know,' she answered and turned to him. 'Because I feel the same.'

It was almost twilight and the bedroom was dim, but James did not bother to light the gas lamps. Instead he took Irina in his arms and held her close, began to kiss her.

She kissed him in return, and they clung together. He slid his hands down her back and onto her buttocks, the silk of the caftan smooth and somehow enticing.

He was even more aroused and stepped away from her, undressing himself swiftly. She did the same, removing the caftan.

They stood in the middle of the bedroom, their eyes riveted on each other. They moved at the same moment, clinging to each other and kissing.

They fell down onto his bed; he held her tightly, his

mouth still on hers. She felt a moment of apprehension. She had not been involved with a man since Vladimir's death. How would she be with James? Would she please him? Would memories of her beloved Vladimir intrude, make her turn away from James? She had no answers for herself, and she felt unexpectedly taut, nervous, yet only a moment ago she had been brimming with desire.

James stopped kissing her, pushed himself up on one elbow and looked down into her face. His expression was loving. He said gently, 'Don't be afraid, Irina. Relax, my sweet girl. All will be all right. With me you are safe.'

She simply stared up at him, saying nothing. He began to smooth his hands over her body, and slowly the tension left her. She fell under his spell.

He slipped out of bed for a moment to fetch protection, and swiftly returned to her side. He spoke soothing words to her, loving words, and began to stroke her body again. He kissed her breasts and then slid his hand down to her stomach. Slowly, tenderly, he began to make love to her; he gave her such intense pleasure that her entire body trembled. Suddenly their passion soared.

Touching each other all over, kissing frantically, their pent-up emotions burst open. He moved onto her, and she grabbed him, put her arms around his back and pulled him closer. And she sighed as she felt him fully inside her. Still fraught with unbridled passion, they moved together, finding their own rhythm. And they did not stop until they reached the pinnacle of sexual ecstasy.

Irina lay with her head against James's shoulder, her eyes closed, although she was not asleep. She was glad she had not failed him, had met his urgent desire and given him pleasure. As he had her. He was a skilled lover, caring and obviously experienced. He knew how to please a woman.

But she did not care about those who had gone before her. Now he was hers, just as she was his.

His voice broke the silence. 'I think we blend well together Irina, don't you?'

'Yes. We're a good match.'

She swivelled her eyes up to his, and a small laugh broke through. 'My sister was right.' She laughed again.

'What do you mean?' He was obviously puzzled.

'Natalie said we were made for each other and predicted we would end up here in your bed.'

'And didn't *you* think that?' he asked, sounding surprised.

'I wasn't sure about *you*. I hoped you wanted this relationship as much as I did.'

James put his arms around her, held her close, thinking what a lovely person she was. And as sensual and erotic as himself. It's a good match, he thought, and yet again, he realized how much she reminded him of Georgiana Ward. Now Irina had replaced her and then he knew that was why he felt the absence of pain. He was no longer alone.

TWENTY

Detective Inspector Crawford had gone to Mrs Culpepper's house in Camden Town twice. On both occasions he had found the house locked up and the street of terraced houses deserted.

Well, what did he expect, he chastised himself. Every person who lived there went to work or would be out shopping.

Now on this Thursday evening, his third trip, his spirits lifted. Mrs Culpepper was obviously home at last. Gas lamps shone through the window of her house.

Telling the hansom cab driver to wait for him, he went and knocked on the door of the small house. Almost immediately it was opened, and he found himself face to face with a middle-aged woman. She was neatly dressed in a navy dress with a white collar and cuffs.

He spoke at once before she could say a word. 'Good evening, Mrs Culpepper . . . you are Mrs Culpepper, aren't you?'

'Yes, I am.'

He put out his hand, said, 'I'm Detective Inspector Crawford of Scotland Yard. I need to have a word or two with you, if you could spare a few minutes.'

For a moment she did not answer, a worried look on her face. Then she said swiftly, 'Could I see your badge, please? I mean, I'd like to confirm that you are who you say you are, sir?'

'Of course.' He took out his police badge and a printed business card. Second-guessing her, he hurried on. 'I actually want to speak to your daughter Milly regarding the period she worked at Tango Rose.'

She took the card and badge from him and then, after studying them, returned his badge and kept the card. 'This is for me, isn't it, Inspector?'

'Yes. Could I come in for a few minutes?'

Immediately she stepped back, opened the door and ushered him inside. 'I don't want the neighbours gossiping. They're no doubt peeping out from behind their lace curtains already.'

He found himself in a comfortable room, with a large alcove at the far side. It was a kitchen, well equipped and as clean as the room they were in.

She now looked at Crawford intently and asked, 'Why do you want to see Milly after all this time? It's a long time since she worked at that bar.'

'Something has come up regarding the attack on James Falconer and Dennis Holden, and I need to check a few facts with her.'

'She's been interviewed before and has told everything she knows, which is virtually nothing. I'll go and get her, though. She's upstairs. But don't upset her, Inspector. *Please.*' She gave him a hard stare.

'I won't, Mrs Culpepper, and thank you.'

The woman nodded and walked through a door which revealed a narrow staircase. Within seconds, she returned. Behind her was her daughter, Milly, a pretty girl with light-brown hair and wide blue eyes. Crawford could see why she'd been popular in the bar.

After greeting her and shaking her hand, Crawford explained why he was there and about the second attack on James Falconer last Sunday night in Soho.

She was instantly taken aback and stood gaping at him, obviously at a loss for words.

He said, 'I hope this last attack is not connected to the other one, but I can't be sure. I need to ask you about a couple of things, Miss Culpepper.'

Milly nodded. 'All right.'

Her mother said, 'Please sit down, Inspector, and you, too, Milly.' They all settled themselves in chairs.

Crawford found it curious that Milly was dressed exactly like her mother, and it struck him that the navy dresses might be uniforms. They obviously worked together.

As if reading his mind, Mrs Culpepper remarked, 'Milly and I work for a young couple, Mr and Mrs Gordon Aspinall. We're nannies to their five children.' A smile touched her lips. 'And quite a handful they are. This is our time off because they've gone to the country today.'

Crawford nodded, and noticing that Milly was growing nervous, he addressed her. 'You were friendly with Denny and James, that much I know. Were they close to anyone else at Tango Rose? What about the owner?'

Milly shook her head. 'Oh, no, Rose didn't bother with them. She paid all her attention to the older men, the big spenders – men of the world, she called them. Denny and James didn't drink; they only had a pint.'

'I understand. So I suppose they came to see you, or perhaps I should say *Denny* came to see *you*, and James tagged along.'

'That's true. Denny and I liked each other, and we started to meet on my free evenings.'

'Didn't anyone talk to them, other customers?'

'Oh no, the other customers were too posh, and older. I don't think they noticed them.'

'I see. So no one at all ever asked you any questions about them. What they did? Where they went?'

Milly stared at Crawford, her brows drawn together in a frown. After a reflective pause, she said slowly, 'Well, Sadie did sometimes.'

'Who is Sadie?' he asked, his interest apparent. 'Tell me about her, would you?'

Milly said, 'She's just another girl like me, lives around here. She went out a few times with Denny, but they broke up.'

'Were there any hard feelings between them? Did either of them bear a grudge?'

She shook her head. 'No, a' course not. They were still friends.'

'What's her surname?'

'*Long.* Sadie Long.'

'Did you ever tell her anything about the two boys?' Crawford asked, almost nonchalantly, not wishing to scare her off.

'No, not really.' Milly shrugged. 'Sometimes she asked me where they went, how they spent their evenings, and she wanted to know if I was serious about Denny. That's it, not much at all.'

Crawford knew she was wrong. Sadie Long was probably the conduit to . . . who?

Mrs Culpepper said, 'Didn't Sadie have a new boyfriend, Milly? I'm sure you told me that.'

Crawford's attention now focused on the mother, his eyes riveted on her.

Milly said, 'Oh, yeah, I forgot. She started going with Patrick Paiseley, that's right.'

'And does he live in the vicinity?' Crawford asked, his focus now centred on Milly again.

'The Paiseleys live round here, and Pat knew James and Denny, but not all that well . . . acquaintances, I'd call them.' Milly shrugged her shoulders. 'He was sort of . . . standoffish,' she confided. 'I didn't really like him.'

'And he never asked about James and Denny?' Crawford's stare was intense.

'No . . . but now I remember something . . .' Milly began and her voice trailed off. Then a moment later, she said, 'Sadie asked me if the boys would be at Tango Rose one Friday night. I told her no, and she asked me about the next night. I said that they would be at the supper Matthew Falconer always gave in the summer. The Special Saturday Supper, they called it, because the whole family attended. Some folks thought they were getting above themselves. Sadie was surprised when I said Denny had been invited. I knew how excited he was, because his father had bought him an off-the-peg suit.'

Crawford remained perfectly still, kept his face expressionless, when he said, 'I might be mistaken, but wasn't that particular Saturday the night the boys were attacked on Chalk Farm Road?'

Milly stared back at him, and pursed her lips. 'Why yes, I think it was. Why? Is that important?'

Crawford said noncommittally, 'Not sure. Now just tell me a bit more about Patrick Paiseley.'

'I don't know much. As I told you, he wasn't a favourite of mine. Sadie was crazy about him. And she tried to comfort him.'

'Oh, why was that? Did something happen to upset him, Miss Culpepper?'

'Well, Denny told me that Mr Paiseley – Patrick's dad, that is – was handy with his fists. From what I remember, one night Mrs Paiseley turned up on Denny's parents' doorstep, who lived nearby. She had been hit by her husband and was battered up something terrible. She went to get their help. Denny's parents were so shocked by how bad she was, they weren't sure they could help her. So Denny's dad, Jack Holden, got her into a hansom cab, and they took her to the hospital. Denny told me that his mother knew a bit about nursing, but they were scared by her injuries, they were so bad.'

'I understand.' Detective Inspector Crawford now stole a glance at Mrs Culpepper. 'No doubt you heard about this.'

'I did indeed, Inspector. Most of us around here knew that Finn Paiseley was abusive. Meg was always being bashed up. I for one will never understand why she stayed with him.'

Mrs Culpepper glanced at Milly. Then her eyes went back to Crawford. 'The sad thing is, Meg Paiseley didn't survive that beating. Anyway, it was her last. She died in hospital a few days later. And the hospital had to report her death to the police. After that, the police arrested Finn Paiseley. And he went to jail.'

Crawford made another note then addressed Mrs Culpepper, 'Anything else you can remember?'

'No, that's about it.' The older woman shook her head.

'At least that poor woman's at peace,' Milly said. 'Sadie told me that Patrick was real upset about his mother's death. *Stricken*, James said.'

'And when was it that Mrs Paiseley passed away? Was it about three years ago?'

'I think so. I know it was the summer,' Milly murmured.

Inspector Crawford stood up, retrieved his hat, and thanked Mrs Culpepper and Milly.

'I hope something I've said has helped, Inspector,' Milly stated, her expression quizzical. 'But I haven't told you much.'

'Every little helps, Milly. It's like a jigsaw puzzle, in a sense. It all comes together to make a whole. Eventually.'

Detective Inspector Crawford went straight back to his office at Scotland Yard. Once at his desk, he went through the set of folders from the closed case file which Mick Owen had given him. He realized at once that the attack on James and Denny had been in late July. Tomorrow he would check on exactly when Mrs Meg Paiseley had died in hospital.

Perhaps a couple of weeks before, perhaps even a month. But he had a feeling the attack had been arranged by Patrick Paiseley. And that it had been directed solely at Dennis Holden. It was *his* parents who had sent Patrick's mother to the hospital, where she had subsequently died. And then the police had arrested Patrick's father, who had gone to jail.

James Falconer had been in the wrong place at the wrong time. He had not been targeted. It was Denny that Patrick had wanted to hurt in order to punish Jack Holden.

Revenge. That had been the motive.

Coming to this conclusion, Roger Crawford made some notes. He could see no way that the attack on Falconer and Keller could have had any connection to the earlier incident.

It must have been Patrick Paiseley who had hired those three bruisers to beat up Falconer and Dennis Holden. Hard to prove but Crawford was planning to try. At least one good thing would come of this.

As for the two men in jail at the moment, they would be grilled by him tomorrow.

With a little luck he might get them to open up and talk. Who had paid them to track and assault Falconer and Keller?

Or had it been a random attack by petty thieves, seizing the moment at the sight of two well-dressed young men? Young men who looked like dandies, which to petty criminals spelled money in their pockets, not to mention watches on their waistcoats and rings on their fingers. Crawford wanted to be sure.

TWENTY-ONE

When he walked into the beautiful large walled garden of Francesca Lorne's house in Chelsea, James had mixed emotions. Instantly happy to see Irina, he was also saddened that her aunt looked so tired and strained.

He went straight to Mrs Lorne, bent over her chair, and kissed her on the cheek.

Looking up at him, Francesca Lorne clasped his hand. Her eyes were weary. 'You're a sight for sore eyes,' she said. 'I'm so happy you could come to tea.'

'So am I,' he answered, his tone affectionate. He then went over to Irina, who was standing near the table set up for afternoon tea. She was wearing a fashionable coffee-coloured day dress of the lightest silk. It showed her figure off to advantage, and suited her colouring beautifully. She and her sister were always beautifully turned out, their Russian ancestry giving their style a touch of the exotic.

They greeted each other, and she said in a low voice, 'I've really missed you.'

'Me too,' he answered.

Turning, he returned to the chair next to her aunt and sat down. Francesca got straight to the point. 'I know

Irina and Natalie have spoken to you about my situation – my husband's decision to leave me – and I want you to know I'm determined to get over it. I'm not a sissy. And I will avoid a scandal.'

James reached out, took hold of her hand. 'I am quite certain you will. You're a strong woman, and whilst I am surprised he would do this in a bad way, apparently Irina and Natalie are not. They seem to think he is capable of anything.'

Francesca smiled for the first time in days, and nodded. Suddenly there was a lighter expression on her face. 'They're correct. I think I would even add murder to the list. He's a real rascal. I should've known he would depart one day. Greener fields and all that.'

Irina had poured the tea and brought two cups over to her aunt and James, then returned to the table and carried over two plates of tea sandwiches. After they thanked her, she went to fetch her own.

Settling down next to them, Irina explained, 'My aunt's husband is an opportunist, James, and he's been involved for quite a long time with a married woman. Now she is suddenly a widow. Her elderly husband conveniently died. He left her rather rich.'

'To my way of thinking, a man like that is best gone and forgotten,' he said to Francesca, then glanced at Irina. 'Don't you agree?'

'I do, very much so. But to be fair to Aunt Cheska, it does hurt a bit to be abandoned in such a nasty way.'

Francesca raised her hand. 'Let's let him *drop*. Once I feel better we shall go abroad to somewhere really nice, travel and have a good time and enjoy ourselves. Get away from London until the chatter dies down.'

'You must get better first, Aunt Cheska, recover your strength,' Irina told her, and stood up, went to the tea table to avoid looking at James, whom she knew would be surprised by her aunt's sudden announcement.

Irina placed small cakes on a plate and fiddled at the table as she heard James say to her aunt, 'And where will you be going? Do you know yet?'

'I am considering going to see Olga in Russia. Her sister, Irina and Natalie's mother, is married to my brother. She's my oldest friend.' Francesca laughed. 'It was I who brought the Shuvalov girls into the Parkinson family.'

Aware there was no way she could now avoid telling James she was going with her aunt, Irina went and sat down next to him. 'Aunt Cheska is *thinking* about taking that trip, James, and she wants me to go with her.'

James turned to find her expressive dark eyes studying him. Although he was startled, he realized that this was not the place to show it. He had no idea what Irina had told her aunt about them. And so he said quietly, 'I think a change is as good as a rest – at least so my grandmother says.'

'Why don't you come with us, James?' Francesca said, looking at him intently. 'I invite you to be my guest. You would enjoy St Petersburg.'

'That's very kind of you, Mrs Lorne, but I'm afraid I have to see my project through. I can't leave it all to your niece. We have to be in Hull.'

Francesca stared at him and nodded, realizing Natalie would not agree to go either. She was diligent and would not neglect her work.

After tea and a lot of conversation about other matters, Francesca excused herself and went into the house. Irina accompanied her, helped her to get undressed and into bed. Her aunt now rested for a while every afternoon;

it seemed to be helping her to overcome her sorrow at this turn of events.

When Irina returned to the garden, she found James wandering around, admiring the flowerbeds and fruit trees. 'Your aunt did a really exquisite job here, didn't she?' he said, as she joined him. 'She's a talented gardener.'

Irina nodded, realizing at once that he wasn't angry. His face was relaxed and there was a smile in his eyes. She took hold of his hand, led him to a wrought-iron bench at the bottom of the garden.

As they sat down, she said, 'I want to explain something. My aunt only told me a short while before you arrived that she wanted to go and stay with Aunt Olga. I had no idea she would wish to go so far away and need me to accompany her.'

'I guessed as much,' James answered quickly, wishing to reassure her.

'If you could come, it would be so lovely,' Irina murmured.

He released her hand. 'No, it's impossible, I'm not a man of leisure with a private income. I have to work. I hope you understand that, Irina.'

'I do, yes, and I'm sure my aunt does as well. Hull has to come first.'

'When do you think you'll leave London?' he now asked.

Irina shook her head. 'I'm not sure. Certain things have to be arranged. Probably next week.'

'Oh! So soon?'

'Yes, but I hope to see you before I leave.'

'So do I, my sweet girl.' He looked into her face, and with a faint smile he asked, 'How long will you be gone?'

'Oh not long at all, I shall take my aunt there, get her settled and then return to London.'

'You can't travel back alone, that's not safe. It's quite a journey.'

'Oh yes, I know. My aunt has already discussed that. If she wishes to stay on with Aunt Olga, my father will come and get me. He'll agree to that, I can assure you.'

James nodded, took out his pocket watch. 'I'm afraid it's getting late. I have to leave to meet my Uncle George.'

Irina laughed. 'So he's back from Scotland.'

'Oh yes, I'm having supper with him and his friend Inspector Crawford. Nice chap.'

'When are you going to Hull?'

'Tomorrow, I'm afraid. So I won't be able to see you until next week.'

Irina nodded, leaned into him and put an arm around his shoulders. 'I do care about you, James. I'm so sorry all this has suddenly happened.'

He held her to him, kissed her cheek. 'It's not your fault. It's nobody's fault. But life does get in the way sometimes, doesn't it?'

James and Uncle George took a hansom cab down to the East End, heading for Chinatown in Limehouse. As they sat together on the same seat, George said, 'I love it down in Limehouse; it's a wonderful part of London. Nowhere like it in the world.'

'You know, I've never been to the East End. I'm looking forward to seeing it.'

'I wish I'd thought to bring you here, especially now you've grown up.'

'That sounds odd, Uncle George. Why didn't you bring me? You took me to other places sometimes, you and Uncle Harry. And why now when I'm *grown up*?'

'It's an odd place, a mixture of things, some good, some bad. But tonight, after dinner, we'll go for a stroll. Crawford knows it inside out. He used to be a copper on the beat down here, and everyone knows *him*. We're safe when he's around.'

'Is it *dangerous* in Limehouse?' James asked, his curiosity aroused.

'"Iffy" is the way I'd put it. But the good things about it far outweigh the bad.'

After that comment, George glanced out of the window and was silent for the rest of the journey.

James, knowing his uncle and the habit he had for falling silent for long periods, remained quiet in his corner of the seat, thinking about Irina. He couldn't help feeling disappointed that she was disappearing abroad so soon into their new friendship.

Eventually they had gone through Whitechapel and into Limehouse, where the hansom suddenly came to a stop. The two men jumped out, and George paid the driver, giving him a generous tip.

Surprised, the driver touched his flat cap, exclaimed, 'Thanks, guv, 'ave a helluva night. A flingawindin!'

James laughed as he and his uncle walked towards the restaurant. 'I've never heard that expression.'

George laughed with his nephew. 'Neither have I. Maybe it's local slang.'

'Or the driver's invention. I don't think we can call it Cockney, can we?' James asked.

'I don't believe so.'

'Oh, look, isn't that the restaurant?' James exclaimed, pointing to Wu Liang Palace straight ahead.

'It is,' his uncle replied.

The two men increased their pace and, within seconds, they were entering the Chinese restaurant, where they spotted Crawford immediately. He stood up, came to meet them, a huge smile on his face.

After greetings were exchanged, the inspector led them down to the back. It was a colourful place, decorated with Chinese lanterns, a great number of small candles and paintings of Chinese women on the walls.

'This is my usual table,' Crawford said. 'Welcome to Chinatown.'

After ordering the special drinks of the house, which Crawford explained were basically a mixture of rice wines, he leaned towards James who was sitting opposite him. 'I have some interesting news for you. I think we've something to celebrate. Inasmuch as I've managed to solve a mystery at last.'

'Is this about me?' James asked. 'About the attack in Soho?'

'In a sense, but it's also about the attack on you some three years ago. On Chalk Farm Road.'

On hearing this James shrank back slightly, and his face turned pale. 'When Denny died,' he murmured, his voice low.

Before the inspector could answer, George interrupted. 'Don't tell me you've discovered who did it at long last?'

'I have.' Crawford paused when the Chinese waiter arrived at their table, served the small glasses of rice wines, bowed and departed as Crawford was thanking him. Lifting his glass, he said, 'Cheers,' and they all clinked their glasses and sipped their wine.

The inspector continued, 'I will explain everything before we order the food. If that's all right?'

'Tell us what you've found out!' George exclaimed. 'I can't wait to hear this.'

'I'll try to make it short and sweet.' He addressed James. 'When you and Keller were attacked in Soho recently, I became quite vexed, remembering the other attack, which I realized had become a cold case. So I dug into it, and soon realized that Milly Culpepper was the only link I had. So I set out to find her. I thought the best bet was to go and ask her mother where she was. I did. And there I found her. Miss Milly Culpepper, at her mother's house.'

Speaking in a quiet voice, and telling the rest of the story carefully and precisely, Crawford filled in James and his Uncle George.

Neither of them spoke until the inspector told them why the attack had occurred and who the perpetrator was.

'I can't believe it!' James cried. 'Paiseley had us beaten up because his father went to jail for savaging his mother? His mother, who died because of her abusive husband. And he hired bruisers to punish us!'

'Can he be tried for murder?' George asked swiftly on the heels of his nephew. 'Dennis Holden *died* of his injuries.'

'I hope so. I pulled Sergeant Mick Owen into the case when I reopened it recently and I met with him several times. He got a warrant and Patrick Paiseley was arrested last night.'

There was a silence at the table for a few minutes. It was James who broke it when he said, 'I will never forget Sergeant Owen's kindness. He and Constable Roy waited at the hospital all night until I came out of my concussion. We were all impressed by that, weren't we, Uncle George?'

'We were, and touched by the way they cared.' George took a sip of wine. 'But why didn't *they* solve it at the time?'

'I asked Owen the same thing. They grilled Milly quite a few times. But she kept saying none of the *customers* had asked about Denny or James. And they kept referring to *customers*. I asked her instead if *anybody* had asked about the boys, and she remembered about her friend Sadie. Also, I believe at the time of the attack she was more than likely terrified, and extremely upset.'

The inspector paused, took a swig of the rice wine, and finished, 'According to Sergeant Owen, she was very, very nervous, hysterical and on the edge of collapse back then. They didn't want to be accused of police brutality or anything like that.'

George nodded. 'Especially because she was a young girl. I understand that, why they backed off . . .' He stopped, shook his head sadly, then let out a long sigh. 'And she hadn't witnessed the attack. She was only working at the bar.'

James's face was serious. 'Milly went out with Denny a few times. She was always kind to us. Poor Denny.' He rubbed his hand over his face. 'At least you solved it, Inspector, and thank you for the work you've done now. So I suppose I was in the wrong place at the wrong time with the wrong person. Is that how you would explain the attack on me?'

'Sadly, it is, in the absence of anything else,' Crawford replied. 'And thank God you survived.'

'And so the attack in Soho is not connected?' George asked.

'No, it's not.' Crawford shook his head. 'Not unless someone is out to get you. And you don't seem to have any enemies. I think it was a couple of petty thieves spotting two likely rich boys, with money in their pockets, watches and rings. The good thing is that they are now in jail. Thanks to you and Keller.'

James said nothing. He couldn't deny the attack had shaken him. London had always been his home but suddenly it seemed a stranger, more dangerous place.

'It's good to know that James isn't a target,' his uncle remarked. 'And I thank you, too, Crawford. From the bottom of my heart.'

TWENTY-TWO

Alexis Malvern sat at Sebastian's desk in the bedroom, writing in his diary.

She thought of it as continuing their story, and it gave her pleasure. It helped to ease her anxiety as well. If she wanted to, she could turn back to the entries he had made, run her fingers over his handwriting.

Outside her window, the gardens were in full bloom and she planned to walk in them later; for now she was enjoying the warmth of the late-summer sun falling through the windowpanes onto her skin as she wrote.

Although she was lost in concentration, the sudden rattle of wheels on the cobblestone courtyard brought her head up with a start. She was not expecting anyone on this July morning. Who on earth could it be?

Running downstairs and through the small entrance foyer, she opened the front door and went outside.

Much to her surprise, it was Claudia. And her heart sank. Pushing a bright smile onto her face, Alexis walked towards the carriage.

'Good morning, Claudia. I didn't expect to see you today. I thought you would be at Courtland.'

'Good morning,' Claudia said in a clipped tone of voice. 'I cancelled my visit for today. *Because of you.*'

They were now walking to the house, and the carriage had gone around to the back, where the trough of water was. The horses always needed to drink after the trip from London.

Having digested the words which seemed to blame her for Claudia's delayed visit to Courtland, Alexis asked, 'What do you mean when you say "because of *me*"?'

Claudia stopped, stared hard at her. 'You didn't come to Lavinia's birthday tea yesterday, even though you accepted the invitation. We waited and waited, and then I got worried, and so did Jane, that you might be ill or perhaps had an accident of some kind. You ruined the birthday party.'

Alexis flushed bright red as she led Claudia into the library, everyone's favourite room at Goldenhurst in Kent.

'I was going to come, but I began to feel overwhelmed with panic and anxiety. That happens sometimes when I have to go out, leave the house.'

'Why didn't you send a message with one of your drivers? Or send a telegram?' Claudia asked, sounding irritated.

Alexis shook her head. 'I didn't think of it.' She sat down and motioned to Claudia to do the same, her face taut, her eyes clouded with tears. 'I didn't really think you would notice.'

'You didn't think of it!' Claudia repeated, looking flabbergasted. 'Are you actually ill, Alexis? Do you need to go to see Doctor Freud in Vienna again? Are you mentally deranged?'

'No, of course I'm not!' Alexis exclaimed. 'I'm just not quite myself at the moment.'

'I'd call that the understatement of the year. You hide down here, doing nothing, mooning for my father.

171

He is dead. Accept that! Come back to London, start living! *He* would want that.'

'It's too hard,' was the only comment Alexis made. She leaned back in the chair, gazing at Claudia, her face without expression.

Claudia stared back at her, nonplussed, wondering how to jerk Alexis out of her stupor, how to push her into returning to London. To start anew, she thought. She was annoyed with her, but also felt sorry for her in many ways.

Taking a deep breath, Claudia continued, 'You must pull yourself together and get back to work. When I first met you, every woman I know admired you for your independence, going to work, competing in business. Young women like me thought of you as a great example, a role model.'

'I didn't know that,' Alexis mumbled.

Claudia said, 'It's a man's world. It always has been, and it always will be. Nothing is going to change. They run everything: institutions, banks, every big business. *Control* is their middle name, and women are second-class citizens. Only recently have a couple of laws changed so that a woman can keep her own inheritance. It used to go to her husband when she married. But you gave so many women hope, fired up their aspirations. You say you didn't realize this, but it *is* true. Come back. Do it again. Give some ambitious women hope.'

Alexis shrugged. 'I suppose I'd forgotten that part of my life. I'm not feeling well enough. And none of you needs me.'

'Please endeavour to revive yourself, Alexis. Women just have to take a stance. We cannot allow ourselves to be so dominated by men. Even the Queen is surrounded by male advisors – the prime minister, other ministers in Parliament. Things need to change on every level. Everywhere, in fact.'

'Does Queen Victoria listen to all their prattle?' Alexis wondered aloud.

Claudia shook her head. 'I don't know. But she did listen to Albert when he was alive. Although I heard they had their rows.'

'Does Cornelius boss you around, Claudia?'

'No, but perhaps he is the exception to the rule. Did my father ever try to control *you*, Alexis?'

'No. He even said I could work after we were married if I wanted to do so . . .' She broke off and closed her eyes.

Claudia gave her a moment, and coughed behind her hand, then said, 'I must go, Alexis. I need to get back to London.'

Alexis opened her eyes. 'I'm sorry I missed Lavinia's birthday. How can I make it up to her?'

'By going back to being the woman my father fell in love with. Pull yourself together, get back your looks and go to work alongside your father. You must know he misses you. Furthermore, you are his heir. It *is* going to be *your* company one day.'

'I will put my mind to it,' Alexis promised.

Claudia nodded and rose. 'I must go to the back, to the carriage, and return to London.'

'I will walk with you,' Alexis said.

Together they left the library, went along the corridor and outside to the stable block. As she headed for her carriage, Claudia turned to Alexis and in a low voice said, 'You're letting my father down. He wouldn't approve of your behaviour, or the way you've let yourself go. Buck up and lose some weight.'

Shocked at her words and her tone of voice, Alexis was rendered speechless. Before she could say anything in response, Claudia had stepped into the carriage and banged the door shut.

As it rolled away, Alexis stood watching her go.

There was no question in her mind that Claudia Trevalian Glendenning was angry with her. And she had travelled a long way to tell her so.

Claudia settled back on the carriage seat and closed her eyes for a few moments. She was glad she had left at that moment. She had said enough for today.

Her tone had been stern, her words harsh, but this technique might work. Certainly being nice had not. Claudia now understood that kindness didn't work with Alexis. In fact, it was almost like colluding with her.

Jane and she had discussed this trip yesterday, when Alexis had not arrived for Lavinia's birthday party at the Grosvenor Square house. Jane had begged her to be tough, and she had taken Jane's advice.

Claudia opened her eyes and sat straighter on the seat, sorry now that she had not brought up Haven House. Alexis had not visited the home for battered women for almost two years.

This charity, which Alexis had founded, had been a huge success so far. Women came to them in droves, desperate to escape their abusive husbands or the men with whom they lived. She, Lavinia, Marietta and Jane spent time there once a week and, fortunately, the money Alexis had given herself and also raised among her friends had lasted. It had been used carefully.

But now Claudia believed that it was time Alexis Malvern came back to Haven House. Jane had promised to make that happen. *Fingers crossed*, Claudia thought, and closed her eyes again, wanting a rest from her constant worry about the woman she had just left.

Alexis found Tilda in the garden, cutting the last few roses with the garden shears and laying them in the flower basket.

'I've been looking all over for you,' Alexis said, coming up to her lady's maid, smiling at her.

'I'm so sorry, Miss Alexis, but when Miss Claudia arrived I decided to come out here. I realized she wished to speak to you in private.'

'She did, and she was annoyed with me. I might go so far as to say she was angry.'

'She did have a ferocious look on her face.' Picking up the basket, Tilda showed it to Alexis. 'These are the last few of your favourite roses. I thought they'd be nice in your bedroom.'

'Thank you, Tilda. It's a lovely gesture. Can you please come and sit with me in the arbour? I need your help.'

'But of course, Miss Alexis.' The lady's maid picked up the basket, put the shears in it, and together the two women walked on the path through the flowerbeds, making for the secluded corner.

'Sit down here, Miss Alexis. We must keep your face out of the sun.'

Alexis did as she was told. Once Tilda was seated, she turned to her maid and said, 'I've lost my looks, haven't I?'

'No, you haven't, but you have been neglecting yourself, I'm afraid to say,' Tilda said, adding, 'We'll soon get them back. You need a few of my special face rubs and several body massages to make you relax.'

'I know I've neglected my hair,' Alexis went on, 'and there are some grey patches or streaks, I should say. How do you get rid of these?' She stared at Tilda, and her eyes grew damp. 'Miss Claudia told me to lose weight. Am I fat, Tilda?'

Tilda hesitated. She knew Alexis Malvern was upset, and she was pleased that Claudia Trevalian had spoken out so clearly. The harsh words which had probably been said had obviously had an effect on her mistress, of whom she was very fond.

Finally, Tilda spoke. 'You have put on weight,' she agreed. 'Mrs Bellamy makes delicious meals and you have to stop eating them. We will devise a special diet for you.'

'She'll be offended,' Alexis exclaimed.

'Not if I explain that you have to eat much less for your health and in order to wear your best dresses.'

'They're not too tight,' Alexis protested.

'I'm sorry to disagree with you, Miss Alexis, but they are. Anyway, you haven't worn them for ages. You live in your silk blouses and long skirts.'

Alexis was about to contradict her and instantly changed her mind. 'A diet, facials, massages. And the grey streaks? What do you use to get rid of those, Tilda?'

'Henna mostly. Special shampoos to enhance the auburn, and perhaps a few new hairstyles. Work with me, Miss Alexis, and I can bring back your beauty and your glamour.'

When Alexis was silent, Tilda continued, 'The biggest problem is your weight, I think. You will have to walk in the garden a lot, do certain exercises, and perhaps go riding *every day*. That will also get you into better shape.'

'It does sound like a lot of work.'

'A big effort indeed. But once you become your old self, and are reborn, in a sense, I can then get your frocks and outfits altered. Then they will fit you perfectly.'

'I understand.' Alexis hesitated, then continued slowly. 'Claudia says I must go back to London, go back to work. But I do become very anxious when I think about that.'

'You mustn't be. And you have to live in London, part of the time at least. I know I have to as well.'

Alexis stared at her maid. Reluctantly she said, 'Then we must try to get me reasonably attractive, I suppose. How long will it take?'

'I don't know, Miss Alexis. That is up to you.' As she spoke, Tilda was well aware that her mistress was genuinely overweight. These pounds would take months to come off.

'You can't give me a date, can you?'

Tilda nodded. 'No. But let's get going today and put all our energy into making you look ten years younger.'

Alexis looked around her, at the beautiful gardens and the farmhouse. This place had been her refuge. But was Claudia right? Perhaps it was time to leave it behind.

TWENTY-THREE

It was a beautiful sunny day in the middle of August. As Natalie Parkinson walked through the cobbled streets of Hull, she smiled to herself, glancing around, feeling a sense of happiness inside.

By nature a true optimist, Natalie's cup was always half full, never half empty. And tomorrow would always be a better day.

Looking up at the perfect blue sky without a single cloud, she nodded. Hull wasn't a permanently rainy city as so many people said. Today the weather was temperate, and she stepped out confidently.

Aside from the lovely sunshine, the brightness of the sky, Natalie was happy because James Falconer was arriving this afternoon. She couldn't wait for him to see the progress the builders had made on the arcade, and the first totally finished shop.

Also, she had met with two potential renters. One was a woman who sold shoes for men and women, the other a man who dealt in estate and antique jewellery.

They were excited about the new arcade in the middle of Hull and were anxious to meet James.

She was also glad he was bringing Peter Keller with

him, because she wanted to find out how *he* really felt about her. They had gone out together a few times, but he was still an enigma to her.

But then she wasn't certain how she felt about him. He was a nice man, kind and certainly well-informed, but shy. His reserve bothered her, although she did not know why.

Turning off the side street, she walked into the busiest part of the city, and her thoughts turned to her sister Irina for a moment or two. She had left at the end of the month, with the group. Her mouth twitched with hidden laughter.

It had become exactly that – a family group. Aunt Cheska had been accompanied not only by Irina but their parents, Maurice and Ekaterina, who had now moved back to Europe.

Even Sandro had been invited and thought of going. But her brother had changed his mind. His deal to design the sets for a new play in the West End had finally come through.

Well, they were in St Petersburg and Aunt Olga had been delighted to welcome them. How long Irina would stay on had not been mentioned.

Natalie felt sorry for Irina and James because they hadn't been able to spend any time alone together before Irina left. On the other hand, James had his work to keep him busy and Natalie wasn't sure her sister really understood his commitment to it. He had spent the last week in London, working with Mr Malvern on the sale of some warehouses in the East End.

When she arrived at their small office near the arcade, she was greeted by her assistant, Lucy Charteris.

Luckily, they got on well, and Lucy was a dedicated worker. She had energy, enthusiasm and a pleasant personality.

Once Natalie was seated at her desk, Lucy said, 'There

was a man here, looking for Mr Falconer. He said his name was Joe. He asked if it would be all right to wait at the building site for him. I told him to do that. I thought you might want to pop over there to see what it's about.'

Natalie frowned. 'What sort of man?'

'I think possibly a builder. He was shaved, nicely dressed and wore a tie and suit. Pleasant in his demeanour.'

Standing up, Natalie answered, 'I'd better go and see what this is all about. In the meantime, don't forget that Mr Falconer is coming up by carriage, and the carriage will be taking you back to London. I won't return until next Friday.'

'I remember everything, Miss Parkinson. I also know I have to cover both of the Malvern arcades in London.'

Moving swiftly across the floor, Natalie said, 'I won't be long.'

'I'll be here,' Lucy Charteris answered with a cheery smile.

When Natalie arrived at the building site, a few of the crew were on ladders, diligently doing their work. They were well advanced now on the first row of five shops.

'Good morning, gentlemen,' she called out in a warm voice. 'You're all doing well! Thank you.'

The men shouted, 'Morning, miss', almost in unison, grinning, and some of them waved a greeting at her.

There was a manager on duty, Bill Jameson, and he hurried over to her.

'Hello, Mr Jameson,' she said, as always greeting him politely. 'I understand there is a man here. He's looking for Mr Falconer.'

'Morning, Miss Parkinson. I spoke with him when he first arrived. I told him I wasn't sure when Mr Falconer would be here. He asked to wait.' Jameson glanced to his right. 'He's over there, sitting at the end of the wall.'

Natalie followed the direction of his gaze and observed,

'He looks mild enough.' With a smile, she excused herself and walked across the site.

The man jumped up when he saw her coming towards him. He threw his cigarette on the ground and stamped his foot on it hard.

'Hello,' she said. 'I'm Natalie Parkinson. I work with Mr Falconer.'

'Mornin', miss,' the man replied. 'Me name is Joe Turner. I answer to Joe most of the time, miss.'

Natalie half smiled. 'How can I help you, Joe?'

'I need ter 'ave a word with Mr Falconer. I worked with 'im at Venables. Foreman, I were, on the ware'ouse crew.'

'Oh, now I know who you are, Joe. He's mentioned you and the other men in that particular crew. He was always touched by your devotion to him.'

Joe Turner beamed. 'So the boss does remember us . . .' The beam turned into an even bigger grin. 'There in't nobody like Mr James. They threw t'mold away when they made 'im. I'm looking for a job, miss. Any chance, do yer think?'

'Perhaps. I'm not sure, Joe,' she answered. She liked this man, and now she knew exactly who he was. She realized he was the salt of the earth. That was the way James had described him to her.

She now said, 'Mr William Venables told me that Mr Falconer saved you and your entire crew from certain death, when he noticed that old warehouse shifting. In the nick of time, Mr William said. It was about to collapse.'

'Aye, that's so. If Mr James 'adn't run in ter ger us out, we'd be goners.'

'Since I don't know exactly *when* Mr Falconer will arrive, I think it would be best if you came back around two o'clock this afternoon. Can you do that, Joe?'

The beaming smile flashed again, 'I can, miss. Thanks ever so much. See yer later then?'

'Yes, you will, Joe. I'll be here working with Mr James for the rest of the day. Once he gets here, that is.'

Joe nodded, his smile intact.

Natalie returned to their office nearby and explained to Lucy Charteris who Joe was. She then started to do her paperwork and wrote a short memorandum to James. It was in regard to the two possible renters who were interested in shops in the arcade.

Much to her surprise, James arrived at exactly noon. He came into the office, a smile on his face. 'I'm early,' he announced, and walked over to Lucy and shook her hand.

Natalie and Lucy laughed, and Natalie said, 'We know how much you miss us and couldn't wait to get here.'

'How right you are,' he answered and looked at Lucy. 'Your carriage awaits, my lady.'

Lucy giggled and stood up, walked over to the cupboard. She took out a light summer coat and a small travel bag. 'So I can go now?' she asked, looking from James to Natalie.

'Of course,' James said. 'The carriage is down on the main road, just a few steps from the arcade.'

'I'll be off then,' Lucy said, and waved as she went outside. 'See you in a week,' she added.

'That's right,' Natalie answered. When they were alone, she looked at James, who was now sitting at his desk. 'Did you drop Peter Keller at the bed and breakfast? I booked a room for him.'

'I'm sorry, Natalie, but he didn't come.'

'Oh,' she said in a lower voice, looking both surprised and a bit let down.

'He did have a proper reason, Natalie. Don't look so

disappointed. His only relative, an aunt, suddenly died. He had to go to the funeral today.'

He noticed the disbelief on her expressive face, and said swiftly, 'There was an obituary in *The Times* the other day. He showed it to me. She was his father's sister and quite a well-known painter. Her name was Angelica Keller. I have it for you in my bag, which I dropped off on my way here.'

Natalie couldn't help laughing. 'I suppose I look like Doubting Thomas, don't I?'

'Not really – let down, maybe. Anyway, he's certainly not avoiding you. He sent many apologies.'

She nodded, then remembered Joe, and told James about his arrival at the office and that she had spoken to him at the site. He was returning at two o'clock to speak to James.

'It'll be nice to see him. I can't imagine why he wants a job, though. I thought he still worked at Venables.'

'Obviously not,' Natalie remarked, and gave him the memo.

After reading the memo James exclaimed, 'How marvellous! To have people coming so soon, before the arcade is finished. This is great news.'

Natalie, standing up, smiled at him and agreed. 'Shall we go and have a quick sandwich at the café on the corner? Before we go to the arcade?'

'What a grand idea! I'm a bit hungry, to tell you the truth.' James rose, went over to Natalie and put an arm out for her to tuck her hand into.

She stood up. 'I'm not really Doubting Thomas. I think I am a bit disappointed. Though I do know that Peter wouldn't use a silly excuse to avoid seeing me. He would tell me the truth.'

'Yes, he would. Come, let's lock up the office and go and have a bite. I can't wait to see the arcade.'

*　　*　　*

At one forty-five, when James and Natalie arrived at the site, James spotted Joe sitting on the wall.

The minute he saw them walking over to him, Joe jumped up, a wide grin on his face.

Once they stood together, Joe inclined his head and said, 'Afternoon, miss.'

'Hello, Joe,' she answered.

James Falconer stretched out his hand, smiling, and Joe took it eagerly. 'Mr Falconer, what a nice welcome. I've missed working with yer.'

'It's so good to see you, Joe. I must admit, I feel the same about you. I hear you're looking for a job. What happened? Why did you leave Venables? You're a great foreman; the men liked you, took your orders well.'

'Me wife were ill, sir, and I 'ad ter stop work ter look after Annie. I were off ever so long, and they let me go.'

'I'm so sorry to hear about Annie's illness, Joe. I do hope she's feeling better now.'

'Much better, Mr James, thank you.'

'I don't understand Venables letting you go, though,' James ventured. 'Mr William always spoke well of you.' He frowned, was puzzled.

'I were off months, sir. I ain't givin' blame. Anyways, I been watching yer arcade risin' up and up. Proud of yer, I am that, sir.' Joe gave James a hard stare. 'If yer don't mind me sayin' so, yer need more protection, Mr James. Mostly Saturday an' Sunday. Yer do, sir, believe me. The place is . . . an easy target.'

James Falconer liked and trusted Joe Turner and knew he was speaking truthfully. He would not manufacture something to get a job. He asked, 'What are you getting at, Joe? Can you explain?'

'I can. Two watchmen, one at each end of t'arcade yer 'ave. Ain't nowt, I been thinkin'. I been watchin' yon place, off and on, and there's lots of folk gazing at it, and walkin'

184

through. Yer need one good guard ter be alert all night, patrollin' it, sir.'

Natalie exclaimed, 'Listen to Joe, I think he's right, James. People are nosy; they look in, and I've seen them trying to walk through after the builders have left.'

James nodded, looked at her, and asked, 'So are the watchmen asleep in their huts? Or what?'

'Perhaps, perhaps not,' Natalie replied. 'But the world is full of clever devils, who could do anything.'

'There's not much they could do here,' James shot back.

Joe cut in, 'They could steal stuff, Mr James. Pinch a tool left behind, a coil of wire, a plank. Folks lookin' for money, they sell stuff.'

'I think you're right, Joe,' James agreed. 'So when can you start?'

'Yer givin' me a job, Mr Falconer?'

James stretched out his hand, gripped Joe's. 'You bet I am, and this shake seals our deal.'

'I'll start ternight, sir, if yer'll tell the boss that's on now.'

'I will speak to him immediately.' James put a hand on Joe's arm and steered him across the arcade, heading for Jameson.

Natalie followed slowly. She felt a sudden sense of relief. She had often thought the arcade was too exposed. When it was finally finished, it would have an iron gate with a lock at each end – full security.

TWENTY-FOUR

William Venables was the first to arrive at the Tamara, at exactly nine o'clock. He was the host this evening, reciprocating James's supper of last week.

Once the waiter had led him to his favourite table, William asked for the wine list and ordered a glass of water.

It was a lovely evening, a reflection of the sunny August day. William enjoyed having James in Hull so much at the moment. He and his father, Clarence Venables, believed James's idea for an arcade in their fine city had been a stroke of genius. There was no doubt in their minds that it would be a resounding success. They admired James's vision, and knew that he was quite brilliant when it came to business.

William's life had changed quite a lot since his cousin James had arrived. His only disappointment had been that James wouldn't stay with them. He had declined gracefully, explaining that the B&B was closer to the arcade and more convenient.

Nonetheless, William and James did spend a great deal of time together, going out at the end of the working week. Hull was called the City of Gaiety for a reason; they enjoyed the variety shows, the music halls and eating out. Of course, the Tamara was their favourite. Saturdays and Sundays were fun.

When Natalie was working in Hull, William enjoyed himself more than ever. He genuinely admired her drive and ambition, and how she handled her independence. And he thought she was beautiful, with her luxuriant chestnut hair and soft brown eyes. In fact, he had quite a yen for her.

The problem was Peter Keller, whom he had only recently met. Natalie seemed to have some sort of understanding with him. On the other hand, from what he had observed, Keller seemed reserved, even withdrawn at times. And William had no insight into him. He did not quite understand the situation between Natalie and Keller, but hoped to find out from James today or tomorrow, when they spent time together.

Natalie attracted him more than any other woman since his fiancée, who had died suddenly some years ago. She was very much his type, and they seemed to see eye-to-eye on many subjects. Given a chance, he believed he could easily fall in love with her.

He longed to have a wife now, start a family and be grounded.

A small sigh escaped, as he thought of his loneliness. James had become his best friend over the past few years and they had spent some good times together. He wished his cousin was here in Hull more.

'My goodness, you look very beautiful tonight, Miss Parkinson!' James exclaimed, staring at Natalie in admiration. He was always careful to address her correctly in public.

He had been waiting for her for several minutes in the foyer of the B&B, and now that she had arrived he was captivated.

Natalie was wearing a fashionable summer frock which suited her admirably. Its background was a light cream, covered in colourful small flowers. It was cut full in the skirt, had short sleeves and a V-shaped neckline. The fabric was light and the frock billowed around her as she walked.

'Thank you kindly, sir,' she said and kissed him on the cheek. 'I think we'd better get going if you want to stop at the arcade to see Joe.'

'I do. And you're right.' Opening the front door, they went outside together and headed for the main street. It was still light and, although the bright sky of daytime had dimmed, it was still blue and cloudless. Dusk had not yet descended.

Walking along at a good pace, and in step, they chatted about the progress the builders had made. James was still a bit surprised – and gratified – that there had been recent enquiries about renting.

When they reached the arcade, they saw that it was empty. The builders had packed up and gone home. They stopped at the small hut where the night watchmen sat. He told them Joe would be walking around the site – on patrol, so to speak.

Within moments they spotted him, and he came over to greet them, his wide grin in place.

'Evening, miss,' he said, inclining his head.

'Hello, Joe,' she responded, with a smile.

He looked at James. 'Good evening, Mr Falconer.'

'Glad to see you, Joe. I have something for you.' Falconer took an envelope out of his pocket and handed it over.

'Thanks, sir, but what is this?' Joe glanced at the envelope.

'I have written you a letter of employment, which allows you to patrol the arcade at will. I have given you the address of the B&B where I live when I'm in Hull, and the address of Malvern House in London. That's our main office. You know where the little office is here.'

'Thanks very much, sir.' Joe put the envelope in the inside pocket of his jacket.

Falconer went on. 'You should know that Miss Natalie Parkinson is my assistant on the Hull project. She stays at the B&B here, and works at Malvern House in London. The other young lady you met earlier has the same address but has now returned to London. I will be here in Hull all week. By the way, the other young lady is Miss Lucy Charteris.'

Joe nodded his understanding. 'So I know where to find yer, Mr Falconer, night or day. Should I be needin' yer.'

'That's correct, Joe. Also, there is some money in the envelope—'

'Oh, Mr James, yer didn't 'ave ter do that!' Joe cut in.

'Yes, I did,' Falconer answered. 'To tide you by for the moment.'

'Thank yer, Mr James. Thank yer ever so much.'

James nodded, took out his pocket watch. 'Oh, we must be going. We are meeting Mr Venables at the Tamara Restaurant. See you later, Joe. We'll say goodnight after supper on our way back.'

Joe grinned, saluted them and wished them a good dinner.

William Venables stood up and waved to them as Natalie and James walked into the Tamara. He was smiling with pleasure to see that Keller was absent, and was mesmerized by the way Natalie looked. Always lovely, she looked unusually stunning tonight.

Spectacular, he thought, as she walked toward him. Her chestnut hair shone like silk, piled high on her head, and her face was creamy-pink and flawless. The smile in her eyes seemed just for him.

Where was Keller? Well, he didn't care. He had her to himself tonight, and he was going to make it clear he wanted to take her out next week. Alone.

As for James, he also looked on top form. William noticed the impact they had made on their arrival. And every woman in the restaurant had their eyes on James. He was handsomer than ever, William thought, as he shook hands with James. He then gave Natalie a light kiss on her outstretched hand.

William helped her to sit down, and then he and James sat on either side of her.

'I've ordered a bottle of white wine,' William announced. 'I know you two have been working all day, and I think a drop of vino helps everyone unwind.'

'How nice of you, William,' Natalie murmured, turning to him, a smile on her face.

'Yes, very kind of you,' James said, then went on. 'Peter Keller sends his apologies to you, William. His aunt died and he had to go to her funeral.'

'Oh, I'm sorry for his loss,' William responded, as always correct and polite. But he was pleased Keller was in London and not Hull.

James started to speak as the waiter came to the table and filled their glasses, and once they had clinked them, he said, 'You'll never guess who came to see me today.'

William glanced at him and said, 'I hope it was someone you were happy to see . . .'

'It was indeed!' James declared. 'Joe Turner, who used to work at Venables.'

'Of course, I know there's only *one Joe* in your mind,' William replied with a small laugh. 'You don't have to add his surname. And he's a good man. Genuine. How was he?'

'He asked for a job and I gave him one. He's going to

patrol the arcade at night. And when the place is finished, I'll keep him on. As head of security. He's had a bit of a difficult time, William. A sick wife, no money. He told me Venables let him go.'

William stared at James and said slowly, 'Yes, Annie became rather ill, and he was off for a long period. We did let him go but, as for money, we made sure he was all right. It was a shame though.'

The waiter returned to the table with menus, and said he would come back in a few minutes.

Natalie looked across at James, before opening hers. 'Irina sends you her best, James. I had a letter from her the other day.'

'Send her my love when you reply,' he answered. 'I suppose she's settled in by now. Is she enjoying St Petersburg?' His light tone betrayed nothing, though she knew he must be frustrated by her absence.

'They all are.' Laughter bubbled up. 'You see, it became a *family* trip. My parents went, along with Aunt Cheska and Irina. Aunt Cheska invited all of us to go. What I mean is, she included me and my brother Sandro. But we had to decline because of work.'

'Your aunt is really very generous,' James observed. After a sip of wine, he went on, 'She's also very philanthropic with all her charities. That's admirable.'

'It is,' Natalie agreed. 'She undertook them when her husband, Edward Forrester, died—'

'I didn't know she'd had a *first* husband!' James exclaimed, interrupting her.

'Oh, perhaps I never mentioned it,' Natalie frowned. 'But, yes, she did. She married Edward when she was eighteen. He was twenty years older than her, but a marvellous man. Extremely successful in business. They'd been married about six or seven years when he dropped dead. Just like that. He stood up from the breakfast table one morning, took about three steps and collapsed. By the time she had run over to him, he was dead.'

'My God, how awful,' James said. 'What a shock for her.'

'It was. It had been a good marriage, and she grieved for some time. Then she slowly got better and picked up her life. In his will Edward had included a clause that said his charities must be maintained by her. But he left his fortune to her. A huge fortune.'

James thought, *So that's where all her money comes from*. Not from Lorne. He felt sure he was right about that, but he knew it was wiser to remain silent. He looked down at his menu, not wanting to ask about Irina, who he felt was unlikely to return any time soon.

The waiter came back, and the three of them glanced at each other. It was Natalie who announced, 'I suppose we're going to order the same as usual?'

William read the menu. 'I will have the caviar and blinis as a first course, and I notice they have goulash tonight. That will be my main entrée.'

'Sounds delicious.' Falconer glanced at his own menu and chose the hot borscht soup, to be followed by poached salmon. Then he said to Natalie, 'I bet you're going to have the borscht soup and chicken Kiev.' A brow lifted questioningly.

'Of course I am. I can't resist my Russian favourites.'

Once they had ordered, they sat sipping their wine and chatting about the arcade and its progress, the Venables wine business; then, out of the blue, William brought up James's twenty-first birthday.

William said, 'I suppose your family is giving a party for your big birthday next year. But I'd like to give a bash for you up here. How do you like that idea?'

'Sounds marvellous,' James answered, pleased at William's show of affection and his generosity. 'We can talk about it more nearer the time.'

William looked happy with this answer. As James seemed to disappear into his own thoughts, he addressed Natalie quietly. 'I hope this is not a rude or intrusive question, but I was wondering if you have an . . . understanding with Keller.'

Taken aback for a moment, Natalie didn't answer for a few seconds, asking herself if she did. No, she didn't; she realized that now. She said, 'No, I don't. Peter has taken me to supper a few times, and we've been at the same events sometimes. But we are only friends. He is very reserved. I thought he liked me, but nothing . . . that is to say, there is no understanding between us.'

William leant forwards a little. 'Then would it be appropriate for me to invite you to supper next week? Just the two of us?'

Although a bit surprised, Natalie looked at William. She noticed the eagerness in his eyes and his hopeful smile. 'Yes, it would be lovely to have supper with you, Mr Venables. Thank you.'

William Venables felt a rush of relief mingled with excitement. Deep down he knew Natalie was just the kind of woman he liked, enjoyed being with. He was going to pursue this relationship and stop dithering about her. He had been attracted to her since the first day he'd set eyes on her. Now the moment was right.

TWENTY-FIVE

It was William who brought up a crucial question, asking Natalie when Irina planned to return to London.

'As soon as she can,' Natalie answered. 'I would say in a few weeks, not much longer.' She looked from William to James, and remarked, 'I wish *we three* could go for a visit. St Petersburg is one of the most beautiful cities in the world, with wonderful things to see.'

James said, 'It's a great temptation to go, but I'm afraid I can't take the time off. I did explain that to Irina when she suggested it.'

William agreed, and then added, 'I would love to see the city. It's built on stilts like Venice, isn't it? And the Hermitage is a wonder.'

Natalie nodded, and was about to say something when the sound of thunderclaps made them all jump. They looked at each other, and it was Natalie who exclaimed, 'I can't bear it if it now starts to rain. I'm wearing a new dress, and we didn't bring any umbrellas.'

James glanced out of a nearby window and shook his head. 'It's not raining yet, but it might. We can stay here a bit longer, wait it out if necessary.'

'Or I'll go and find a hansom,' William said. 'It's been

a hot day and, up in these parts, rain and storms often follow.' He grimaced. 'I'm afraid that Hull is considered a Rainy City, as well as the City of Gaiety.'

There was another thunderclap, and then total silence. Again James looked outside and told them, 'No rain, we're all right.'

William beckoned to the waiter and asked for the bill. Once he had paid it, he turned to Natalie and said, 'Thunder often intrudes and, as often as not, it doesn't rain. I'll finish my wine and we can be off.'

'I'm reassured,' she murmured, and then smiled. 'Thank you. It's been a lovely evening.'

'Yes, a real treat, old chap,' James said. He had noticed the flicker of interest between them and the quiet conversation, and smiled inwardly, hoping their prospective supper date worked out well. He had recently begun to think they were made for each other. But they had to know that themselves. He felt a bit sorry for Peter Keller, but his colleague had been too reserved, too cautious with his interest. Too busy, perhaps, with all the travel for Malvern's. James hoped his friend would take it on the chin.

There was a sudden flurry at the door of the restaurant. As he looked down the room, James saw Joe standing there, gesturing to the waiter, glancing around, looking for him. He was chalk white and obviously upset about something.

James jumped up and hurried across the room. 'What's wrong, Joe?' he asked, staring at him.

'An explosion,' Joe said in a low voice, pulling James toward the door. 'The arcade. The arcade's on fire. Come on. Let's go, sir.'

Shock rolled through James, and for a moment he was frozen on the spot. Finally he said, 'Go on. Go back there. I'm coming after you in a moment.'

Joe simply nodded and left the restaurant.

James went back to the table and, although he was shaking inside, he said quietly, 'The arcade's on fire. It wasn't thunder. It was an explosion. I've got to go!'

He left and began to run after Joe, who was speeding down the road. James was filled with alarm, knowing that he was facing a huge disaster.

His fear pushed him forward. He had long legs and stamina, and had always been a good runner. He sprinted on, worry prominent in his head.

It did not take James Falconer long to catch up with Joe, who nodded, and ran on. James ran next to him. When they came to the end of the side street, went out onto the main road, he saw the huge blaze ahead. *Oh God! His arcade!*

To his relief, he suddenly saw the firemen, whom he identified by their uniforms, holding hoses, along with half a dozen policemen. They were dealing with the fire between them.

Falconer grabbed Joe's arm, brought him to a stop. 'They're on the job. Just tell me what happened,' he gasped, out of breath, sweating. 'How could the arcade start burning?'

Joe stopped, nodded, attempting to breathe more evenly. He too was perspiring hard, and barely able to speak.

Joe leaned against a shop door and finally managed to get some words out. 'I don't know who did this, Mr James. I been on duty since eight, like yer told me ter be. Not a soul in sight. I patrolled. Talked ter both watchmen. Then boom! It were like a bomb gone off.'

'You saw no one, Joe?' James asked, his voice a little more normal as he leaned next to Joe.

'No.' Joe shook his head. 'I met yer at two. Then I went 'ome. Annie give me dinner. Saw yer at about nine, when yer came by.'

196

'Someone did this,' James said. 'If it was a bomb, it was somehow placed earlier today and detonated from somewhere else.'

'But 'ow can yer do that, Mr James?'

'Not sure. Did you go for the police? Who got the fire brigade in? Was it quick?'

'Police patrol on duty come right away. They 'eard the blast. They took over. I knows one of 'em, Andy Coles.'

James nodded. 'Let's go!' He started running, followed by Joe, who soon caught up with him.

Within a few minutes, James was running right into the throng of men, followed by Joe, who motioned to the others to let Falconer through. The police and firemen did so.

Suddenly, there he was, standing in front of his beautiful arcade, a big part of his dream. It was blazing along one side; the flames still shooting up into the dark sky, illuminating it with brilliant light.

His heart clenched, and he stood there helplessly. Tears rolled down his face; he couldn't hold them back, and he felt as if his heart had just broken. 'Oh God, no!' he cried out. 'My arcade is gone! Destroyed.' He felt a hand on his arm and looked down and saw Joe, still as white as bleached bone, tears on his cheeks also.

Joe said, 'Yer'll start over, Mr James. I'll 'elp yer. An' we'll find the bleedin' bastards who set t'fire. Arson, sure as bloody 'ell, it is. We'll ger 'em.'

The Chief Constable of the Hull Police Force, Joe's friend, Andy Coles, joined them quietly. James immediately wiped his cheeks, took out his handkerchief, patted his face with it and blew his nose.

With his usual determination, he took control of his flaring emotions. Turning to the policeman, he extended his hand. 'I'm James Falconer, Chief Constable. This is my arcade. Or rather, I'm building it for the Malvern Company.'

'Sorry to meet you under such terrible circumstances, sir. We're here to help. Let's move to the side, please, sir. The firemen need to move in closer to the blaze.'

The fire was burning on the left side of the arcade where the frame structures were. As James continued to stand watching the blaze, he began to realize that the right side *was untouched*. Relief flashed through him. He felt a bit better.

He mentioned this to Chief Constable Coles, who nodded. Coles explained, 'I hate to use the word *lucky*, but you have been in one sense, Mr Falconer. It's a warm night, no wind to blow the flames across to the other side, where you have a finished area. I think it's safe there.'

'But the left side is a furious fire,' William said, and introduced himself to Coles. He and Natalie had been allowed through to join James. 'It blazes on.'

'They'll get it under control. We're proud of our fire brigade, as you're well aware I'm sure, Mr Venables. Being a resident.'

Natalie said, 'I'm Mr Falconer's assistant, Chief Constable. How do you think this happened?'

'We won't know that until the firemen kill the fire and examine the ruined part of the arcade. But I believe this to be arson, a criminal act,' the chief constable explained. 'Not much doubt.'

'Where are the two watchmen who sit at each end of the arcade? I hope they're not injured,' James said worriedly, looking at the police chief intently.

It was Joe who jumped in to answer first. 'I gor 'em out quick. They're over there with two policemen. Safe as 'ouses, sir.'

'Thank God no one has been injured.' James turned to Coles. 'What started the fire? Do you have any idea?'

'The chief of the fire brigade, the chap over there who's manning the big hose, says it was probably a bomb.

But a badly made one, perhaps. However, it's done plenty of damage, I'm afraid to say.'

'Dynamite?' William asked, his curiosity aroused.

'Most likely, Mr Venables.'

'I thought dynamite wasn't easy to get,' William remarked, staring at the chief.

'That's true. The manufacturers sell only to demolition companies. But there's always somebody ready to steal it, sell it for a few bob.'

Natalie asked, 'I don't understand anything about dynamite. What is it exactly, Chief?'

'It's an explosive. The best there is, and it's often used to blow up old buildings, or used in quarries. I only know that it is composed of nitroglycerin or ammonium nitrate. Maybe other things. But it's powerful. The chief of the fire brigade could give you more information, Miss Parkinson.'

'Thank you,' she answered and moved closer to James. He looked down at her, his face fraught with tension, a terrible sorrow flooding his eyes. She said quietly, 'We'll rebuild, James. Take heart. We're all here to help you.' Wanting to lift his spirits, she added, 'Don't forget you have a *posse*. And thank God the right side is seemingly untouched. Part of the arcade is there.'

'Thank you for comforting me, Natalie, and for being here. Who could have done this?' he asked hoarsely.

'God knows. The chief does believe it's arson, though.'

'How could they get past Joe?' James shook his head.

'I don't think it was done today,' Natalie said in a low voice. 'It might have been placed there earlier and then set off from afar. Ask the chief what he thinks.'

James did so, and the chief nodded. 'I came to that conclusion earlier, sir.' He added, 'But I can't be certain, not about dynamite.'

'How do you explode a bomb?' William asked.

'A bomb made of dynamite needs a fuse. The fuse has to be set alight with a match.'

'I see. So the arsonist has to physically light the fuse?'

'No other way, sir. And it'd better be a long fuse, otherwise the arsonist will get himself killed, Mr Venables.'

'I understand,' William said, and suddenly began to cough.

There was now a great deal of smoke in the night air, accumulating as the fire was being doused and dying out in some areas. The stench of the smoke was stronger, and Natalie began to rub her eyes, as did Joe.

William came up to James and put an arm around his shoulders. 'Whatever you need, just ask me. I am here for you. Look, would you and Natalie like to come home with me, spend the night? You are both very welcome.'

James swung to face his cousin. 'That's so kind of you, William. Right now I want to stay here. I must stay here. It's my duty to wait until the fire is finally out. I know the firemen have managed to get it under control. However, I can't leave until I know that the other side of the arcade is safe. At least that will be good news.'

'I understand,' William answered. 'I wonder if Natalie wants me to take her back to the B&B.'

'You could ask her, but I'm certain she will insist on staying here,' James said.

She did. They all stayed, grouped together around James. Finally the fire died out at four o'clock in the morning, and there was a huge sigh of relief.

'Let's meet here at noon,' the chief said. 'Hopefully we might have some answers for you, Mr Falconer. My men and the firemen will examine the ruins looking for clues. They're all experienced and very diligent.'

When they all met late the following morning at the partially ruined arcade, they were overwhelmed by the stench of smoke which still lingered.

The left side of the arcade was totally ruined. It was a pile of rubble, fallen bricks, planks and bits of timber, and broken masonry. There were several small craters amongst the rubble, but the fire was out. And there was mud across the outside area.

James was in better shape. Although he hadn't slept, he was relieved to see that the right side of the arcade was totally unharmed. It would need cleaning because of the smoke, but it was intact. Part of his dream lived on still.

Natalie and James arrived together. Joe showed up a few minutes later, as did the two watchmen. The last to arrive was William, with his father, James's Uncle Clarence. Both of them carried hampers of hot tea, hot soup, and a selection of sandwiches to be shared later.

They grouped together in the undamaged right side of the arcade. After Clarence Venables was introduced to everyone, it was the police chief who spoke first.

Andy Coles addressed them, sharing the information the police already had. 'We're fairly certain this was a bomb blast, and we believe the arsonist entered the arcade through a grate on the outside of the arcade's main brick wall. On the left. There is a visible grate there which can be levered off with a strong tool, and a ladder going down into the underground area. That is where there are water pipes and a sewage system.'

After clearing his throat, the chief continued, 'The shops share a water closet. The bomb was placed in the underground sewer, on a ledge, and a fuse was attached. The remnants are there. We found them earlier this morning. Any questions, please ask me.'

'Are you saying the bomb was put there earlier, and then the fuse was set off later?' James enquired.

'That's what the chief of the fire brigade believes. He thinks the arsonist returned, perhaps late last night, immediately before the bomb blew.'

'But Joe was there,' William said.

'He was mostly *inside* the arcade,' the chief pointed out. 'The arsonist was on the outside of the main brick wall, the outer wall. If he had set everything up earlier and levered off the metal grate, that would have made it easier for him to lift the drainage grate and go down into the sewer a second time.'

Much to everyone's disappointment, the fire brigade and the police found no incriminating evidence whatsoever. They worked together with great diligence for several days, going over the damaged part of the arcade, seeking clues. Nothing was forthcoming.

'It's like looking for a needle in a haystack,' the chief constable told James. 'We've gone over the underground sewage area and found nothing to lead us to the arsonist. The remnants of the bomb tell us nothing.'

'What you said before is that the arsonist set up, left the arcade, then returned to light the fuse late at night,' James remarked. A brow lifted. 'But no one saw him. Even Joe missed him.'

The chief constable nodded. 'Remember the drainage gate is on the land outside the main brick wall of the arcade. Nobody in the arcade could see him because the wall blocked their view. Whoever the arsonist is, he had to be lithe, fast and a good runner. Because of how quickly the fuse would burn.'

William stared at the chief constable, and said, 'Yes, I went and looked at the grate.' He grimaced. 'He got away with it, didn't he?'

Andy Coles shook his head. 'I won't admit to that yet, Mr Venables.' He glanced across at James and, after a slight hesitation, he said, 'I can't imagine the motive behind the bombing. What reason did this person have to destroy part of the arcade? Do you have an enemy in Hull? Someone who wants to do you harm, Mr Falconer?'

'Not that I know of . . .' James broke off and looked reflective, as if he was searching his mind for a name. Once more he said, 'No. I don't have any enemies here. I hardly know anyone.'

'There is one other thing I want to clarify,' Coles said. 'A bomb made of dynamite cannot be set off from afar—'

'Certain bombs can be, though,' William interjected. 'I did a bit of research and discovered a bomb can be put into a package and left on a doorstep, as if the postman delivered it. Then, whoever picks it up and moves it around will be blown to smithereens.'

'That is correct, Mr Venables, but that kind of bomb is undoubtedly not made of dynamite. A bomb made with that particular type of explosive *must* have a fuse, and that fuse has to be lit by a flame . . . a match. As I told you before.'

William nodded vehemently. 'We understand that now, Chief. And by the way, we know how hard your men have worked, how long their hours have been. Don't we, James?'

'Of course we do!' James exclaimed. 'And I'm always hopeful that a bit of evidence will turn up. And thank you, Chief Constable. And please thank all your men for us.'

James stood in front of the ruins of his arcade. His vision, his idea, all his work, destroyed. He had persuaded Mr Malvern to put up the money, and now they faced a huge bill for a sodden, charred ruin.

The police and the fire brigade had found nothing to help them track down the culprit. James had his own suspicions. But voicing them would only bring disgrace on the Venables family. With no evidence to back them up.

His dream seemed further away than ever.

TWENTY-SIX

It was Wednesday 5 November, and this night, all over England, bonfires were being lit in hamlets, villages, towns and cities. On top of each bonfire was an effigy of Guy Fawkes; he was the conspirator executed for his role in the Gunpowder Plot. Still remembered, although it had taken place back in 1605, with roaring fires and outside suppers. His attempt to blow up Parliament and kill King James I was to avenge the persecution of Roman Catholics in England. It failed, and yet became an historical event thereafter.

At Courtland, the bonfire was built, and the village would be joining the house's inhabitants to light it and mark the date.

'Can you imagine that's almost three hundred years ago,' Alexis said to Tilda, who was helping her dress for the evening event in the gardener's yard beyond the stable block.

'"Remember, remember, the fifth of November, gunpowder, treason and plot." Those were the words I learned in school,' Tilda told her.

Alexis laughed. 'So did I. I expect every child who went to school did as well.' There was a pause, then she said,

'I'm glad I accepted Miss Claudia's invitation to come and stay on for the whole week. She's been very nice since Marietta's marriage, warm and welcoming. It was a lovely wedding. And I was flattered to be a godmother to baby Nicholas.'

'I know that, Miss Alexis, and she's made several comments to me that she is happy about the way you look. Almost your old self, she said to me.'

'Except I still need to lose more weight, Tilda,' Alexis protested. 'I really do.'

'We all put it on so easily, Miss Alexis, but it's surely very hard to get off. You are doing so well, my lady, and your hair is looking lovely.'

'I'm determined to battle it through,' Alexis remarked, and stood up from the dressing table.

Tilda helped her on with a moss-green fitted jacket that matched the long straight skirt. With this tailored but dressy suit she wore a burgundy silk blouse, which tied with a large bow. Alexis left the bedroom, followed by Tilda, who was carrying a full-length moss-green cape for Alexis to wear outside.

Lady Jane and Lord Reggie were waiting for Alexis in the front entrance hall. Alexis thanked Tilda, and then went to join them.

'Good thing you wrapped up well,' Jane said, kissing Alexis on the cheek. 'It's a bit nippy this evening.'

Lord Reggie put an arm around Alexis and hugged her to him. 'Let's hurry. The others have gone ahead to be there when the villagers arrive.'

The three of them crossed the garden and went into the block where the horses were stabled. As they walked at a good pace, Lord Reggie remarked: 'Having a bonfire for the villagers is an ancient custom, started by Sebastian's ancestors. And how he enjoyed it himself, especially the fireworks. Don't you remember?'

Lady Jane and Alexis both nodded and smiled at the memory.

A few minutes later they arrived at the gardener's yard, where Claudia and Cornelius were already standing with Lavinia, Marietta and her new husband, Anthony Gordon. Their wedding had been a success and they had ignored any gossip about the early arrival of their baby.

Alexis was always pleased to see them together. They were beautiful young people, and so very much in love it was touching. She knew that Dukey's solution had worked and avoided a bigger scandal. She could see that it had been the right course of action, however much it had made her feel excluded. And now that she was godmother to the baby, her place in this family she loved was secure.

A few minutes later Aunt Thea arrived, just as the villagers were trooping up the side path from the village of Courtland down the hill.

It was Cornelius who took charge once everyone was grouped around the huge pile of wood, twigs and rolls of paper. Perched right at the top of this pile was the effigy of Guy Fawkes that the villagers had made and which Lavinia usually said looked like a scarecrow. Once again, the same words left her lips.

Cornelius handed Reggie and Anthony boxes of matches, and then stepped over to Jake, Tom and Larry, the under-gardeners, and gave a box to each of them. 'Now we must set the paper at the bottom of the pile afire. Within minutes there will be a huge blaze.'

As the entire pile flared up into the night sky, the villagers laughed and clapped, cheered and sang the old ditty. And when the legs of the effigy caught the flames, louder cheers echoed in the yard.

Mr Frome, the head gardener, was in charge of the fireworks and was assisted by the other under-gardeners, Ellis, Alan and Fred.

Armed with the Swan Vestas, they set alight all kinds of fireworks – from Catherine wheels to flares – which filled the black sky with fantastic patterns in a spectacular display of colour and light.

Everyone clapped and sang. Some of the villagers did jigs, and there was much laughter and enjoyment. When the fireworks were over, Claudia and Cornelius thanked the villagers for coming and told them to go and enjoy the baked potatoes, roasted chestnuts and other food on the buffet table that Mr Frome had set up.

The family walked back to the great stately home. Within minutes they were sitting down at the dining table, where a country-style dinner was served.

Claudia had asked the two cooks to make legs of lamb, all kinds of winter vegetables and baked potatoes.

To start she had suggested a hearty soup, followed by oysters. After the first courses, the haunches of meat were carved by Kingsley and the two under-butlers. The maids handed around the vegetables, while the footmen served various wines from Sebastian's impeccable cellar.

It was a jolly evening, with much chatter, laughter, jokes and reminiscing. It was a companionable group, and Alexis glanced around the richly coloured dining room, gas lamps casting pools of yellow light over the family. She caught her breath at how much she had missed this. It was wonderful to have been made to feel so welcome.

The following morning, after breakfast, Alexis went into the library, where Lady Jane sat reading a newspaper.

'Do you mind if I join you?' Alexis asked. 'I promise I'll be as quiet as a mouse.'

Jane laughed. 'Of course you can. I'm just glancing at the newspapers. That's all.'

'Where's Reggie?'

'He went upstairs to find his spectacles. He just dodged out for a minute or two.'

Alexis exclaimed, 'The Artful Dodger, that's what Sebastian called him at times . . . he would say Reggie just knows how to dodge out when he's asked to answer an awkward question.'

Jane couldn't help grinning at these words as she picked up *The Times* and opened the paper. Alexis followed suit, and found another one to flick through.

When Lord Reggie returned a few minutes later, Alexis said to him, 'I forgot to tell you, the strangest thing – a local estate agent wrote to me, informing me that someone wanted to buy Goldenhurst. Apparently there was a rumour, locally, that it was for sale.'

Jane put down the paper and stared at her, frowning. 'How odd. Imagine a rumour like that starting.'

'It is, but at least I know that if my father cuts me off without a shilling, I've an asset I can sell.'

Immediately recognizing this was the moment he had long been looking for, Reggie discarded *The Chronicle*. He said in a serious voice, 'You cannot sell Goldenhurst.'

'I don't intend to. I'm only telling you what happened regarding the estate agent,' Alexis explained.

Reggie took a moment, rearranging the thoughts in his head, wanting to be clear so that she truly comprehended what his words meant.

At last he said slowly, 'What I'm saying is that you cannot *ever* sell Goldenhurst, even if you wanted to do so. The house is *entailed*.'

Alexis, taken aback, had a perplexed expression on her face. 'I don't think I understand you, Reggie. What on earth do you mean?'

'"Entailed" is a legal term. An entailed estate has a predetermined order of succession.' When she simply gaped at him, he went on, '"Entailed" means to limit the inheritance of a property to a specific succession of heirs.'

Alexis sat digesting what Reggie had just said, and the puzzled expression remained on her face. She finally asked, 'Are you saying that I can't *ever* sell Goldenhurst throughout my lifetime?'

'No, you can't. Nor can you leave it to an heir. When you die, the house automatically goes to a member of the Trevalian family. Let's say Claudia, or a child of hers. Or either of her sisters. And it is an unalterable inheritance. That's really what "entailed" means.'

'But why would Sebastian do that? I mean he left me the house in his will, even before we were married. Why did he do *that*?'

'I've absolutely no idea, Alexis. Truly I haven't. And remember, Goldenhurst was his, paid for with *his* money. Sebastian spoke of many things to me. We were best friends, but he never discussed his will.'

'Why haven't you told me before?' she asked.

'In the beginning, when he died so suddenly, so unexpectedly, you were out of your mind with grief. If you recall, you did not come to the reading of his will. You were ill in bed and sedated. You were hysterical with grief.' Reggie shook his head, looking sad. 'I perhaps should have told you after the reading, but I was a little afraid of bringing up his name, never mind explaining all this after you went abroad for treatment.'

'It's not your fault, I realize that,' Alexis said in a low voice. 'Can I ask you a few questions?'

'Yes, and I'll attempt to answer them if I can.'

'Let's say I do get married one day. Then I eventually die. I can't leave Goldenhurst to my husband?'

'No, you cannot.'

'What if I have a child, an heir? Does that same rule apply?'

'It does. That's what entailed means. It goes to whom-
ever Sebastian has chosen to inherit his property. A
Trevalian.'

'So it's only on loan to me, while I'm alive?'

'That's another way of saying it. And yes, that's the
situation.'

She stood up, putting a hand up to her throat.

'Why would he leave the house to me when we were
only engaged?'

'I don't know. I can only hazard a guess.' Reggie cleared
his throat, and continued, 'He fell madly in love with you
the moment he set eyes on you. He was a widower for
ten years and although he took out various women, I had
never ever seen him behave in the way he did with you.
It was a *coup de foudre*, as the French say. He was struck
by lightning, in other words.'

'But he couldn't have known he was going to die,' Alexis
interjected.

'I agree. However, I do think he wanted to give you
something substantial, in case there was a problem, a
tragedy of some kind . . . maybe an accident, whatever.
It's hard for me to understand what he did myself.' Reggie
sighed. 'I think in his mind it was some sort of protection
for you for as long as you were alive, and if perhaps he
wasn't alive.'

'I think I understand,' Alexis murmured, looking from
Reggie to Jane, but sounding baffled.

Jane's face was without expression. She too was rather
startled.

'Let me say something else. If he had lived we would
have been married, and more than likely we would have
had children. So when I died, who would have been the
heir to Goldenhurst?'

'Your first child by Sebastian. Or Sebastian himself, if
he were still alive. Remember, you would have become a

210

Trevalian, and it was deeded to a Trevalian.' Reggie shook his head. 'That's the best way I can explain it.'

'I still think it was a strange thing to do, Reggie. Don't you?' Alexis pressed.

'I'm not sure what to think. However, just remember, it is yours for your whole life, Alexis.'

Alexis nodded, and stood up. 'Thank you, Reggie, for explaining this to me. I must go up to my room and puzzle through it.'

Alexis sat upstairs on one of the couches in her bedroom, staring out at the gardens and thinking about Sebastian, wondering why he had entailed the house. She had listened carefully to everything Reggie had told her, and she understood fully what entailment actually meant. She shook her head. She felt that Reggie was as baffled as she was – and Jane, too, had appeared slightly stunned.

Sebastian hadn't trusted her to do the right thing. As this thought entered her mind she closed her eyes, pushing back the tears. She had loved him so truly, and with all her heart. She would have protected him with her life. Surely he had known that?

If he had not suddenly and unexpectedly died at forty, they would have married, and more than likely had children. And when he died, his heir would have inherited Goldenhurst. That was the law. Perhaps he had had a premonition that he might die young, and not have an heir, and had wondered what her life would become without him. That she might marry again, have a child, and leave Goldenhurst to her child? A son or daughter who was not a Trevalian?

He could have had that thought, of course he could, she decided, and did not like the sudden rush of disappointment that flooded through her. He wasn't like that, not at all. He had always been generous and kind, and a man who was loyal to those he loved.

211

Nonetheless, he had entailed the house that she thought of as her home, and although she could live in it for her entire life, it would go to Claudia, or another Trevalian, when she died. She felt the tears trickling down her cheeks, and tried to shake off the hurt feeling inside . . . but she knew it would not go away . . . not for a long time. Perhaps it would remain with her forever. She would not ask Claudia anything about her father's will, nor discuss this matter. She would explain that to Reggie and Jane later. Now she would attempt to pull herself together, and put this unexpected knowledge behind her. She was a visitor here for the weekend and she must mind her manners and be a good guest. Keep face, no matter what.

PART FOUR

Taking Chances
London
1891–2

TWENTY-SEVEN

Henry Malvern knew that James was going to celebrate his twenty-first birthday tomorrow on 27 May. He also knew that this brilliant young man was itching to strike out on his own.

But Henry understood that he couldn't allow James to leave Malvern's. Not just yet.

On this sunny morning in May, he sat in his office overlooking Piccadilly, wracking his brains, struggling to find a solution to his dilemma. He needed a really worthwhile inducement which would persuade James to stay. Six months, Henry decided, I need him next to me for six more months. I'll pitch for that and perhaps he might even be persuaded to stay for good.

Malvern and Falconer, Henry said to himself. It didn't sound bad at all.

There was, of course, one other way to go. He could drag his daughter back to London, screaming and objecting though she might be. He would instruct her to learn everything she could from Falconer. With six months to do it. He would then tell Falconer he could go out on his own, start his own company. He knew the young man was restless.

Sighing under his breath, Henry got up and walked across to the window, looking down at Piccadilly. As usual it was filled with traffic – hansom cabs and carriages, men pushing carts, horses pulling wagons. Men and women hurrying along, pushing and shoving to get ahead. Newsboys shouting out headlines. Always bad news as they waved their newspapers. The shouts of the pie men selling their food. What a cacophony of sounds came in through his open window. And a variety of smells.

What should he do? Henry asked himself, his mind focused on James Lionel Falconer. Now was the moment to decide.

Promote him – but how? Make him managing director? Or reward him in another way. Certainly Falconer deserved it. He had worked at Malvern House for only three years but he had been devoted, diligent and totally committed. More than that, he had become Henry's trusted deputy. He had pushed the company to modernize, anticipated change, encouraged them to take risks or to rationalize.

Henry nodded to himself. The company had grown and prospered under James's management. He was a born businessman. A genius, in a sense.

As for Alexis, she had been absent for most of this time. While she still wrote and visited, she had obviously lost interest in the Malvern Company. He did not wish to leave his heiress without money. *Half* of Malvern's shares would amount to a great deal. Furthermore, she would inherit his personal fortune, and his late brother Joshua had left her all his wealth. Plus she had a trust from her mother and the house in Kent, left to her by Trevalian.

There was no doubt in his mind that Alexis would be a very wealthy woman.

He would talk to Falconer later today and try to assess the young man's feelings.

* * *

After Henry Malvern returned from a business meeting with his accountant Edgar Williamson, he stopped off at James Falconer's office.

'Will I never be able to convince you to take a break for a bite to eat?' Henry asked, standing in the doorway.

James jumped up at once, and had the good grace to chuckle. 'I don't think so, sir. Nobody can.'

Henry walked into the office and closed the door behind him. 'I'd like to talk to you for a few minutes,' he announced. 'If I'm not interrupting anything important?' He raised a questioning brow as he spoke.

'Of course, Mr Malvern,' James answered. 'Please, do sit down.'

Henry did so. 'First a question. How did we make such a big profit in the Wine Division this quarter? I just saw the papers you put on my desk on Monday night. Very impressive.'

'I suppose the first answer is that we now employ honest men in Le Havre. And Armand is a very good manager. Also, we had a big sale.'

Astonishment flashed across Malvern's face. 'A sale of wine? I've never heard of that before! Who did we sell to, Falconer?'

'The Balkan countries. They had been buying a lot of our champagne, white wines and sweet dessert wines, but not the red. When Keller was in Le Havre a few months ago, Armand showed him cases and cases of red wine stacked up. He asked Keller if he could cut the price a bit.' James paused, shuffled the papers on his desk and found the page he wanted.

'They were good burgundy wines, but did not move. Keller brought down the price, and then, on the spur of the moment, he told Armand *to cut the price in half*. Armand did so, and that huge bulk was gone in less than a week. The sale was repeated about ten days later, with

217

a red that was quite highly priced and moving slowly –
and that too went fast.'

'And yet we still made a profit?' Henry looked doubtful.

'Yes, because Armand then apparently brought in some
slow-moving whites and cut the price. Also, we had more
space in the warehouses and could ship in a new batch
of champagne. Somehow it all balanced out in our favour.'

'Well, well, good news indeed.' Leaning forward slightly,
Malvern pinned Falconer with his gaze and said, 'Even
though I am now in much better health, I don't want you
to think about leaving. I want you to stay on for another
six months. Will you?'

James was not surprised one iota about this request.
He had been expecting it. He did want to leave and start
his own company, fulfil his dream – he wanted that more
than ever. On the other hand, he had feelings of guilt
about the burning of the arcade in Hull.

The arsonist had never been found. However, James
harboured a suspicion, one he had never been able to
voice to anyone. He already felt responsible for encour-
aging Mr Malvern to expand and commit to the arcade.
That it had been reduced to a ruin before a single shop
had opened had been devastating. Thankfully their insur-
ance firm had paid out and made rebuilding it possible.

But in his darkest moments, James couldn't avoid feeling
he had somehow attracted the arson attack. No one else
felt this, he knew that. But he had his own view. And it
was one he would have to keep secret.

The good news was that the ruined left side had been
cleaned out of rubbish and was already open, along
with the right side. The arcade had been rebuilt in record
time, thanks to his idea of using two building firms
working together, and with Joe as the manager of both.
At night Joe's team of guards surrounded the entire
arcade and there had been no more incidents.

The project had been an enormous effort, and a lot of people were employed on it. The financial outlay for the company had been massive, and quite a strain at the end of the previous year. But it had succeeded. The arcade had opened in January and business was booming as the summer drew closer.

And yet James still somehow felt responsible for the fire, and all that costly rebuilding. So he remained silent, hesitating.

Henry Malvern, not knowing any of James Falconer's worries and qualms, jumped in and said, 'If you will agree to stay for the next six months, I will appoint you managing director. Immediately. And as a reward for all you've done for Malvern's over the past few years, I will give you shares in the company . . .'

Henry paused and, amending his first thoughts as another idea came to him, finally said, 'The number of shares I would give you would increase with each year you spend with the company.'

'How very generous, Mr Malvern. I would certainly like to be the managing director, and the offer of a gift of shares is extremely kind and very tempting. But how would I be able to leave if I accept those shares?'

Henry Malvern studied this unique young man, trying to second-guess him, surprised by the hesitation he was showing.

Falconer said, 'I think I would like to stay for six months, to see through certain projects, sir. And to know that you could manage without me.'

'That makes me feel better already, Falconer. Your presence gives me confidence. But what about the shares? Are you rejecting my gift?'

'No, sir. I am going to think about accepting, and I will let you know in due course.'

Malvern nodded. 'Fair enough. I agree to your terms.'

'Anyway, Miss Alexis might decide to come back, sir.'

Henry Malvern laughed hollowly. 'That would be the day! Hell would freeze over before she did that! No chance.'

Falconer nodded. 'Well, you never know what can happen. Sometimes life surprises us.'

After Henry Malvern went back to his own office, James thought about the offer his boss had just made. It was indeed generous.

He didn't mind working for another six months, and being managing director gave him total power at Malvern's. More or less.

But taking the gift of shares somehow tied him to the company. That was his feeling. And he wanted his freedom, to do as he wished. His own retail empire remained prominent in his mind.

He sighed, put his papers in order and locked them in his desk. Last night he had decided to take tomorrow off. His own birthday treat to himself. And he had just decided to leave early – *now*. He wanted time to think about several things. And about Irina, stuck in St Petersburg because her aunt Olga had been in a serious accident and needed her.

He couldn't help wondering where that left him. How much longer would she be in Russia? It had been months.

When he arrived back at the flat on Half Moon Street and opened the front door, he saw several envelopes on the inside mat.

Picking them up, he noticed that one was addressed to him. His heart missed a beat. He recognized the hand-writing immediately. The envelope had been addressed by Georgiana Ward. A small rush of happiness filled him as he went upstairs. Calm down, he cautioned himself. It's probably just a birthday card.

He opened it eagerly once he was inside the flat. It was indeed a card wishing him a happy birthday. However, there was a small note on the other side of the card. Georgiana had invited him to come and see her about an important matter. Whenever he could in the next few weeks. She had asked him to choose a date and given him her address so he could write back to her.

He sat down in a chair, still holding the card. He was excited to have heard from her at long last. He would write to her later this week and go to visit her as soon as he could. Why ever did she wish to see him, and what could the 'important matter' be?

TWENTY-EIGHT

Esther and Philip Falconer considered a twenty-first birthday to be the most important anniversary in a person's life. 'Coming into manhood or womanhood' was the way Esther put it.

She also believed it should be a family affair, and that everyone who could should chip in to make it the best. And she would always add, 'No, not the best. *Better.*'

For one moment Harry thought of offering his own restaurant, the Rendezvous, as the venue, closing it for the evening, telling his steady customers that it was a private event. But almost instantly, he changed his mind. James's eighteenth birthday party had been held at the Bettrage Hotel in a private room. Nothing less would do for his twenty-first.

Harry's brother George agreed with him, and so they worked out how much they would each give to their parents. When they explained this to Matthew, James's father and their eldest brother, he insisted on matching the amount.

George, who had collected wines as a hobby for years, also offered to provide the wine for the birthday party. It was with a huge smile that Philip was able to announce

222

to his sons that Lady Agatha and the Honourable Mister had already gifted them the wine, to honour James.

As it so happened, James was a particular favourite of Lady Agatha's. For years she had been giving him magazines and books, and there was always a birthday present from her of some kind.

'So this year it was the wine,' Philip remarked. Esther had added, 'And thank you, boys, for helping to pay for the private room. The food and the tips we can easily manage from our savings.'

And so, on a sunny evening on Wednesday 27 May 1891, George and James walked together up Curzon Street heading for the Bettrage Hotel in Mayfair.

Uncle and nephew did not talk very much as they walked along at a steady pace. George was mentally writing a new piece in his head; James was thinking about sending a telegram to Georgiana Ward, instead of writing a letter.

By the time they had reached the famous hotel, he had made up his mind. He would send the telegram, and no doubt she would send one back. That would be much quicker. He was so intrigued by her invitation that he couldn't wait to go to Ascot where she lived.

Philip and Esther were already standing in the private room, near the table which had been set up as a bar, with waiters standing behind it. Hurrying over to his grandmother, James kissed her on the cheek. Holding her at arm's length, he exclaimed, 'You should always wear deep purple, Grans. It's decidedly your colour.'

'James is right, Mother. How regal you look. Royal purple! And your hair is beautiful,' George complimented her.

Esther smiled, thanked them.

Both men shook hands with Philip, and remarked how smart his tuxedo looked on him. After thanking them, he said, 'I can certainly say the same about you two.

You're a couple of toffs. I think there's nothing quite as elegant as a man in a black tie. I'm glad Esther insisted on our wearing them tonight.'

'I want to thank you, Grans, and you, Grandpa, for allowing me to invite my friends. It's very generous of you to have them at such a private family event.'

Philip nodded, smiled, and so did Esther. He then said, 'I understand from Rossi that they're your *posse*.' A laugh escaped. 'I must say I do like that curious name. Rossi explained that it means really close friends.'

Before anyone could respond, Natalie appeared in the doorway of the room, accompanied by William. He had come up to London for the party, not wanting to miss it. Lucy Charteris, Natalie's assistant, was right behind.

After introductions had been made, and drinks served, Matthew and Maude strolled in, with Rossi and Eddie hovering in their wake, and came across to embrace their son James.

Detective Inspector Roger Crawford and Harry were the last members of the group to walk in, both apologizing profusely for being a bit late.

James thought it was a lovely gathering, people he cared about. His family, as always, and those friends who had shown how much he meant to them over these last months. *A great posse indeed.*

His eyes roamed around the room. Suddenly he felt as if he were standing outside, looking in through a window. And, for a fraction of a minute, he saw each person objectively, and he was amazed.

How good they all looked, attractive, nicely dressed, being friendly with each other, moving around yet attentive. Laughing and chatting.

What pleased him the most was the sudden knowledge that every one of them wanted to celebrate his birthday, share the joy with him. How lucky he was to have a family like his – family meant everything to him. And his friends did, too.

Natalie, a staunch supporter at work; William his dearest male friend, always ready to help him if he could. Detective Roger Crawford, who had gone out of his way to make sure he was safe, that he hadn't been targeted by someone. And finally, Lucy Charteris, Natalie's assistant, who had proved to be another diligent and loyal colleague.

He was many times lucky, no two ways about that.

His eyes stayed on Lucy, and his face suddenly changed, a smile pushing through. His uncle Harry had just made a beeline for her and was being his most charming self. And she was charming Harry back.

Well, you just never know, James thought. You could meet your soul mate anywhere, anytime. And certainly when you least expect it. Lucy was blonde, a pretty English rose.

As if the window he was staring through had melted away, he found himself in between Rossi and Natalie, one on each side of him, eager to talk.

'We want to ask you a question,' Rossi said in a firm, no-nonsense voice.

Natalie took hold of his arm. 'Only *you* can answer it,' she asserted.

James looked from one to the other, and said, 'Ask away. I'll do my best to answer it.'

It was Rossi who took the lead. 'Why didn't Peter Keller come to the party? Or didn't you ask him?'

Inside James was amused, knowing full well that Natalie probably believed Keller's absence had to do with her.

Keeping a straight face, he replied, 'He was invited, but he had longstanding plans to go to Le Havre, then down to a vineyard in Provence, and back to Le Havre. Armand was going with him to the vineyard, so it was all too difficult to rearrange. He's extremely busy, as you know, still getting the wine business back on its feet. There was nothing personal about it.'

Natalie nodded. 'I thought perhaps he might be upset with me, because of William.' She threw him a questioning look.

James said, 'Not at all, as far as I know. He likes you a lot, but I'm sure he's still gun shy.'

Rossi asked, 'What are you referring to, James?'

'I understand he had a relationship with someone that he considered to be serious. And, quite unexpectedly, the lady broke it off. There was never a proper explanation, I gather, and then she went to live in America.'

'Oh how awful!' Natalie exclaimed. 'I think that explains a lot. He was a bit cautious with me, and I worried about our relationship. But when I look back there never really was one. He was a bit remote.'

'William isn't. He cares about you,' Rossi announced in a confident voice.

James glanced at his sister alertly. He realized Rossi and Natalie had become close friends and decided to leave them to their confidences. 'If you'll excuse me, ladies, I must move around, work the room.'

Esther and Philip, with the help of Harry, had planned the menu. The first course was seared foie gras on thick slices of warm sautéed apple, to be followed by a scoop of lemon sorbet to cleanse the palate. The main course was duck cooked in an orange sauce with tiny roasted potatoes.

Dessert was James's favourite, strawberries Romanov, but there was also a birthday cake with twenty-one candles which he had to blow out. He did so amid much laughter.

The wine flowed, with champagne for the birthday cake, and everyone commented on the delicious food. A grand meal.

There were short speeches, accolades, jokes and teasing. The supper was a great success, which pleased his grandparents, who had set out to make it the best birthday ever for their grandson. After all, there was nothing quite like a twenty-first birthday party . . . it must always be special so it could be remembered forever.

Everyone stayed on, to relax together, and coffee and tea were served. Philip offered after-dinner drinks and took a cognac for himself. And so did his three sons.

'There's nothing like a drop of Napoleon at the end of a superb supper,' Harry said.

'Now is the perfect time to open your presents,' Rossi announced, and she and Natalie began to bring them over to James. He had told everyone not to buy anything for him, but they had not listened.

There was an elegant delphinium-blue cravat from Natalie, and a gold tiepin with a small pearl at the end, ideal for the cravat, from William. Lucy had found a silk handkerchief which worked well with the cravat and would go in his top pocket. Inspector Crawford gave him a smart satchel for his papers, made of soft black leather.

After opening them all, James said, 'Thank you. Thank you for my presents and for making this a wonderful birthday.'

As he said this, he looked at his grandparents, smiling, and then smiled once more at his entire family.

Slowly he walked around the table, kissing cheeks and shaking hands, being his usual charming self.

Eddie, never one to be left out, exclaimed, 'I hope you liked my painting, James?'

'I did. It's one of your best.' He glanced at his mother, and then his sister. 'And your white shirts are the epitome of elegance . . . definitely to keep for special occasions.'

*　　*　　*

James and George walked back home to their flat on Half Moon Street. It was a balmy night, without a wind, and the midnight-blue sky was scattered with stars. Uncle and nephew were not in a hurry, and George smoked a cigarette, enjoying the stroll and dissecting the evening. The journalist in him came out in its usual way.

'Did you notice that Harry seemed rather taken with Lucy?' George threw James a knowing look.

'I certainly did,' James responded and grinned. 'He didn't waste much time.'

'He beat me to it as usual,' George mumbled. 'Anyway, Natalie's more my type. But I think she's taken. I noticed William . . . hovering a lot.'

'I believe they might be an item. And probably serious, or at least on the way to being so.'

'Mmm. Lost out again, I have. By the way, when is Irina coming back from Russia? She's been gone a while now.'

James let out a long sigh. 'I don't know. Her aunt Olga had an accident and needs her for a bit longer.' He half smiled. 'At least I had a birthday card from her, and she seems to miss me.'

'I'm sure she does. Don't worry, old chap. She'll be back.'

'I got a promotion this week, Uncle George. Mr Malvern appointed me managing director of Malvern's. I'll be running the company. He wants to slow down, take it easy.'

'My God, why didn't you tell us all at the party? Everyone would have been thrilled to hear this fantastic news. Congratulations, James. Well done. And you've earned it.'

'Thanks, Uncle George. It's true. I've worked like the devil, and put in long hours. But to be honest, I didn't expect such a big promotion.'

'I wish you'd told us at the dinner. But never mind, I'll announce it to the world. In my paper.'

'You'd better check that out with Henry Malvern first,' James cautioned. As always he never wanted to look as if he was boastful or promoting himself.

'Leave it to me,' George answered. 'I'll handle it with kid gloves.'

TWENTY-NINE

The first thing James did the following morning was to send a telegram to Georgiana Ward. He said he could come to see her, at any time convenient for her, at her home in Ascot.

The thought of her kept playing in his mind, despite the demands of the day. But his work kept him extremely busy, and his feet on the ground.

Mr Malvern made the announcement to the staff that he had appointed James Falconer to be managing director of the Malvern Company. The news was well received by the staff and the heads of various divisions, proving to Henry Malvern that he had made a good decision and that James was popular within the company. Edgar Williamson, his accountant, very much approved of him.

As for James, once the excitement of the day and the congratulations had died down, he found his thoughts returning to Georgiana Ward and his visit to her. He dithered about whether or not to take a present. And if so, exactly what? He dismissed a box of chocolates, and flowers, and settled on a silk scarf from Rossi's small shop in the Malvern arcade just before Trafalgar Square.

Within minutes, he had slipped out of the office and

was walking down Piccadilly, and soon hurrying inside her shop. Her face filled with smiles when she saw her brother, and she rushed forward to greet him.

'James, hello! Don't tell me you've come to buy something.'

'I have, Rossi, you know I'm a big fan. I'm looking for a silk scarf for an old friend I haven't seen for almost three years.'

'What colouring? Blonde, brunette or raven?'

'Dark hair, yes, raven, and blue eyes that have a hint of violet.'

Rossi went to a shelf and took out a tray of scarves, showed him several. He settled on a longer style rather than a square, and the shade of blue reminded him of pansies.

'This is the right one, just perfect, Rossi. Incidentally, I am going to need some more merchandise for my own little shop in Hull.'

'I'll make a selection for you. I know what your customers like. When are you going up there again?' Rossi asked as she carefully wrapped the scarf. 'This weekend?'

'No, no, I'll be in London all week . . .' He paused, then said in a low tone, 'Mr Malvern has just promoted me. I'm now the new managing director.'

'Oh, my goodness, James! How wonderful!' Rossi exclaimed, staring at her brother, truly happy for him. 'Congratulations.'

There was a moment or two of silence, and then Rossi asked, out of the blue, 'How is his daughter doing?'

'Quite well, but she's more or less retired. She is living in Kent, doesn't come in . . . not often, anyway.'

'I've always thought she was a bit odd,' Rossi stated, tying the ribbon into a bow on the box.

To say the least, James thought, but he decided not to

comment at all. He paid his bill, kissed his sister's cheek, picked up his package and left with a smile and a wave of his hand.

Back at his flat, there was a reply waiting from Georgiana Ward. Her suggested date for lunch was for the coming Saturday, 30 May. Her carriage with her driver, Drummond, would come for him at ten o'clock. He could hardly wait.

James dreaded those nights when he knew that sleep would be evasive, and he endeavoured to tire himself out early, get into bed and go into a deep sleep at once.

But the events of the last few days kept him wide awake, his mind turning constantly. It had been a few days of constant changes. He had a new title and a new job with more responsibility. William had confided his deep interest in Natalie; he was happy for his cousin, but uncertain what it would mean for either William or Natalie in terms of where they lived or worked. Harry had hooked onto Lucy, and he had heard from Mrs Ward. And, of course, Irina was still far away in St Petersburg.

He missed her, wished she would come back. They'd had a brief relationship and got on well, yet they had not spent enough time together to understand the nature of their friendship.

He was lonely, and that was the one emotion he loathed, the sense that he didn't have a close friend. Well, there was William, but they were not always in the same town, and now Natalie had entered the equation and William was preoccupied with her.

Georgiana Ward's birthday card had given him pleasure . . . he was delighted he would see her in a couple of days, yet what would that mean? Perhaps nothing at all. And the differences between them were too important to ignore. He drew a blank there.

And what of his own ambition – his little shop and the idea of his own retailing business. What did Mr Malvern's offer mean for that?

A long sigh slid out of him, and he turned onto his side, hoping to fall asleep. Eventually he did, but dark dreams haunted him all night, and left their imprint on his mind. They lingered the next morning.

Good things had happened and he was grateful. He had so much, if the truth be known – a fantastic family, genuine friends, and success at work. And yet there was that emptiness inside him, something he could not quite fathom. Would it never go away?

Lady Jane walked across the impressive foyer of their elegant townhouse on Chesterfield Street in Mayfair, heading for the breakfast room.

As she approached the door, she heard her husband chuckling. Since he was alone in there, she realized he must just have read something in his newspaper that amused him.

Coming in silently, she paused at his side, leaned forward and kissed his cheek. 'Good morning, Reggie.'

Lowering the newspaper, he looked up at her and nodded. 'As beautiful as always, my lovely Jane. Good morning.'

'What's so amusing in *The Chronicle*? I heard you chuckling.' She sat down opposite him at the round table and placed a serviette on her lap.

At that moment, Mr Grant, their senior butler, appeared. After they exchanged greetings, he brought the teapot over to the table, poured a cup for her. 'Will you have your usual breakfast, m'lady?'

'I will, Grant. Thank you.'

Once they were alone, Reggie said, 'There's a great story in the business pages which I approved last night, and I was laughing because I realized it might upset or annoy someone we know when I just read it again.'

'Oh! So what's the story?' Jane asked, her eyes focused on her husband, her curiosity apparent.

'I won't read the whole piece to you. I'll give you the gist of it. That's all right, isn't it?'

'Of course,' Jane answered and took a sip of tea.

Reggie chuckled once more, and said, 'Henry Malvern has just made James Falconer the managing director of the Malvern Company. I don't think this announcement will sit too well with Alexis, do you?'

'You're right, Reggie. I think she will be furious. I wonder why Henry Malvern did this. Perhaps he's retiring. You know he hasn't been well.'

'He's not retiring. He's now the chairman of the board, but the day-to-day running of the company is in the hands of Falconer.' He shook his head, and a sad expression flickered on his face. 'What a fool she's been.'

'I agree, but let's not forget she's still her father's heir and will inherit the company when Malvern dies,' Jane observed. 'And all of the power is Falconer's. Even if he were to leave, I don't believe she could run the business.'

'That's a given, my dear.' Reggie sighed, folded the paper and laid it on the table.

They fell silent. A few seconds later Grant arrived, removed the newspaper and served them breakfast. Grilled tomatoes on toast for Lady Jane, and eggs, bacon and a pork sausage for His Lordship.

After a few bites of food, Jane said, 'I've been meaning to ask you, Reggie. Do you know who might have started that rumour about Goldenhurst being up for sale?'

He shook his head, and went on eating, not looking at her, intent on his breakfast.

Jane, her eyes narrowing, saw an expression on her

husband's face she knew so well. *Glee*. That was the way she thought of it.

She exclaimed, 'Reggie, *you* didn't do it, did you?'

'Do what?' he asked, sounding puzzled, and finally he looked across the table at his wife.

'You know what I mean, don't pretend you don't. *Goldenhurst*. Remember her innocent remark . . .' Jane stopped, her mind racing. 'Her remark gave you the perfect opening to bring up the entailment of the house. Alexis got upset about that, and I think she still is a little miffed. *Did* you set this up, Reggie?'

'Certainly not,' he answered in a mild tone, endeavouring to look innocent.

Jane saw the glee in his eyes again, and she said, 'It's made her buck up, and she's in better shape, physically at least. Go on, Reggie, tell me the truth.' She chuckled. 'You can tell *me*, I won't split. I'm your wife, men confide in their wives.'

'Only some do, not all men. They've too much to hide,' Reggie announced.

'I know there are some genuine buggers around,' she shot back.

'*Swearing*, Jane! That's not like you.'

'Perhaps I know a lot more than you do about some men . . . who are your friends, by the way.'

'Oh, oh, do tell, darling,' he said in a teasing voice.

'I can't. You see, I never break a confidence.'

Reggie studied her, loving everything about her. Her looks, her warmth, her sterling character and her integrity. He said in a more serious voice, 'Remember the phrase, "Who will rid me of this troublesome priest?" regarding a king and Thomas à Becket?'

Jane nodded, already understanding what had probably happened. Reggie had made a comment and someone had acted.

Reggie took a sip of tea, cleared his throat, and explained, 'I happened to say in front of someone that I wished Goldenhurst were up for sale, that I'd buy it just to get Alexis out of that house and back to London. A friend spread the rumour without my knowing. I was only told later.'

'Who was it, darling?'

'Oh, Jane, come on. You know I can't break a confidence.' A mischievous glint entered his eyes. 'Anyway, no harm was done. No one was hurt, and it had the desired effect, didn't it?'

'Yes, it did. I'm really hoping and praying she finally starts coming up to London.'

'She probably will do that, Jane. However, being in London doesn't necessarily mean she will go to Malvern's.'

Jane merely nodded, seeing the truth in that. It also occurred to her that it had to be a *friend* who had acted on Reggie's comment, and an *educated* friend who knew English history like Reggie did. Someone who knew that it was Henry II who had uttered those fateful words, 'Who will rid me of this troublesome priest?' in reference to Thomas à Becket. He was later murdered, in Canterbury Cathedral in 1170, by four knights in service to the king, knights who had taken his words seriously.

'I can tell you one thing, Jane,' Reggie said, interrupting Jane's meandering thoughts. 'It was James Falconer's uncle, George Falconer, who brought me the Malvern Company story. But he asked me to put another journalist on to actually check it out with Malvern, and then write it.' Reggie smiled at her. 'He's such a nice chap. He didn't want to write it because he didn't want anyone to think the story was biased in any way.'

'Falconer, I mean James, is such a nice young man. I've never quite understood why Alexis was so mean about him.'

'And inexplicably rude to him when he came to deliver the letter from her father. I felt like boxing her ears.'

'And so did I.' Jane stared at her husband, and finished, 'Let's just sit and wait. There are bound to be fireworks between those two.'

THIRTY

The trip to Ascot was easy and pleasant, once Drummond, Mrs Ward's driver, had got them out of London, where the traffic was heavy. The usual rush and push of a Saturday morning, with people crowding the streets, made the going slow and difficult.

James relaxed in the brougham, which was roomy and comfortable, his mind less troubled today. He realized that his tautness and anxiety had lessened because he was thrilled to be seeing Georgiana Ward. He had never imagined he would hear from her again, still less have a meal with her.

He thought of his grandmother's words, often uttered when something unexpected happened. 'Always remember, James, you never know when life is going to rear up and hit you in the face.' Grans had usually added that sometimes it was a bad thing, but as often as not, a pleasurable one. Certainly seeing his lovely friend was a happy event, especially since it had come as such a surprise.

James hoped she was well. The terrible fogs of London, caused by smoke from the many chimneys, had troubled her and led her to leave the city permanently.

He also hoped her sister Deanna had not passed on.

Georgiana had always been worried about her and her heart condition, another reason for leaving London.

Glancing out of the carriage window, he saw from a signpost on the roadside that they were about to enter Ascot. He sat up straighter in the carriage and continued to watch the countryside flying by, as Drummond drove the carriage horses at a quick trot. The time had passed quickly on the roads.

It was not long before he noticed the driver slowing the horses down, and saw they had turned into Honeysuckle Lane, which was where Mrs Ward lived. Within a few minutes, the carriage was going through tall iron gates. On the stone wall, a plaque announced that this was Heathcote House. It was a short, tree-lined drive, and in a couple of seconds the carriage was drawing up to a small but beautiful manor house, painted white, with dark-green shutters at the many windows.

As James climbed out of the carriage, the front door opened. He glanced towards it, and smiled. Standing there, waiting to greet him was Mrs Mulvaney, Georgiana Ward's lovely housekeeper, who had always been friendly.

'Welcome, Mr Falconer,' she said, opening the door wider. 'It's so nice to see you, sir.' She beamed at him.

'And you, too, Mrs Mulvaney,' he replied and shook her hand.

'Mrs Ward is waiting for you in the conservatory,' she went on. 'Please, do come in, sir.'

Smiling, James did so, liking the entrance foyer with its pale-peach walls, doors painted white and tall pots of green plants on a side table.

He followed Mrs Mulvaney down a short corridor which led him into the conservatory.

'Here we are, Mrs Ward. Mr Falconer has arrived.'

Georgiana was standing at a window looking out into the garden, and she swiftly swung around. 'Thank you,

Mrs Mulvaney,' she said, and walked forward, staring at James, her face lighting up, her violet-coloured eyes sparkling.

As the door closed behind Mrs Mulvaney, James hurried over to Georgiana Ward and took hold of her hand, clasping it tightly. So breathless with excitement at seeing her again, he could hardly speak.

They gazed at each other for a long moment, and finally he managed to say, 'I can't tell you how wonderful it is to be with you, Mrs Ward. I've missed you.'

'I, too, have missed you, James, and I was thrilled when you agreed to come here.' She let go of his hand, stood on tiptoes, and kissed his cheek. 'Come. Let us sit down over there on the sofa. Mrs Mulvaney is bringing us a pot of tea. You must need it after the trip. Do you want to freshen up, James?'

'No, thank you, and a cup of tea will do the trick nicely.'

Sitting next to her on the sofa, staring at her intently, James saw at once that she looked in blooming health and had hardly aged. She was ten years older than him, but did not look it. Before he could stop himself, he exclaimed, 'You haven't aged a day, and it's been years since I've seen you.'

Her raven-coloured hair was as luxuriant as ever, piled up on her head, and delicate amethysts hung from her ears and sparkled on her finger. Her complexion was as clear and flawless as the day he'd first met her as a teenage boy, her figure as youthful.

Georgiana laughed lightly, and corrected him when she said, 'About three years, James. That's all.'

He grinned. 'Well, it seems longer to me.'

She nodded. 'I know.' Settling back against the cushions, she remarked, 'It's been quite a week for you, hasn't it? Your twenty-first birthday and a very big promotion at Malvern's.'

His eyes widened slightly, and then he said swiftly, 'Ah, you read about *that* in *The Chronicle*, I'm assuming.'

'I did, and I was so happy for you. You're achieving everything you set out to do, and I'm proud of you.'

He took hold of her hand, now relaxed and at ease with her, and said, 'I'm happy you're proud of me, it means a lot. Everyone has been complimenting me, except someone did say I was too young for the job at only twenty-one.'

Georgiana let out a huge laugh and shook her head. 'How stupid! Age doesn't have anything to do with success . . . it's talent, drive and ambition that count. And I'd like to point something out. We had a man who was prime minister of England at the age of twenty-three – William Pitt the Younger. So, puff-puff to that silly person who said you're too young.' She waved her hand, as if brushing someone away dismissively.

Mrs Mulvaney came in with the tray of tea, and poured for them.

'Thank you,' Mrs Ward said. 'And we're going out for a walk around the garden before we eat, Mrs Mulvaney. I want to show Mr Falconer our pretty little plot.'

'Yes, of course, madam.' Mrs Mulvaney smiled, nodded and was gone.

After sipping the tea, James looked at Georgiana, his expression serious. 'You said on my birthday card you wanted to speak to me about an important matter. What is it?'

'We'll get to that shortly. After we finish our cups of tea, I want you to see the garden. I call it my little plot, but it's a bit more than that. It's a small estate, really, with an orchard, a bluebell wood and some fields.'

James said, 'It sounds lovely, and the air is fresh . . . healthy. And you do look in good health.'

'I am, thank goodness, and Ascot's peaceful. Just a little

village, actually. The only time it's really busy is in June when the royal races are running.'

'How is your sister?'

'Doing much better, I'm glad to say. There's nothing like clean air.'

Georgiana stood up, and said, 'Let's go outside, James.'

He also rose. Spotting the present he'd dropped on a chair when he had rushed to greet her, he went to pick it up. 'I was in such a hurry when I arrived. I forgot to give you this little present.'

He handed it to her, and she thanked him, a half-smile playing around her mouth. As she opened it, he realized the scarf would match the frock she was wearing.

'Oh, how lovely it is, James. Thank you so much. My goodness, how did you know I'd be wearing blue today?'

He shook his head. 'I didn't, but you do wear that colour a lot.'

He stepped over to her, took the scarf from her and put it around her neck, pulled her gently toward him, the scarf still in his hands. They were now face-to-face, close enough to kiss. And they did. It was a loving kiss, rather than passionate. And automatically, they pulled apart. They were in a glass room, visible to all.

Georgiana, smiling, took off the scarf and placed it in the box. She walked to the French doors and beckoned James out onto a stone-flagged terrace. It was a sunny day, and he saw at once how lovely the garden was, filled with flowerbeds and lawns.

Looking down the garden, he saw a stand of trees and a gazebo painted white. At that moment, a young woman came out of the gazebo. James recognized her. It was Sonya, who had lived with Mrs Ward for years and been trained to be a lady's maid.

Georgiana came and stood next to him, called, 'Coo-ee, coo-ee!' and waved to Sonya. Within seconds a small child came out of the gazebo. Sonya took her hand. But when she saw them, the girl broke free and flew down the path, her legs running as fast as they could.

'Oh my God, she's going to fall!' James exclaimed, his heart tightening. 'She's running too fast. She'll hurt herself.'

'She's always running,' Mrs Ward said softly.

James rushed forward onto the flagged path and, as the child hurtled towards him, laughter on her face, he noticed her fair colouring.

A peculiar sensation rushed through him. When she stumbled to a stop in front of him, almost hitting the ground, he bent down and caught her in his arms. Just in time, thank God, he thought.

She was still laughing as she stared at him.

He stared back and saw the blueness of her eyes, the fairness of her hair. The dimple in her chin. Rossi's dimple. And he knew.

The little girl touched his cheek with her tiny hand. 'Pa,' she said. 'Pa . . . pa.'

Still holding her in his arms, James stood up and turned around. He saw Mrs Ward sitting in a chair on the terrace and walked towards her. The child had her arms around his neck, her face close to his. When she kissed his cheek, looked at him, merriment flooding her face, he felt a surge of emotion.

Holding her tightly, he stood in front of Georgiana Ward, and said, 'She's mine, isn't she? She's my daughter.'

'She is, James.' She looked up at him, her blue eyes steady.

'What is her name?'

'Lionel Georgiana Ward. But I call her Leonie.'

He couldn't help smiling. 'A boy's name for a beautiful little girl like this?'

She laughed. 'Everyone calls her Leonie. And I wanted her name to be at least one of yours.'

243

'She's about two years old, isn't she?'

'Yes. She'll be two in September.'

'What was she trying to say? Papa?'

Georgiana nodded. 'She can only say a few words, half words really. I told her that her papa was coming to see her today. I've talked about you to her, and she listens, but probably doesn't understand most of it.'

'She seems to understand *Papa*, doesn't she?'

Georgiana caught the emotion echoing in his voice, and agreed.

'So Leonie's the important matter you wanted to discuss?'

'Yes. Not really discuss. But I wanted you to know of her existence, that we have a child together.'

'Why ever didn't you tell me before, Mrs Ward?' James asked, a surprised note in his voice.

Georgiana gave him a hard stare, and said carefully, 'Although you have often called me *Mrs Ward* when we've been making love, you really must stop doing it. *Right now*. Leonie won't understand that when she's older.'

James couldn't help laughing, remembering how she had chastised him in the past about the use of her surname. 'I promise I will call you by your Christian name . . . *Georgiana*.'

He sat down in the chair next to her and settled Leonie on his knee. The child immediately nestled into him and he bent over her, kissed the top of her head. Then he asked again, 'Why now? Why are you telling me about her all of a sudden? Bringing me here to meet her, *my daughter*?'

'Because you're now twenty-one. Also, I began to feel guilty, I believed you *should* know. I wasn't being fair to you. After all, you are an adult. And I thought I should also be fair to Leonie. I can't acknowledge it publicly, but I would like her to know her father.'

'I understand . . . I just wish I'd known all along. That's the real reason you left London?'

244

'It is. But the other reasons were important. The awful fogs affecting my lungs and my sister Deanna not being well.'

'Does your family know about Leonie?'

'My mother died years ago, and my father passed away just before Leonie was born. He had developed an illness of the brain, so he didn't know about Leonie. My sisters do, and they adore her.'

'Do they know Lionel Georgiana Ward is also a Falconer?' he asked, a slight edge to his voice.

'They do indeed. But they know it is a secret, between us.'

'I wish it didn't have to be a secret.'

For a moment she was taken by surprise.

Clearing her throat, she said, 'It must be.'

'Should I marry you?' he asked, his face serious.

'No! I don't want any scandal attached to you. It doesn't matter about me. No one really knows me in Ascot, and those who do think my husband just died recently. But I must be sure you are protected, safe – clean as a whistle, so to speak. In these strange times we are living in, under the rule of Queen Victoria, people are judgemental. It seems to have become worse, the longer the queen has been in mourning for Albert. I'm older than you . . . it might look as though you married me for my money, or got me pregnant. Haven't you noticed our society is very hypocritical – and prudish?' She paused for a moment.

'James, you are on the rise in your career. You will achieve your dream. I will not become a burden to you. And I have no need to marry.'

'You would never be that,' he told her, and looked down at Leonie.

Georgiana stroked her head. 'She is your child, and you can come and see her whenever you wish. I am happy you will know each other but I am part of your past, not your future. Now, I think we'd better have something to eat. I thought out here. Is that all right?'

'Of course, and can Leonie stay with us?'

Georgiana smiled. 'I think she might protest rather forcibly if I tried to prise her away from you.'

Rising, she hurried back into the conservatory. Leonie watched her leave, and then settled back, nestling against James, contentment on her little face.

Once alone, James thought about Georgiana and the way she was so protective of him. He knew she was a woman of some wealth; her late husband had seen to that. So she had no need of financial help. And even though she was obviously adamant about not marrying him, he knew Leonie was safe in every way. She would be their secret.

Nonetheless, he was determined to be a part of his daughter's life, even if not outwardly known to be her father, and he would be ever watchful of her. She was part of him, and a Falconer.

THIRTY-ONE

Meeting the daughter James did not know he had fathered
was the biggest shock – and yet also the biggest thrill – he
had ever experienced.

As he hurried down the Malvern arcade at the far end
of Piccadilly, his mind was full of thoughts of his child.
In point of fact, he thought about her at some moment
every day. As always, business was at the forefront of his
mind, his ambition and drive intact. But now he had
Leonie as well.

He had been visiting her periodically in Ascot for just
over three months, and this coming Saturday, 12 September,
she would be two years old. Georgiana had invited him
to come for the small party she was giving. He would
finally meet her sisters Deanna and Vanessa. He was happy
about this and planned to buy some toys to take as
birthday presents for his child, who had captivated him.

When he reached Rossi's small shop, he stood regarding
it for a few minutes, looking at the single window, the
name above the door. It was her name: *Rossi*.

His eyes shifted to the shop next door, on the right,
actually the last one at that end of the arcade. Double-
fronted windows, obviously much larger, and perhaps

soon to become available, according to gossip Rossi had just heard.

Opening the door of his sister's shop, the bell tinkled as he went in. Rossi was coming around the counter, with a happy smile lighting up her face when she saw him.

'James! At last! Where were you? I've been trying to reach you since Friday,' was her way of greeting him.

'Hello, my beauty,' James responded and gave her a hug. 'I had to go away for a couple of days. But here I am now. Fresh as a daisy on Monday morning, and all ears.'

Sitting down in one of the two chairs, he gave her a bright smile. 'Tell me, Rossi,'

Taking the other chair, Rossi said quietly, 'I've heard rumours that Mrs Galbraithe next door has been taken ill, seriously ill, and won't be coming back—'

'So the shop will be vacant,' James cut in.

Rossi shook her head. 'Apparently her sister, who is currently running it, wants to keep it for herself.' There was a pause as Rossi stared at her brother. 'Can she do that?'

'Absolutely not. It is Mrs Galbraithe who signed the lease, and no one can just take it over like that.' He snapped two fingers together and grimaced. 'I met her sister once, and I thought she was an unpleasant sort. Aggressive. Hardly a welcoming shopkeeper.'

Rossi said, 'You always wanted me to have that shop, James.'

'I still do. I want you to have both shops. And they will have a new name. FALCONER will be on the sign above the doors.'

'I thought it would be my name,' Rossi exclaimed, her face changing. 'Why my last name?' she asked, her voice rising.

'*Our* last name. And the shops are going to be the beginning of my retailing empire.'

Startled, Rossi said almost angrily, 'You're managing

director of Malvern's now – isn't that enough for you . . .?' She stopped abruptly, realizing he was staring hard at her, and those blue eyes were icy.

'I don't owe you or anyone else an explanation, Rossi, but let me inform you that I will not be staying at Malvern's forever. I plan to move on. And fairly soon, to start my own company. Its name will be Falconer and that's it. I am giving you an opportunity to be part of my dream. I would let you run the shops in this arcade. Take it or leave it.'

The cold look in his blue eyes and the stern expression on his face told Rossi she had just made a terrible mistake, and she felt like kicking herself. James was a law unto himself, and everyone bowed down to him. And not only in the family. Everyone he met, or so it seemed to her, revered him, kowtowed to him.

After a moment, blinking back unexpected tears, Rossi said, 'I'm so sorry I said that. I didn't mean it the way it sounded.'

Knowing how much she regretted her words, James brushed his irritation with her aside. 'Let's move on, Rossi. Will you run this shop and the one next door?'

'Of course, you know that, and I want to be part of your dream, your success. But what about Mrs Sutton? That's the sister's name.'

'I will look at the lease, and then Natalie will come and see her. If I remember correctly, there is a clause I put in all of the new leases. If someone becomes incapacitated and retires, the lease reverts to Malvern's. Her sister can't just take over. Or any other person, for that matter.'

Rossi nodded her understanding, wondering why she had worried about Mrs Sutton. Of course, her brother had thought of everything. He always did.

Taking a deep breath, Rossi now asked, 'What other merchandise will we sell? Mother and her team can't make enough product, even with my help.'

'I realize that. Natalie told me the other day that she is still storing a dozen or so evening dresses made by Irina, and so we would sell those, and pay Natalie the money to hold for Irina—'

'Is *she* ever coming back?' Rossi interrupted.

'I don't know. But it's been so long now, I've come to doubt it. She was always very drawn to Russia. Anyway, going back to the merchandise, I thought you might try your hand at making silk drawstring evening bags in beautiful fabrics, and we'll have a shoe boutique within the shop next door. *Evening shoes*. We can also have jewellery. I've heard of a manufacturer in Paris who makes spectacular pieces out of crystal and semiprecious stones. I think we'd do well with that kind of thing.'

She nodded, wishing yet again she hadn't answered him back in such a nasty way.

James rose, went over and kissed her cheeks. 'Stop worrying, Rossi-possi,' he murmured, using a childhood nickname. 'I'm not angry. And I have a meeting at noon with Mr Malvern, so I must be off.'

Walking back to Malvern House at the other end of Piccadilly, James thought about Rossi's retort of a few minutes ago, and felt a trickle of disappointment. There was also a hint of sadness within himself. He hadn't expected *that* from her. He had spoiled her, looked after her, always been kind, and he had to admit now he *had* been taken aback by her comment.

He felt a hollow laugh rising and swallowed it. Hadn't his grandmother always warned him that the most dangerous place to be in this world was in the middle of a large family? 'Too much floating emotion,' Grans had explained, and she'd been correct.

He had wanted to tell everyone about his gorgeous little daughter, but had instantly discarded that idea.

However, early this morning, when he was shaving, he had considered confiding just in Rossi. Now he was relieved he had remained silent. *Tell no one.* That had always been his motto. Yes, best to say nothing. Ever. He heard his grandmother's voice echoing in his head: 'A still tongue and a wise head.' Leonie Falconer, as he thought of her, would remain a secret.

When James knocked on Mr Malvern's door, his boss called out, 'Come in, Falconer.'

James walked in, a smile on his face. 'Sorry I'm a few minutes late, sir. But I had to stop off at the arcade to see Rossi.'

'Morning, Falconer. Anything wrong over there?'

'No, sir. Rossi had heard rumours about Mrs Galbraithe being ill, not coming back. Natalie will take care of everything.'

Henry Malvern nodded. 'I have some interesting news for you. Alexis has been in London for a week, staying with me, and seems so much better, more like her old self. And she told me at the weekend that she is going to come back to work here at Malvern's. What do you think about that?'

'I think it's great, Mr Malvern,' James exclaimed, meaning it. Her arrival meant he could finally jump ship, go out on his own. He felt a rush of excitement.

'It is, yes. But I'm afraid I'm facing a problem. You have reorganized Malvern's to such an extent that it won't be the same place to her. She won't be able to run it. She has to learn to do that. And only you can teach her, show her the ropes, Falconer.'

James sat back in the chair, his brain racing, wondering how to make the most of this sudden and most unexpected event. He groaned inside, knowing how she hated him and how unpleasant she could be.

After another few seconds, James said, 'You and I had an agreement, Mr Malvern. You asked me to stay for six months, and I said I would. I've only three months left now.'

'I don't think that's enough time to train Alexis, do you?' Malvern asked, staring hard at James, his look intent.

'I agree,' James said. 'There's a whole new system in place now, which has proved to be very successful and has made Malvern's the very best, sir.'

'I know, and I'm grateful to you.' Malvern leaned across the desk, focusing on him. 'I would make it well worth your while. I would want you to sign an agreement saying you would stay for one year, to train my daughter. I would be prepared to give you a large bonus, Falconer, for doing this.'

James hesitated. 'A year is such a long time, and she's not very friendly. Would she want to work with me?'

'She will have to, if she wants to inherit Malvern's. I will speak with her, Falconer. She will listen to me this time around, because she knows if she can't run it as you do, I have no alternative but to sell the company.'

'Have you told her that already?' Falconer asked, curious about her reaction.

'I have indeed. I'm not prepared to leave anything to chance. If she comes back here next week, she knows she has to toe the line, do as she's told and be serious. I know she understands there's a lot at stake and, seemingly, even surprisingly, she appears to want to *work*.' He emphasized the last word, then added, 'And she is very much against my selling the company.'

'All right, Mr Malvern. I agree to stay for another year, and I will sign the written contract. But I have several conditions, sir.'

Henry Malvern was not at all surprised, knowing full

well he was dealing with a very clever young man. 'So, tell me what they are, would you please?'

'I would like Miss Alexis to sign the contract as well as you, just in case—'

Malvern cut in, 'Just in case I'm ill or disabled in some way? Or have dropped dead?'

'Yes . . . I would also like a clause in the contract that guarantees she takes my advice. I don't want to waste my time.'

'Agreed, and very smart of you, Falconer. Any more?'

'Yes. What would the bonus be?'

'I'd pay you twice your salary, which I just raised, remember?'

James thought for a moment. 'I will have to put in a lot of time, sir, to get Miss Alexis up to scratch. I would like to be paid three times my current salary.'

'Done,' Malvern said, glad he hadn't asked for more.

'One other thing, sir. I would like to have the lease of Rossi's shop in the arcade renewed immediately for ten years. And the lease of the shop next door for the same ten years. Because Mrs Galbraithe won't be coming back, Mr Malvern. As I told you, she's ill.'

'Can Rossi afford these two leases?' Henry Malvern asked with a frown.

'No. But I can. I will call the two shops Falconer, and I will start my retailing company in your arcade, sir.'

Henry Malvern gaped at him, and then he smiled, began to laugh. 'My goodness, Falconer, you certainly think fast on your feet.' There was a short silence and an admiring look in Malvern's eyes, when he said, 'I will be very proud if you start your retailing empire in my arcade.'

'Do we have a deal, sir?'

'We do, Falconer,' Malvern answered, laughter in his voice.

THIRTY-TWO

Lady Jane sat in her study upstairs in their townhouse on Chesterfield Street in Mayfair, checking some of the new menus she had created. She knew Reggie would enjoy her choices, and the different mix of foods she had put together.

The sudden knock on the door made her jump, and she jerked in her chair, called, 'Do come in, Grant.'

The butler did so and inclined his head. 'Miss Malvern has arrived, my lady, accompanied by her lady's maid.'

'Where have you put them, Grant?'

'In the green parlour, m'lady.'

'Very good. Please tell Miss Malvern I will join her in a few minutes, and you can show Miss Tilda to the servants' parlour. Please ask Cook to offer her some refreshments.'

'I will, m'lady.' Grant closed the door quietly.

Jane stood up, went into her boudoir next door, and glanced at herself in the mirror. Satisfied she looked tidy, she went downstairs.

Alexis had opened the French doors and gone out onto the terrace. Jane joined her, and when Alexis swung around, she caught her breath in surprise.

'How lovely to see you here in London,' Jane said. 'And

looking so *stunning*. Congratulations. You've done a wonderful job on yourself.'

Alexis laughed, stepped closer, and kissed Jane on each cheek. 'Claudia telling me I was fat was a great motivation, you know. And, as I told you a few weeks ago, you and Reggie helped me to pull myself out of the stupor I was in. So, thank you for that. I do believe you saved me from another breakdown.'

'We love you, Alexis, and were worried about you.' Eyeing her again, even more intently, Jane said slowly, 'You look ten years younger, like you were when we first met you with Sebastian. Actually, you've looked this well for several weeks. But today you are very glamorous. That was always something I admired about you, Alexis, your natural glow.'

'Thank you, Jane, for these compliments, and thank you for being my friend and standing by me. You and Reggie have been so good.' Alexis suddenly choked up, felt her eyes growing moist, because they had been the most supportive and true friends. Unconditionally.

'It's a bit warm out here,' Jane remarked, linking her arm through Alexis's. 'Let's go inside. I thought we could eat in the morning room – so much cosier than the big dining room.'

Walking across the grand foyer together, Jane stopped suddenly, and said, 'This lilac suits you so well, and enhances your colouring. How perfect it is with your red hair.'

'Tilda picked it out of a bunch of frocks that had been too tight. Now it fits me again. It was hard getting the weight off, but well worth the effort. And all my clothes fit me now. Tilda has given them an updated look with a few alterations. Anyway, I have some news for you.'

As they sat down opposite each other at the oval table, Jane glanced at her questioningly. 'You're not going off travelling abroad somewhere, are you? I couldn't bear it if you were going away when you've just returned to town.'

'I am going somewhere actually, Jane.' Alexis paused, and said rather proudly, 'I'm going back to work.'

Jane stared at her, caught totally unawares and truly startled by this announcement. After a moment, finding her voice, she asked, 'You do mean you're going back to Malvern's, don't you?'

'I do. My father is thrilled, as you can imagine.'

Jane nodded. 'And what about James Falconer? How does he feel about this move on your part?' she asked somewhat pithily.

'I suppose he's happy. It's Falconer who is going to teach me how to run Malvern's. My father has given him a contract for a year, plus a big bonus.'

Jane took this extraordinary information in her stride, and exclaimed, 'Goodness, they must both believe you're very serious about your work.'

'I am. What else have I to do? I'm not a big socialite, never have been. Work is the thing I do best, and I enjoy it. Look, I have to have a purpose. I can't just hang around. Life has to be meaningful.'

'I understand that, but you could help out at Haven House. You will, won't you?' Jane gave her a long look. 'We need your input.'

'I know. I am coming to the next meeting . . . in a few days. I have been neglectful of my charity as well as neglectful of Papa. He's needed me and I've been absent. I'm really rather ashamed of myself. I haven't behaved as I should have, as his only child.'

Grant came into the morning room carrying two plates on a tray. Alexis nodded when she saw the oysters, a favourite of hers. 'I see you're spoiling me already, Jane.' Alexis stared at her friend. 'And they're a good starter, if you like shellfish. And not fattening.'

'What are you going to do at Malvern's?' Jane asked curiously, pushing the small fork under the oyster in its shell.

'Falconer is to take me from division to division and train me how to head up and run each of them, should I ever have to take it over. I might have to one day.'

'Are you actually up to this, Alexis? I mean, you don't like Falconer . . . how do you plan to get on with him?'

'By being nice, polite, attentive to my work and doing what he says.'

Jane looked at her intently, her eyes narrowing, amazed at Alexis and what she was saying. Yet she believed her. Alexis wanted her father's company, after all. And she *needed* Falconer. So she would have to toe the line, kowtow to him a bit. Now Jane decided she was brave to take this on. 'I wish you well,' she murmured. 'And always remember, Reggie and I are here for you, to help any way we can.'

After enjoying a cheese soufflé and mixed berries for dessert, Jane and Alexis went back to the green parlour. Grant served them coffee, which they had decided to have outside on the terrace.

It was a glorious day, a bright-blue sky without a blemish, and no breeze at all. Jane said, 'How nice it is out here, and it's already mid-September.'

'An Indian summer kind of day,' Alexis volunteered. 'And the air seems quite fresh for once. Not so many fires in our homes.'

Jane nodded, and was silent, continuing to worry slightly about Alexis working with James Falconer. In order not to sound as if she was lecturing her, Jane decided to bring her husband into the conversation.

After a few sips of coffee, she glanced at Alexis once again, taking in her beauty and vivid colouring – the red hair, emerald-green eyes and alabaster skin. Quite an amazing comeback. She now said, 'Returning to the subject of your being helped in your work by Falconer, I want you to know that Reggie really admires him. So much so, he offered Falconer a job at *The Chronicle*. In management, of course. It's his uncle George who's on the newspaper.'

Looking surprised, Alexis asked, 'When did Reggie do that?'

'The first day he met him, when Falconer brought that letter from your father. To Goldenhurst.'

'My goodness, Reggie must have been impressed. He was rather fast on the draw, wasn't he?'

'Indeed. But I must amend that a little, Alexis. Reggie had run into Falconer once before, in fact, when he was with his uncle George. I should add that Reggie's job offer to Falconer still stands – he would hire him in an instant.'

'I realize I have to learn how to run Malvern's, Jane. And I will be a diligent student. Actually, my father trusts him implicitly, and I cannot ignore that.'

Jane nodded, smiled warmly and was filled with relief that Alexis was obviously very serious about the company. She was also still impressed by the way Alexis had pulled herself together, gone back to being the woman she was before Sebastian's tragic, very sudden death. He was far too young to die.

Alexis interrupted her meandering thoughts when she said, 'I'm thinking of buying a house, Jane.'

'A house!' Jane exclaimed, staring at her. 'Don't you want to live with your father?'

'I am doing so at the moment, as you know. But I'm used to running my own place now, being independent. And it was his idea, actually. I too was as surprised as you obviously are.'

'I'm amazed. Have you found one?'

'Yes, last week. It's on South Audley Street, on a corner, of medium size. Rather nice, not too big.'

'You'll need to get a staff together. Perhaps I can be of help.'

'I'd love that, Jane. Mrs Bellamy, my housekeeper at Goldenhurst, has a cousin, Vera Fox, who has agreed to become my housekeeper. And she knows of a couple of good butlers. I'm to interview them tomorrow. I've hired Mrs Fox.'

'Gosh, you've been quick!'

'I think my father wants me to be independent, to have my own home, an establishment that's new and fresh, which I can run myself as I want.' She laughed. 'I'm quite excited about it, and about decorating it.'

'As I said, I'd love to help.'

'I will show it to you tomorrow, if you're not busy. It's empty, and I have the keys. The papers are being prepared, but they accepted my offer. I can go into the house whenever I want, to take measurements, all that.'

'What a great project – I'll be thrilled to give you a hand.'

'Then you shall.'

James sat at his desk, gathering together papers, making a small pile of them, then placing them in a folder for Peter Keller. It was turning out to be a busy day.

Rising, he hurried across the room and wrenched open the door, causing Alexis Malvern to stagger and fall against him. Dropping the folder, he grabbed her and held her tightly with both hands, preventing her from dropping to the floor.

They were both so startled by this strange encounter that neither of them could speak for a moment. They just clung together, stupefied.

It was James who pulled himself together first. He righted

her carefully, making sure she was properly balanced on her feet.

He stared at her. God, she was beautiful. Beyond belief.

She stared back, still disconcerted by this odd accident and discovered she couldn't look away. His eyes were so blue, they were mesmerizing.

She blinked and took a deep breath. 'I was just about to knock,' she murmured by way of an explanation.

'It was my fault,' he answered swiftly. Taking her arm gently, he led her into his office. 'I'm afraid I have a bad habit of rushing around, and wrenching doors open too quickly. I'm so sorry. I hope you're not hurt?'

'No, I'm not. I'm fine, thank you.'

'Come and sit down for a moment, to recover your equilibrium.' He led her across the room to a large window, in front of which two chairs and a small table stood.

She did as he asked, and watched him as he picked up several pieces of paper and a folder, which he placed on his desk.

Her reticule? Where was it? She then saw it still hanging on her arm. Letting out a sigh, she leaned back in the chair, attempting to relax.

A moment later he was leaning towards her, offering her a glass of water. Taking it from him, she thanked him, and began to drink. He sat down in the other chair and drank some of his own water.

After a while, he said, 'I didn't know you had started to come to the office. I thought it was to be next week.'

'Oh, it is, you're quite right!' she exclaimed. 'But I had a bite to eat with Lady Jane at midday, then we had to go and look at the outside of a house, which took all of twenty minutes. She had to leave me for another appointment afterwards. I had time to spare, so I thought I would come and say hello to you . . . and apologize for being so rude to you when you came to Goldenhurst. So, I'm sorry, Mr Falconer. I wasn't very nice. I have no excuse for being so beastly. However, it was a bad period of time for me.'

James, though taken aback, said in an even voice, 'Thank you for apologizing, Miss Malvern, and for taking the trouble to come here today. It's very nice of you.'

'I wanted it to be . . . well, a fresh start, since we are going to be working together, and for a whole year.'

She smiled, her green eyes sparkling with eagerness, with life, with warmth.

He inclined his head, wondering how on earth he was going to cope. He was experiencing that strange tension in the pit of his stomach again, blinded by her incredible natural beauty.

In the light from the window, her auburn hair was like a burnished helmet around her alabaster face. She was ravishing. And so desirable.

Suddenly realizing she was gazing at him intently, he cleared his throat and asked, 'Do you wish me to introduce you to Peter Keller? Some of the other division heads?'

'Oh, no, no, not at all. It's not necessary. Actually, I came to see just *you* . . . to make amends, as I explained a moment ago.'

'You have done so, and we'll leave the introductions for next week. But since you *are* here, I would like to ask you a question. I'm not certain whether or not Mr Henry has told you that you will have to travel. To Hull, where the new arcade is a huge success, and to the arcades that you know in Leeds and Harrogate.'

'He did mention it in passing. That doesn't present a problem at all. He also explained that your contract finishes at the end of the year, after which you will leave Malvern's, and I will become managing director.' She paused and hesitated, before asking, 'Do you think I'll be ready?'

Without hesitation, he answered, 'Absolutely. When you worked here before you were excellent. Nobody better. You're very clever and intelligent. You'll pick everything up very swiftly. You'll see the changes I've made are not very huge. But they have succeeded.'

'I'm glad you have faith in me, Mr Falconer,' she said, and stood up. 'I must leave you to get on with your work.'

'Yes, and I must give these papers to Keller.' Taking them from the desk, he went on, 'Are you going to see Mr Henry now?'

'Oh no, he's not here. I believe he had a meeting at midday in Mayfair, and then went home.'

'Is your carriage waiting outside?'

'Yes, it is,' she answered, and wanted to offer him a lift but didn't dare.

'Then I'll escort you downstairs,' he said in a firm voice. 'I'll just give this folder to Keller. He is in the next office to me.'

Once he had handed the folder to Keller, he left his office immediately. Alexis was waiting in the corridor and, putting his hand under her elbow, James walked with her down the staircase. Neither of them spoke, caught up in their own thoughts. About each other, although they did not know this.

After he had handed her up into her carriage, she lowered the window and her eyes locked on his.

'I will do everything you want me to do, Mr Falconer,' she promised. A small smile suddenly flickered on her mouth and was gone.

'I sincerely hope you will, Miss Malvern,' James answered, before turning and going back into the Malvern building without a backward glance.

When he was inside, he leaned against a wall, taking a few deep breaths. How would he be able to handle this situation? This woman spelled trouble. She had a terrible effect on him, aroused him in a way no other woman ever had.

He had never forgotten that trip to Paris, and how he had believed she felt the same as he did. Only to be discarded and avoided on their return to London.

Their odd collision in his doorway just now had been an accident, due to their timing. But oh, how it had thrilled him to hold her in his arms, her body pressed close to his, feeling that rush of desire, that stirring in his loins, the oncoming erection, which he had managed to control as he moved away from her as fast as possible.

He must endeavour to put distance between them when dealing with other matters. That was a given. And he must think with his head, not his heart. It occurred to him that he must include other people when he informed her about each division. *The division heads must be present.* That was important.

The contract was the key to his future, the beginning of his dream, his retailing empire. Nothing could get in his way, or block his rise. Not even Alexis Malvern.

THIRTY-THREE

What a relief it was to be in the cool, dark carriage. Alexis closed her eyes, trying to calm herself and gather her scattered senses as they drew away from Malvern House.

She was embarrassed and dismayed to recall how rudely she had behaved towards James Falconer when he had arrived at Goldenhurst to deliver her father's letter. Her manners had been appalling that day. He hadn't deserved that humiliation in front of Reggie and Jane. In fact, he hadn't deserved any of her other slights and bad behaviour. Actually, he had been perfect in every way during their encounters. It was all her fault. She was totally to blame, and why she had been so mean she had no idea.

Of course, now he had the upper hand as managing director of Malvern's. Although her father had explained he was easy to work with, he also pointed out that James was tough and ran a tight ship. 'Don't be surprised if you hear his private office called "the lion's den", which often happens. But I can assure you that his roar is worse than his bite.'

Alexis had smiled at this odd reference to his office. *Lion's den* indeed, she thought, as the carriage moved along Piccadilly, pushing through the heavy late-afternoon traffic. He had been calm, charming and well mannered, and had accepted her apology at once. Batted it away genially.

She suddenly laughed to herself about the way she had tumbled into his office. A total accident. She had been thrown against him unexpectedly, and now she realized how much she had wanted to be held by him. In fact, she had forgotten how good-looking he was. He was a real *matinée idol*, as the newspapers often called the very handsome young men who starred in stage plays in the West End. And he surely had an actor's voice, melodious and cultured.

I like him, Alexis thought. Her mind still focused on Falconer. No, it's much more than that, she decided. She was physically attracted to him, and rather strongly at that. A sigh trickled out of her as she admitted she really wanted him. Instantly, she saw a difficult time ahead. She must put him out of her mind and concentrate on learning how to run the business which one day would be hers.

She must also make an effort to go to Haven House, the charity she had started several years ago. And she *would* go because she had promised Jane. Claudia would be pleased, too, for her to be back on the team.

There were no two ways about it, Alexis knew she had to become truly involved with Haven House again, now that she had returned to London. But she must be on top of her form to be of any use to them. She was angry with herself that she had let those poor battered women down, and all because she had mooned too long for the man she loved who had died too young.

The women who came to Haven House did so because they had nowhere else to go to be safe from the men in their lives who abused them, treated them badly in the most horrendous ways. They needed to be taken care of, given comfort, both physically and mentally, and helped to become whole again.

She remembered how pitiful they had been, and yet how soon they had come alive again, knowing they were safe from harm, had food to eat, and decent clothes to wear. Yes, physical wounds healed fairly quickly, but the mental wounds took longer. The women needed to talk, to get things off their chests, to have someone who would *listen* to them, allow them to vent, to express their feelings.

Alexis knew she was not a psychologist, but she had been treated in Vienna by Dr Freud, and had learned a lot from him. She was equipped to handle some of the more terrified women, who were lost, felt helpless, unable to start over.

That would be her goal. To help those women who needed her the most. To help them to start again, to make new lives for themselves.

Her thoughts returned to Claudia. Always her closest friend, the daughter of Sebastian, who had had to become like a mother to her sisters after their real mother had died. She had run the house and been her father's hostess. And had done it all very well without complaint.

Thankfully, they were still friends, after Claudia had driven down to Kent to give her a strong lecture about her behaviour and missing Lavinia's birthday party. So Claudia had been tough with her, but the combination of toughness and yet true concern for her welfare had worked. Alexis had listened and had begun to see herself as she really was. *Fat.* And also she understood she had neglected herself; let her looks go to waste in the worst way.

There's nothing like the truth, she decided. I will always tell the truth in the future. Even if the truth hurts.

Tilda was so thrilled to be back in Madame Valance's elegant salon – amongst lovely clothes – that her excitement was infectious. Alexis hurried over to join her when she beckoned, smiling broadly. Tilda was holding a lime-green silk gown, and put it against Alexis's body.

'This colour is marvellous for you, Miss Alexis,' Tilda said. 'And look at that purple velvet jacket over there.'

Alexis followed the direction of her gaze, and nodded.

'It's so elegant, and it must go with that draped purple skirt made of taffeta.' As she spoke, Alexis walked over to the outfit spread out on a long banquette, eyeing it critically.

At this moment, Madame Valance returned with several dresses over her arm, accompanied by her two assistants. After placing the outfits on the banquette, Madame Valance joined Alexis. Tilting her head slightly and smiling, the couturière said, 'I'm so happy to see you in London, Miss Malvern, and looking so well. I can't wait to see you in some of my latest creations.'

'They all look wonderful, madame,' Alexis responded, smiling at her. 'I love this velvet jacket and the skirt, and the lime-green silk gown is a colour that suits me. I'd like to try on both of those, and perhaps you have some suits, the kind I could wear to work.'

The designer nodded. 'I do, shall we go to a dressing room, mademoiselle?'

'Oh yes, let's do that,' Alexis agreed warmly. Suddenly she was glad she had given in to Tilda's pleadings to go shopping for new clothes.

She had been a little reluctant at first, but Tilda had talked her into it. In Kent she hadn't really needed fancy, stylish dresses and outfits, but once back in London she had to be as elegant as she had been in the past.

The grey-and-white jacket-and-skirt suit she was

wearing looked good on her, because Tilda had remade the jacket, brought it more up-to-date, and a large white silk rose on one of the lapels added a chic touch.

In the past, when she worked for her father, everyone had commented on her sense of style, and her good taste. Of course, she didn't have much competition, as women who worked in offices were few and far between. She could only think of one other woman who went into an office every day, and she had inherited a bank. Like Alexis, that particular lady had been an only child.

When Tilda had finished helping her to get out of her suit, Alexis stepped into the lime-green dress, and waited as Tilda fastened the buttons down the back. Her maid stared at her when she had finished and exclaimed, 'My goodness, Miss Alexis! Just look at yourself, here in the mirror.' Tilda took hold of her arm and led her across the fitting room. 'Look how the lime green makes your eyes look even greener, and your auburn hair even lovelier. That's your crowning glory, it really is, Miss Alexis.'

Looking in the mirror, Alexis instantly knew why Tilda had been so startled. The lovely silk gown with a high frothy neckline, long tight sleeves with semi-mutton-chop shoulders, a slender tight skirt with a frill at the hemline, fitted her perfectly. And Tilda was right, her auburn hair appeared to shine.

Nodding her head, Alexis said to Tilda, 'Shall we see what Madame Valance thinks?'

Tilda laughed. 'She will be proud of her design, I know that, and happy that you are going to purchase the dress. You are, aren't you?'

Laughing, Alexis said, 'I certainly am, and I think I will like the purple velvet jacket and taffeta skirt as well. The skirt looks unique.'

Tilda opened the door of the fitting room, and Alexis

walked out, smiling when she saw the beaming face of the designer.

'*Mon Dieu!*' Madame Valance exclaimed. 'I must have been thinking of you, Miss Malvern, when I sat at my drawing board. The gown was made for you and only you.'

Sitting having a cup of tea with her father at their house in Mayfair, Alexis was explaining to him that she had been to Malvern House. And told him why. He looked the happiest that she'd seen him since she had been home, and this gave *her* a sense of happiness.

'Well, done, darling. You've shown your true colours to Falconer, and to me. I think it was a wise move, a clever move, even though I know it was sincere on your part. You want to start with a clean slate.'

Alexis nodded. 'At least he doesn't appear to hold a grudge.'

'He's not that type. He's down to earth, matter of fact. No side to him. Everyone treated with charm and grace. No wonder the staff love him,' Henry said, picking up his cup. 'You'll get on with him all right, Alexis. You really will.' Inside his head, Henry hoped it would go beyond that, become something . . . permanent.

A little later, Alexis went upstairs to her suite of rooms. She found Tilda ironing a dress in the wardrobe room which opened off the boudoir.

She looked up at the sight of Alexis, and said, 'Good afternoon, Miss Alexis. Did you enjoy tea with Mr Malvern?'

Alexis nodded. 'I did. I told him about the office this morning. I think it will be a challenge, but I need a challenge. It'll do me good, Tilda, working. Would you help me out of my clothes, please?'

Tilda did so, placing the jacket, dress and underwear on a nearby chaise longue. She then slipped a silk robe on Alexis, and asked, 'Do you want a massage, Miss Alexis?'

'Thank you, Tilda, I'm fine. Instead, I'm going to have a soothing bath.'

Alone in the bathroom, Alexis took off the robe and hung it up. Then she went and stood in front of the cheval mirror in one corner. Staring at her naked body, studying herself, she slid her hands over her breasts, viewing them intently. They were full, quite voluptuous, but firm, did not droop at all. She smoothed one hand across her hip, and was glad she had dropped the weight. Yes, she had a lovely figure once again, and smiled, wondering if Falconer would like her body.

Turning away from the mirror, Alexis went to the bath and turned on both taps, filled the tub. After throwing in lavender bath salts, Alexis lowered herself into the tub of water.

Closing her eyes, she relaxed, letting the water lap around her. It was warm and soothing. As she lay there in the quietness, she let her mind wander, and inevitably she finally came back to the man she had seen earlier today.

James Lionel Falconer.

She placed her hands on her stomach. Thank God it was now flat, not blown up and bulging as it once had been. She allowed her hand to slide down to her mound, and touched herself gently. Then she simply drifted with her erotic thoughts, visualizing Falconer undressed, touching her, kissing her and eventually taking her to him. Making love to her.

Oh yes, she did want that, wanted him. What about him? Maybe he wouldn't want her, in view of their past, the unpleasantness. He was a sensual man. She was certain of that, and no doubt he liked women. He was so handsome. Women must have thrown themselves at his feet. Still did, no doubt. She felt a sudden rush of jealousy, and then smiled ironically. What right did she have to be jealous? No right at all.

She knew quite a lot about men, their moods, their desires and their needs. And Sebastian had taught her a great deal about pleasing a man, bringing him to ecstasy, pleasuring him.

She might have to seduce Falconer at some point. And she would do so with much expertise. After all, she had been taught by a master.

THIRTY-FOUR

Two things were important to James Falconer when it came to his wellbeing: *sleep and schedules.*

As usual both of these imperatives had been drilled into him by his grandmother. 'Good sleep is important for your health,' she had explained when he was twelve. 'It cures most things that might ail you. So when you go to bed, put all your troubles to one side and just relax. Sleep like a log.'

As far as schedules were concerned, she had told him that they would make his life much easier to handle if on Monday he made a list of things to do for the entire week. And so he had done that. He still did it, because it made his week manageable. Now he took out the small notebook he kept in his jacket pocket and opened it. He had written *MONDAY* on the new page earlier, but had not put anything else down.

Staring at the page, he wrote one line. *This coming Sunday. Ascot.* He smiled to himself, thinking of his little daughter Leonie. He loved his visits to see her and Mrs Ward . . . *Georgiana*, he said under his breath. It was odd, the way he so often thought of her as *Mrs Ward*.

Of course, it went back to their days in Hull. He sighed.

272

A lot of water had flowed under the bridge since then. He would always be fond of the older woman who had been his first lover, but he knew she had been right to refuse the idea of them marrying.

He was proud of his child. She was beautiful with her bright-blue eyes, *his* eyes, and she was happy, always laughing. He detected a quickness in her, and intelligence.

Georgiana was a good mother and was bringing Leonie up very well. Leonie was safe in Ascot. And he had her under his eye at all times.

He now wrote: *Saturday: Family.* He knew his grand-parents would be free to have supper with him, and with his parents and siblings. Lady Agatha, for whom his grand-parents worked, was suffering with arthritis and had gone to Madeira by ship, seeking warmth in the sun. His grand-mother suffered with arthritis in her right hand, and he had promised to get her a special ointment from an apoth-ecary in Chinatown. He would talk to Roger Crawford tonight. Uncle George had invited him to supper with the inspector at Wu Liang in Limehouse. The special Chinese apothecary was not far from the restaurant. They would walk over there after they had eaten.

James made a note in the book about supper with his uncle, and looked across at the door, hearing a knock.

There was another one, and as he called, 'Come in,' Natalie's face appeared and she came into the room, closing the door behind her.

'Sorry, I'm late, James,' she said, smiling. 'The train was late getting into King's Cross and traffic is a bit heavy this afternoon.'

'It's all right, Nat,' he answered, smiling at her, glad to see her back at the London office after a week in Hull. She was as hardworking and diligent as always, and his right hand in many ways.

Sitting down in the chair opposite, she said, 'William sends his best.'

James got up and walked around his desk, looking at her with a certain curiosity. 'Is this becoming serious?' he asked, his voice low. 'You and William?'

'In a way, yes,' Natalie answered. 'There are certain issues . . . but not yet. They might develop though.'

Returning to his chair, James leaned across his desk and gave her a long, knowing look. 'Location,' he observed. 'You living in London, and him in Hull. That's it, isn't it?'

'That's the main problem. It truly hasn't become an issue. Still, I think it could.' Natalie shook her head and then leaned back in the chair, staring at James, her eyes quizzical.

He was reflective for a few seconds, and smiled. 'Leave it alone for the moment. Let things take their course. Life has a way of sorting everything out.'

She nodded. 'I would find it hard not to work, and not to be in London part of the time. That most especially. It's my home.'

'I know. So would I.' James paused, then said, 'You'll never believe who came to see me today.'

'I won't, I suppose. So please tell me.'

'It was Alexis Malvern,' James said, amusement in his voice.

Natalie was so surprised that she was unable to answer immediately. Then she asked, 'Why? What did she want? To say that she's changed her mind about coming back to work?'

'No, just the opposite, in fact. She came to apologize for being rude to me in the past, for her bad behaviour, for neglecting her duty to her father and the company. She was very sincere.'

Natalie's eyes narrowed. 'Was she really?' she asked in a doubtful voice.

'Believe me, I know her, and she meant it. I think she came to her senses recently, and realized she had to get out of Kent.' James sat back in the chair, and finished, 'I believe she has been in a long depression about Sebastian Trevalian's death. Something, or perhaps someone, pulled her out of it.'

'That's possible, I suppose,' Natalie murmured. 'Is she starting back next Monday as planned?'

'She is, and I've more or less formulated a plan – a schedule, if you like – for her. I can't teach her about every division since I have to run the entire company. So I will first give her a month with Peter Keller, since she knows a lot about the Wine Division, has been to Le Havre, knows Armand and those in the Paris office. What do you think?'

'I absolutely agree. Of course that's the answer. After a month with Keller, you'll move her on to Goring, so she can learn about the warehouses, correct?' Natalie raised a brow.

'Exactly. A month with each division head, and I'll spend time with her each week, checking her out.' He laughed lightly. 'And the year with her, training her, will pass quickly. I can leave the Malvern Company, and properly run Falconer.'

'Can I come with you?' Natalie asked, sounding suddenly sad, looking at him woefully.

'Of course, you can, if you really want to—' He broke off, grimaced, and continued, 'At this moment I only have a dream . . .'

She interrupted him and said, 'I will make things right with William. I know I can. As you just said, life takes care of itself.'

He nodded, and gave her a loving look. 'You're a good woman, Nat, a true friend and a wonderful colleague. I do have a plan to start something down here. And of course you can work at Falconer once I get it going at full speed. And we'll tackle the William issue later.'

'Thank you, James, and listen, I owe you an apology too. I haven't been entirely honest with you about Irina . . .' Her voice trailed off when she noticed how he had tensed in his chair, and his expression had changed.

'What are you trying to say?' he asked, sounding more puzzled than annoyed.

'She begged me not to tell you, because she didn't want you to be upset or distracted, but she was injured – as well as Aunt Olga – in the accident with the carriage. Her left leg and her left arm were broken. I'm afraid she's still recuperating.'

'Oh, Natalie, I'm so sorry to hear this. How terrible for Irina, but I'm happy to know she's improving. You must send her my best for a speedy recovery. And I will write to her too.'

'I should have told you the truth, James. I shouldn't have listened to her. Again, I apologize. I wasn't fair to you.'

'And I accept your apology, my dear Natalie. I understand you were in a difficult situation. And now you've told me.'

'Thank you.' Natalie looked at him. 'I don't know when my sister will come back. Perhaps it would be wise for you to move on.'

'I believe so,' James answered, his voice mild, light. 'I've a lot of work to keep me well occupied.' He didn't want to say he'd come to the same conclusion some months before. Irina Parkinson was utterly delightful but the more time had passed, the less he had heard from her. 'So tell me about Hull.'

'It's all working extremely well. The arcade is a big hit, no question about it. Mr Malvern should be grateful to you. I call it a cash cow. It's one of the biggest money earners in the company.'

'I know, and he is grateful,' James said, and then added, 'By the way, Alexis Malvern is coming back to be trained to do *my* job. So she won't be bothering you about running the arcades.'

Natalie started to laugh, and then said, 'I think I realized that, James. Anyway, I've always got you to look out for me, haven't I?'

'You do indeed. I've always got your back.'

'And I hope I have yours.' Natalie tapped her fingers on the desk. 'Next time you come up to Hull there's something I want to show you.'

'At the arcade site? Everything is all right, isn't it?' He instantly sounded concerned.

'Yes. However, I think I've found you something special—'

'What do you mean?' he interrupted, staring at her intently.

'A little shop. One you could rent. We could easily find someone to run it. It would be the beginning.'

THIRTY-FIVE

Alexis stared at the calendar on her desk at her office at Malvern's. It was Friday 23 October, and she had worked here for just over a month.

How the time had flown, and she had certainly learned a lot. She fully understood why they called his office 'the lion's den'. James could be hard-headed, ruthless, tough, unmoving; he was so disciplined and he expected everyone to be exactly the same.

He rarely lost his temper, however, so the atmosphere was calm. She realized, in the first few days, that he had cut the staff in half.

When she mentioned this to her father, he had explained that James thought it took only one person to do one job, not three. 'He runs a tight ship,' her father had added, and had given her a huge smile, obviously delighted by this decision on Falconer's part.

She herself smiled at this moment, thinking that her father had been right all along about James Falconer. He really was a brilliant businessman, always out to win, and loyal to Henry Malvern. And a demon for work.

As she had watched him from time to time, she had recognized he was a genius at handling people. He gave pay rises where he thought they were deserved, let people have an occasional Saturday off, and did a variety of favours for everyone. Kindness worked. Charisma, a natural, pervasive charm and perfect manners went a long way in this world, and he was loaded with the lot.

She herself had fallen under his spell a little bit, and often found herself working harder just to please him.

And he was generous with praise and compliments to every member of staff for a job well done. Even to her, sometimes. His warm words pleased her.

For the past few weeks she had been working with Peter Keller and had enjoyed being in the Wine Division. Keller had asked James if she could stay on for another two weeks, and he had agreed. Keller needed some special tasks done.

Once a week she spent a day with James Falconer, going over everything she had worked on, telling him the outcome of the decisions she had made and why she had made them. He, in turn, gave her his opinions of her progress, and he was always pleased, congratulated her, which made her feel she was pulling her weight. This was the longest time he spent with her, first thing every Monday morning, reviewing the past week.

In many ways it was trying for her, not because of her reporting in, but because of her longing for Falconer himself. She felt a powerful attraction to him; there was no question in her mind and in her heart about that.

In fact, if she were scrupulously honest with herself, she had fallen in love with him on the trip they had made to Le Havre and Paris two years ago. She had believed there might be a life for her after all, and was pulled to him, needed his presence.

But once back in London she had begun to feel guilty about Sebastian, and had fled to Kent. Originally, her motive had been to straighten herself out, put her grief behind her, and start all over again. With James Falconer, if he was willing.

Then something strange had happened. She had begun to turn against him, and even now she did not understand why this had happened. She also realized she might well still be in Kent if not for Claudia, and also Jane and Reggie.

Claudia had told her the truth about herself and her foolish behaviour. Jane had steadied her when she had been flummoxed by Reggie's announcement that the house in Kent was entailed.

Sebastian's decisions and actions about Goldenhurst and his Will still came back to haunt her. This was because she truly was puzzled about it, did not understand his reasoning.

Jane had warned her not to mention anything to Claudia about the entailment. When she had asked Jane why not, Jane had told her that Claudia had been at the reading of the Will and knew about it anyway. 'Just let sleeping dogs lie,' Jane had cautioned. 'Just get on with your new life.'

And she had done that. When she had gone to apologize to Falconer, it had been out of shame and disgust with herself for her rudeness. Every word had been sincere.

Seeing him again, after so many months of absence, was something of a shock. And so was her emotional reaction to him. A rush of desire for this man, a need to know every part of him, to *be* part of him, took her by surprise. He was charm personified, and more handsome than ever.

For a while she had believed this unexpected physical and emotional attraction would recede, just go away with familiarity, but it had not. In point of fact, she dreaded Monday mornings because she was always filled with desire for him, a need to touch him, to tell him she loved him.

She never said anything and conducted herself with decorum. As the days had passed, gone into weeks, she had become aware that he was having a difficult time, too. She had caught the several odd looks he gave her, his caution when they were together, trying not to get too close to her, and ending their meetings quickly.

When she had confided in Jane earlier in the week, Jane had given her a peculiar look, and then she had smiled knowingly.

'Hasn't it occurred to you he might be in love with you?' Jane had asked.

'Partially. What I mean is, why would he fall in love with me when you consider how badly I've treated him? I've humiliated him,' she had responded.

'Go and look in the mirror, my dear. You're a very beautiful woman. Any man would want you. Anyway, you went to see *him*, apologized to him. That must have pleased him, boosted his ego no end,' Jane had pronounced.

She had explained to Jane that his ego didn't need boosting, and that the secretaries looked at him like he was a god. This had amused Jane, who had reminded her that Falconer was a bit of an Adonis.

Jane had not been able to come up with any suggestions that day, and had merely pointed out that things had to run their course. They had gone on to speak about Millicent Plymouth, the designer who was helping her to decorate her new house. She was clever and had good taste, according to Jane.

Sitting up straighter in her chair, Alexis thought again about Falconer, wondering how to solve an unsolvable situation. The office was the wrong place to have any kind of conversation with him, especially one of a personal nature. Also, he was busy, and constantly surrounded by people.

A thought crossed her mind. How on earth was she

going to learn to be like him? That was why she was there: to be trained to be managing director. For a moment she was scared, and then pushed that thought to one side. She had a year to learn.

Unexpectedly, it occurred to Alexis that she must find a way to get him alone so that they could be at ease with each other, more relaxed than they were at work. How to do that? Alexis pursed her lips. For once in her life she had no idea.

There was a knock on the door, and it immediately opened. There he was, walking into her office. James Falconer.

'Do you have a minute?' he asked, striding forward, standing in front of her desk.

'I do, and please sit down, won't you?'

He did. 'Your father asked me to come and see you regarding your house. Basically, he thinks you might need help with certain things. So, here I am. Do you want me to take a look around?'

'Well, actually . . . yes, I do. Certainly. Oh yes. Yes.' She was so flustered she almost stuttered.

'Are you able to do it now? It's turned five, and I happen to be going home. We don't live far apart. In fact, if you've got your carriage, you could give me a lift.' He raised a brow, his blue eyes riveted on her.

'Why, yes, of course. I was thinking of leaving shortly.' She was shaking inside.

'Then let's go, shall we?' He stood up.

She locked her desk, grabbed her handbag, and followed him out of her office, her chest tight with anxiety.

Alexis's driver Josh directed the carriage at a medium trot through the traffic of Piccadilly, heading in the direction of Mayfair.

Inside the carriage, Alexis sat in one corner, Falconer

in the other. Neither of them spoke. Eventually, much to Alexis's relief, Falconer said, 'Is your house in good condition or does it need a lot of restoration?'

'It's in good shape inside,' she answered, surprised that her voice was steady. She was still shaking inside, and anxious, although speaking normally at least. 'Outside the house looks like nothing, but the rooms are lovely, in fact,' she added.

'I like building projects,' he confessed, his voice as steady as hers. 'I learned a lot when we had to redo part of the arcade in Hull. After the explosion.'

'My father told me how hard you'd worked, and what a splendid job you did.' When he did not respond, she went on, 'The arsonist was never found, I understand.'

'No, he wasn't. More's the pity. But the Hull arcade is proving a huge success. That's the most important thing.'

'Yes, of course.'

'Your father told me your house is on South Audley Street, but he didn't say exactly where.'

'Close to Mount Street,' she answered. 'And it has a mews at the back, with a carriage house and a flat above for a driver.'

'Will Josh be living there?' Falconer asked, sounding suddenly anxious.

'Yes, of course,' Alexis replied.

'I'm glad to hear that. I don't like the idea of women living in a house in London without a man being around.'

'I understand,' she murmured. So he was *concerned* – and about *her*. That instantly told her what she had begun to think lately . . . that he was as much interested in her as she was in him.

They fell silent for a while, and again it was Falconer who broke the quiet inside the carriage. 'I like Mayfair. It's like a little village, in a way. And I'm on Half Moon Street. Your father's home is on Chesterfield Hill and Lord

Reggie is on Chesterfield Street. We're all in very close proximity.'

'That's true,' she said.

A few moments later, Josh was bringing the carriage to a halt. As they alighted, Alexis said, 'Here we are. Josh, will you please come into the house and help Mr Falconer light the gas lamps.'

'Of course, Miss Malvern,' her driver answered, climbing down, then stroking the horses' noses, calming them as they suddenly became restless, their hooves clattering on the cobbles.

The three of them walked to the front door, and Alexis took a bunch of keys out of her handbag. After opening the door, she stepped into the medium-sized entrance foyer. The two men followed her.

She handed a box of matches to Josh, and one to Falconer. 'There are gas lamps in this hall, Mr Falconer, and perhaps you will attend to the lamps near the fireplace in here, Josh.' As she spoke she walked into the drawing room, the sound of her footsteps echoing in the empty house.

Attending to the gas lamps in the foyer, Falconer said, 'It's larger than I expected.'

'It's a good size for me,' Alexis answered. 'I will have to have a staff, and there is a servants' floor at the top, with plenty of bedrooms of medium size on the floor below. It's the reception rooms down here that are generous in size.'

'So I see,' Falconer said as he went into the drawing room.

Josh said goodnight to him, and then handed the matches to Alexis. 'Shall I wait for you, Miss Malvern, or come back later?'

'Oh no, that's not necessary.' She smiled faintly. 'I'm only a few minutes from home, and I know Mr Falconer

284

will be kind enough to walk me back. You might as well go and have your supper, Josh.'

'Yes, miss, thank you. Goodnight then.'

'Goodnight, Josh,' she said.

'Yes, goodnight,' Falconer called from the drawing room, and went back to studying the details of the interior.

Alexis locked the front door after Josh had left and returned to stand next to Falconer.

He turned to face her, and said, 'I like this room. It can be really beautiful if it's decorated well.' Leaving her side, he went over to the two tall windows. 'Lovely silk draperies, full-length, will set just the right look. And the fireplace is an Adam, I'm sure.'

'Oh, do you think so? How lovely if it is. You seem to know a lot about architecture.'

'A bit.'

'Thank you for following my father's suggestion and coming to help me. I appreciate it.'

His eyes did not leave her face when he said quietly, 'It was the reverse, to be honest. I went to your father and asked him if you needed help. His answer was yes and I should go and see you. So I did. An hour ago. And here I am.'

She gazed at him, unable to speak, her chest tight. So *he* had initiated this meeting.

'You see, I needed to speak to you privately, alone, and I didn't know *how* to get you alone with me. Until I remembered this house you'd just bought, and I had the idea of offering my help.'

'What do you wish to speak to me about?'

'An important matter which I must discuss *now*. Is that all right?'

'Yes.'

'I am in love with you and I've realized I have been since the very first time I set eyes on you – three years

285

ago now – when we went to Le Havre looking for Percy Malvern. I walked into your father's house to pick up you and Tilda, to go with Josh to France. Do you remember?'

She nodded. 'It was a Sunday afternoon,' she managed to say.

'You are the most beautiful woman I have ever seen. And during the trip I knew that I loved you and always would. I thought you felt the same. But you disappeared to Kent. And eventually I buried my feelings, closed the door on them and you, in a sense. But when we had that funny accident, when you fell into my office and into my arms, *I knew I was still in love with you.* I am really at my wits' end. It is very hard for me to be anywhere near you because of my overwhelming feelings.'

Alexis stood there, still unable to speak, stunned by his words.

He said, 'What I need to know is whether you have any interest in me or not. If you share my feelings.'

She walked, half stumbled towards him, tears trickling down her cheeks, and put her arms around him, clinging to him.

Falconer looked down into her face, wiped the tears away with his fingertips. 'Tell me, Alexis. Tell me how you feel. If you don't love me as I love you, I will understand, and I won't trouble you again.'

She gazed up into those dazzling blue eyes and recognized the yearning in them, and she exclaimed, 'I'm in love with you, James. And I have been for years – like you, from that Paris trip. But for some reason I blocked you out. Of course, I'm in love with you. I love you with all my heart.'

He bent his head and kissed her on the lips, and she kissed him back, pressing herself against his body. They stayed like that for a long time, kissing passionately, and holding onto each other as if afraid something might rip them apart.

Eventually, they separated, stood gazing at each other, unable to look away. He touched her cheek gently, and asked, 'Why were you crying?'

'Emotions, knowing you felt as I did. *Relief.*' She stared at him, and said, 'I want to make love with you . . .'

'So do I, Alexis. I don't suppose there's a bed here . . .'

'Yes, there is. But I don't think there are any bedclothes.'

'I don't care! Do you?'

'No.' She glanced around, looking for the candlesticks she had seen a few days ago. Spotting them, she hurried across the room. 'James, please come and get a candle, and I'll take the other. I'm not sure about the gas lamps in the bedrooms.'

Falconer came over. He took the box of Swan Vestas out of his pocket and lit the two candles. He gave one to Alexis and together they mounted the stairs.

Alexis led the way into the master bedroom, exclaiming, 'Oh, look, the street lamps outside are shining light into the room.'

She put the candlestick on the mantelpiece, and made her way to the bathroom. Here she found a pile of towels that Millicent Plymouth had put there yesterday.

She carried them out and placed them on the bed, then went to Falconer, who stood watching her. As she drew closer, he reached out and grabbed hold of her, pulling her into his arms.

He said against her cheek, 'I really am in love with you, Alexis, and I always will be. Don't start this with me unless you feel the same. You see, I'm not playing a game, I'm playing for keeps.'

'And so am I. I want you forever, James.'

Alexis gave him a flirtatious glance and began to remove

her jacket, and then her blouse. 'Get undressed,' she said to him, and he did so.

Within seconds they both stood naked in the middle of the room and moved at the same moment, rushing into each other's arms.

He held her face in his hands for a moment, kissed her on her forehead, and slowly began to pull the pins out of her hair. The abundant auburn locks fell down around her shoulders which, in the candlelight, looked like alabaster against the auburn curls.

Alexis moved back into his arms, and pushed her body next to his. Her arms went around him, and she slid her hands down his back and onto his buttocks, pressed him closer. 'I want to learn every part of you,' she whispered.

He did not speak. Instead he kissed her passionately, and they moved together, half stumbling to the bed. They fell onto it, still in a tight embrace. He continued to kiss her, his tongue touching hers, which to James was a true sign of absolute intimacy.

He pushed himself up on an elbow and looked down at her. How glorious she was, looking back at him, with her eyes full of desire and love. He suddenly knew she was as sensual as he was.

Reaching up she put her hand against his cheek, and said softly, 'Touch me. Touch all of me. I want you to know all of me, James.'

'And I want the same.' He stroked her neck and her voluptuous breasts. He let his hand trail down her stomach and onto the mound of auburn hair between her legs.

Within seconds they were inflamed and fully aroused, and went into a frenzy of touching and kissing, until he slid onto her and took her to him almost roughly. Alexis cried out, filled with pleasure as he entered her and made her his. To her they had become one entity.

James was in total command, loving her completely,

filled with passion, his sensuality taking him to new heights with her. She was as uninhibited as he was, and satisfied his every need. Ecstasy and rapture enveloped them.

They were unable to let go of each other. They lay in a tight embrace under the towels, talking quietly in the bedroom illuminated by the dying candles and the pale light from the street lamps outside.

Suddenly, Alexis said, 'I was so afraid you wouldn't forgive me for the horrific way I treated you. And especially that day Jane and Reggie were present. I must have been ill. That's the only explanation I have.'

'I'm certain you were,' James replied, holding her tighter. 'I believe you were in a deep depression without really understanding it. I remember thinking that when I came to Goldenhurst with your father's letter.'

'How could you know? Did I appear to be ill?'

'In a certain way, yes. You were pale, looked worn out and sad – perhaps *lost* is a better word,' James explained, his voice soft, soothing. 'You weren't at all glamorous, although I realized you were in riding clothes. I suppose you seemed apathetic to me, like you couldn't make an effort. But I must admit I was puzzled by your dislike of me. I thought perhaps you were jealous of my relationship with your father. Your hatred just didn't make sense.'

'That did occur to me, too,' Alexis replied. 'And also I probably was terribly unhappy, still grieving for Sebastian. But obviously I fell into bad ways. I let myself go, couldn't be bothered. I just drifted along, had no purpose.'

'What pulled you up, pulled you out of it? Or should I say *who*?' he asked, loving her so much, wanting to truly understand her.

'I believe it was Lord Reggie, in one way, and Claudia, Sebastian's daughter, in another.'

'Tell me more. I want to understand you and know everything.'

Alexis sighed. 'Claudia was angry because I accepted an invitation to her sister's birthday party and then didn't go.' She told him about Claudia's visit and everything she had said, and how it had affected her.

'Well, she was very tough with you,' James said gently. 'But obviously she did you a very good service by actually telling you the truth. Her words made the right impression. And Lord Carpenter? What did he say to help you?'

Alexis let out another long sigh and recounted what had happened the morning she had learned that Goldenhurst was entailed. When she began to explain what entailment actually meant, he stopped her.

'I know what an entailed house means, so you can stop there. And this upset you, did it?'

'I think, looking back, that it did. Maybe because I couldn't understand *why* he did that,' Alexis admitted. 'Don't you think it was strange, James?'

'I'm not sure what I think. It was a lovely gesture of Sebastian's to put you in his Will, before you were married – protecting you in the way he did. The entailment may seem odd, but I believe he was a businessman at heart. He was a banker, after all.'

She was silent for a moment, and then said, 'I'm not angry, nor really *that* upset . . . just perplexed.' She nestled close to him, and whispered, 'We can always go there, to be alone, you know.'

Startled, James exclaimed in a low tone, 'But wouldn't it be hard for you to be there with me . . . would memories of him intrude . . .?' He let his voice trail off.

'No, I don't think so . . . well, how do I know? I think I've grieved for him for a long time and now I've recovered. That's why I was able to come back to London . . . and to you.'

'To *me*?' he said. 'Why do you say that?'

'Because I came to my senses and understood that I had fallen in love with you in Paris. I had then shut you out because I felt guilty about him. I was so wrong, James.'

'Talking of being alone, how are we going to manage that? I mean, I share a flat with Uncle George. We can go there when he's away—'

'And come here when the house is finished,' she interrupted.

'But you'll have staff,' he pointed out. 'We can't create a scandal. People can't know.'

'So we can always go to Kent for a weekend.'

'We'll work it out,' he promised. 'Now, about the office, we are going to be totally discreet. Nothing will change. We have a routine, and we'll stick with it. No gossip about us.'

'I totally agree,' Alexis said, her voice as firm and serious as his had been. 'No gossip, no scandal. And I promise you, I won't mention anything about our relationship to anyone.'

THIRTY-SIX

James Falconer stood outside on the steps of Malvern House, glancing around, looking for Josh and the carriage.

It was a cold day in January 1892, and he could smell snow in the icy air. He shrugged deeper into his overcoat. He was about to start walking when he heard Josh's voice. 'Over here, Mr Falconer, behind you, sir.'

As he swung around, he spotted the carriage and hurried up the street. To his surprise, he saw Alexis peering out of the open window of the carriage.

Before he could say a word, she exclaimed, 'Get in the carriage!'

He did so, frowning. 'What are you doing here? You're supposed to be in bed, nursing that cold,' he said. 'It's an icy day, and we don't want you to catch pneumonia, now do we?'

Alexis looked at him steadily, her green eyes sparkling, and then she took hold of his hand. 'Good afternoon, James darling. And you don't have to worry about pneumonia. I'm better, much better. In fact, I'm *good*, really *good*.'

As the carriage set off up Piccadilly towards Hyde Park Corner, Alexis placed James's hand on her stomach.

She leaned closer to him and whispered in his ear, 'I'm pregnant. You've given me a baby, James!'

'Oh my God,' Falconer exclaimed, and gazed at her lovingly, his blue eyes shining with delight.

'And the reason I'm out on an icy day is because I've been to the doctor. I've been feeling under the weather for some weeks, so I decided I'd better make sure before I made any announcements. Aren't you thrilled, Mr Falconer?'

'I am indeed, and now perhaps you'll agree to become Mrs Falconer. I've asked you so many times I was beginning to think you'd changed your mind. I could have just walked off, you know.'

'No, you wouldn't have done that. You're a Falconer, and Falconer men are honourable.' She leaned into him, and added, 'And so many other delicious things . . . like being so sensual and very sexy.'

He shook his head, laughing, full of happiness. After a moment, he asked, 'How pregnant are you? I mean, when will the baby come?'

'I believe we made the baby that first night we spent together in my empty house. In October last year. We're having a summer baby, James.'

James put his arms around her and held her close, his eyes suddenly moist. Finally, a family of his own. Leonie he had sworn to keep a secret. Not even Alexis knew of her existence. But this child, he could acknowledge. This child would be celebrated.

He turned to kiss the woman he loved.

'Will you marry me, Alexis darling?'

'It will be my great pleasure, James. I would love to be your forever wife.'

'I think we had better make it sooner rather than later, don't you?' he said, a hint of anxiety in his voice.

'Yes, I agree, James, and I really don't think it should

293

be a big wedding. Just our two families and a few special friends.'

'That makes a lot of sense,' James said. 'And we can talk about it over supper. If I'm going to be invited into your house.'

Alexis laughed, and removed his hand from her stomach. 'You can touch the baby whenever you want, and now let's get out of the carriage. We're already in South Audley Street. And of course you're invited to supper – and breakfast, as well.'

James loved the way Alexis had decorated the house. It was totally different to Goldenhurst, which had always seemed rather cold to him. They had gone there a lot, because of the need they had to be alone together, and to love each other.

During the week they avoided being in the same room as much as possible. They were clever about hiding their feelings and were the epitome of discretion. Not one member of the staff had guessed they were involved in any way at all. They went to the office, did their work, and sometimes she gave him a lift in her carriage, especially in bad weather. Mostly they played it safe, arrived alone and left alone. Sometimes they met at her house, her father's house, or at his flat in Half Moon Street. Not so much to make love, but simply to be together. They found it excruciating to be apart, had a great need for each other's company. They had a lot in common. Falconer discovered they were totally in tune and compatible in every way.

Now, as they entered the house, it started to snow, and Alexis was laughing as they stood in the entrance foyer. It was elegant, and welcoming. But at this precise moment, she was thinking of the night they had come here and made love for the first time in a cold bedroom. And made the baby, she thought, convinced this was so. However, she kept quiet as she took off her coat.

'Let's go into the parlour,' James said, after giving his overcoat to Hunter, the butler, who had been highly recommended by Lady Jane. In turn, Hunter had brought in Maud Feltham, a lovely young Cockney, who had a great gift. She was a fabulous chef and created wonderful meals. James knew Alexis treasured Maud, enjoyed her food, plus her sharp Cockney wit, and her rhyming slang. She made them laugh a lot when they saw her in the house.

The fire was blazing in the parlour, a comfortable room filled with overstuffed sofas and armchairs in colourful red and green fabrics. Millicent Plymouth had found some special Georgian antique chests and a matching table. But James knew that it was Alexis who had used her knowledge to pull everything together to make a whole. And that *whole* was splendid. The greens and reds stood out against pale buttery-yellow walls and echoed colours in the paintings. It had been a wonderful place to visit at Christmas, just after she moved in.

Alexis had chosen pale-pink silks and satins for the drawing room next door, highlighting these with blue and lime green. These two main reception rooms were traditional in style. James preferred them to those cool, sleek, empty rooms at the house in Kent. But it had been a godsend when they had an urgent need to make love and nowhere else to go but Goldenhurst.

Alexis had seated herself at a small writing desk, where she found sheets of notepaper and a pencil. She went and sat in a chair near the fireplace, where James was standing with his back to the fire.

'Let's make the list,' Alexis said. 'So what's the name of the groom?'

James chuckled. She always managed to make him laugh

with her curious style of humour. He played along with her. 'James Lionel Falconer,' he said with a straight face. 'Unless it's some other chap.'

'And what's the name of the bride?' Alexis asked.

'Victoria, Empress of the World,' James answered teasingly.

'So her name is Alexis Helen Malvern.'

'I didn't know you had a middle name,' James responded. 'My Helen of Troy, known as a great beauty, which you are; a woman over whom men fought battles.'

'The bride's father is Henry Malvern, and that's it for the bride's side. Now to the family of the most handsome man in the world. Come on, give me their names, my darling Falconer.' She laughed, winked at him.

'All right, here we go. And let's be serious and do the list quickly. I want to toast you and the baby.'

Alexis looked at him, realized he *was* serious, and nodded. 'Parents, Maude and Matthew Falconer; grandparents, Esther and Philip Falconer; uncles George and Harry; siblings Rosalind and Edward. Is that it?'

'Yes, unless we include the Venables from Hull. William's parents,' James said. 'Marina is my great-aunt, my grandmother's younger sister. What do *you* think, Alexis?'

'Why not? William is so nice, and he's been a good friend. And I think you must ask Natalie. She's devoted to you.' Alexis paused. 'Do you think we have to ask anyone from the office, such as the division heads?'

'I don't really know. It could get problematical if some people feel left out, slighted, don't you think?' James looked thoughtful. 'Why don't we ask your father? Let's hear what he thinks.'

'I agree. Also, there are two people at the office who might be hurt – Peter Keller and Lucy Charteris. What about them?'

He nodded. 'Of course, you're right. I'm sure Keller in particular would be genuinely hurt.'

'After we've discussed it with Father tomorrow, I must send out invitations immediately. I'll get the best calligrapher and have them done by hand, and delivered by hand.'

James nodded. 'We will have the wedding at your father's church, won't you?'

'We will, and he will give me away. Who will be your best man?'

'Uncle George. Oh, and I would like to invite Detective Inspector Roger Crawford. He's been a real friend. And what about your friends? Lady Jane and Lord Reggie?'

'I agree. They must all be invited, as well as Claudia and her husband Cornelius. Oh wait, they have gone to New York on some bank business. They left last week. So that's our list. Now what about that toast?'

James looked across at her, his blue eyes moist again. He could hardly believe all this was happening. Their child was growing inside her. She was so happy, as was he. And another miracle was their marriage. No wonder he felt so happy. What a lucky man he was. And quite unexpectedly, he realized, he was about to start a new life.

The Reverand Silas Asten, the vicar of the local church where Henry Malvern worshipped, stood at the altar waiting to perform the wedding ceremony.

Waiting there with him were James Lionel Falconer and his best man, George Falconer. Both men looked handsome in their morning suits, with white waistcoats and white carnations in their buttonholes.

As the organ began to play Mendelsohn's 'Wedding March', all heads turned as the bride, Alexis Helen Malvern, walked down the aisle on the arm of her father, Henry Malvern.

It was Saturday 6 February 1892, at four o'clock in the afternoon. And the marriage service was about to begin.

There were gasps of delight and many moist eyes as the bride walked gracefully towards the vicar.

She looked more beautiful than ever. Her shining auburn hair swept up, her face flawless and radiant with joy and her green eyes sparkling.

Her gown was simple, made of white satin, the boat-shaped neckline trimmed with white fur, which also edged the long sleeves. She wore a small diamond-and-emerald tiara, which held her veil in place, and small emerald earrings.

On her left hand was the diamond engagement ring that James had given her.

Slowly, sedately, she walked down the long room and, as he watched her coming towards him, James was filled with love for her. He had always thought of her as the love of his life. And indeed she was. Although he had once believed he would never have her as his wife and that he had lost her.

When Henry brought Alexis to him, tears filled James's eyes as he took her hand in his. He saw that she too was crying, as well as her father, all extremely emotional because of this union.

The vicar cleared his throat, and the bride and groom took control of their senses, as disciplined as always.

They listened to the vicar and answered his questions, and before they knew it he was pronouncing them man and wife.

Turning to Alexis, James lifted her veil of white lace and kissed her. They smiled at each other and went on smiling for the rest of the day and into the evening.

Once the ceremony was over, the organ began to play,

and the bride and groom walked down the aisle to the church entrance.

Here they stood waiting to greet their guests, clutching each other's hands.

'I love you so much,' James said, then added, 'I can't believe you're mine, that there is suddenly a Mrs James Lionel Falconer.'

'Well, there is, and it's me,' Alexis said, looking at James, her love for him shining in her eyes. 'And I'm your forever wife, remember that.'

The drawing room of the Malvern home in Mayfair had been totally transformed the day before the wedding. All the furniture had been removed, except for the piano, and the room had then been filled with small gold-painted ballroom chairs.

All of them would be taken, because everyone on the couple's list of guests had accepted their invitations.

White flowers were everywhere, including orchids, lilies, roses and carnations. Some were banked under the windows, others filled out corners, and great bouquets stood on wooden stands on either side of the fireplace, where a fire burned brightly.

To one side, at the far end of the room, a small trio composed of a guitarist, a harpist and a pianist were next to the piano, waiting for the bride and groom. As they came in, the trio started to play, and Alexis and James were suddenly surrounded by family and friends, toasting them with glasses of champagne being passed around by the waiters.

James turned when his grandparents and parents arrived. They had all been captivated by Alexis's charm and beauty when they met her. Especially his grandmother, Esther Falconer.

'You're lucky. You found the right woman for you,'

Grans had told him. Now she said again, in a different way, 'The new Mrs Falconer is of our ilk now, and she will be a wonderful addition to our family, James. She's the best.'

His parents had taken to her, and of course his uncles had teased him. They had asked him how he of all men had managed to catch this raving beauty.

Lady Jane and Lord Reggie came to join them, friendly and warm, and obviously most approving of James.

At one moment, Henry Malvern joined them and asked them to gather the Falconers and the Venables to have their photographs taken. They did, trooping into another room. Afterwards, they joined the guests once more in the reception room.

It was a happy evening. Everyone was enjoying themselves, laughing, chatting and having a good time. The supper, which had been cooked by Mrs Feltham, was delicious, and the wines that Henry Malvern had chosen were superb. Waiters were constantly refilling crystal goblets, other waiters bringing plates of food.

Glancing around at one moment, Alexis saw again how lovely the women looked in their elegant gowns and jewels.

After the wedding photographs had been taken, Great-Aunt Marina helped Alexis to take off her veil, with Tilda assisting, and replace the small diamond-and-emerald tiara which had belonged to her maternal great-grandmother. Now she would be able to dance with James. She could hardly wait to be in his arms.

As the supper continued, there were a number of toasts and speeches between courses. First to stand up was Henry Malvern, the father of the bride, and then James's father, Matthew. He was followed by Uncle George and then Uncle Harry. They gave amusing short speeches about their handsome nephew, teasing him a bit with humour, jokes and affection, making all the guests laugh.

When James stood up, the room became totally silent. He gave an eloquent speech, much of it directed at Alexis. Then he took hold of her hand and led her onto the dance floor for the traditional first dance of the evening.

James held her firmly in his arms, and Alexis gazed up at him, as usual mesmerized by the brilliance of his vivid blue eyes.

She smiled inwardly, aware they made a most handsome couple, and that all eyes were focused on them. She spotted the Trevalian sisters, Lavinia and Marietta, the latter's husband Anthony Gordon, and his brother Mark. They were all sitting together with Aunt Thea, who was accompanied by Marmaduke Gordon. Alexis was happy she had invited them.

As they moved around the dance floor, James Falconer saw the future as he gazed into his wife's eyes. There was a new lightness of spirit in him. An absence of pain. The emptiness was gone. The future was theirs.

It had just begun.

EPILOGUE

James felt a tingle of excitement as he fitted the key in the lock of the small shop in Hull, and opened the door, stepping inside.

When Natalie had handed him the key earlier, he had experienced that same little rush of expectation, and eagerness to view the building.

He stood in the middle of the floor, looking around, noticing that this one room, the main room, was rather spacious, and he envisioned it filled with clothes and fancy handbags and all manner of other goods. He smiled to himself. At last he would have a shop. Not anything like Fortnum and Mason, of course, but it was a beginning. You had to start somewhere.

It needed sprucing up, lots of fresh white paint on the walls and ceiling, highly polished floors and the doors needed a new coat of paint. Yes, he could soon get it into shape, and would enjoy working on it. Natalie had said they would help – his *posse*, as she called his small group of friends.

James opened a door and went into the back of the shop. There were two storage rooms for goods, filled with shelves, and a small office. He was already well pleased with this unexpected find, and the rush of excitement returned. He was going to rent it. What a fool he would be to turn it down.

One of the things which pleased him most was that it was in Hull. He loved this busy city. The folk who lived here liked to enjoy themselves, have a good time. And it was one of the great seaports in England, with ships carrying goods all over the world; while other ships from other countries sailed in with their imports. The flow of ships hinted at adventure.

He enjoyed going down to the docks with his cousin William Venables, and he had loved the few trips he had made on one of the Venables' ships, sailing over to Le Havre. Uncle Clarence had begged him to go to work for their wine importing company, but James had declined, although he had been tempted. But he had his loyalty to Mr Malvern to think about, and then there was his dream.

His dream of his own business – a shop like Fortnum's, and an arcade of shops like the Burlington Arcade in Piccadilly. He liked beautiful things, clothes for women, jewels, Savile Row tailoring for men's clothes. Luxury, glamour, sumptuousness. He sometimes wondered where his liking for such things came from. He had no idea. Certainly, he hadn't been brought up with it. He had had truly humble beginnings. On the other hand, he had an imagination, a certain vision and his grandmother had exposed him to Fortnum's, the arcades and magazines passed on by Lady Agatha.

As he left the shop, and locked the door, he stepped back into the road and looked at the shop. And in his mind's eye he saw the name above the door. FALCONER.

Coming soon and available to pre-order now

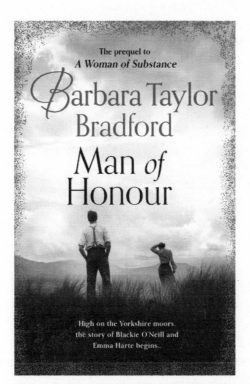

The world first met Blackie O'Neill, lifelong
friend of Emma Harte, forty years ago in
A Woman of Substance.
In *Man of Honour*, the true Blackie O'Neill
is revealed for the first time . . .

If you enjoyed *In the Lion's Den*, be sure
to read the first of the House of Falconer novels,
Master of His Fate

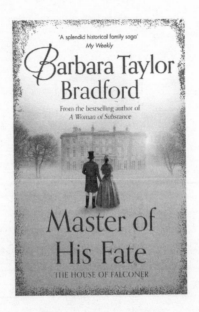

London 1884: James Falconer works as a
barrow boy in a flourishing London market
owned by Henry Malvern. But James hungers
for more. He dreams of building an empire of
stores like Fortnum and Mason and believes that
Henry, and his daughter and heir Alexis, could
offer him a way to climb beyond his beginnings.

Also available is the *The Cavendon Chronicles,*
a sweeping historical series full of
intrigue and drama

CAVENDON HALL

Two entwined families: the aristocratic Inghams and the Swanns who serve them. A stately home: the grand Cavendon Hall, nestled in the Yorkshire Dales. And a society beauty: Lady Daphne Ingham, the most beautiful of the Earl's daughters. But life as the families of Cavendon Hall know it – Royal Ascot, supper dances and grouse season feasts – is about to alter beyond recognition as the storm clouds of war gather...

THE
CAVENDON WOMEN

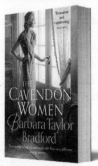

The Cavendon estate is under threat: the aftermath of the Great War has left it facing ruin. And now four young women from both sides of the house must shape its future. But as the roaring twenties burn towards the Great Depression, nothing will ever be the same again...

THE
CAVENDON
LUCK

The great house of Cavendon Hall has stood on the Yorkshire moors for centuries. But when war looms, sons, husbands and brothers are called up to fight; trials and tragedies strike the great house itself. And the women of every generation and background must rise to meet the terrible threat posed by Hitler. The Cavendon Luck has held for a long time. Can it hold in the face of this greatest threat of all?

Secrets
of
Cavendon

The year is 1949. The Second World War has exacted a terrible price at Cavendon Hall. The aristocratic Ingham family is at odds with its loyal retainers, the Swanns, for the first time. And when Cavendon's secrets start to rise to the surface, young and old alike are threatened. Can the generations unite to save the family name and their future?